ALWAYS A CHOICE

ALWAYS A CHOICE

Copyright © 2023 by Rana Schenke.

All rights reserved. Printed in the United States of America. No part of this book may be used or reproduced in any manner whatsoever without written permission except in the case of brief quotations embodied in critical articles or reviews. This book is a work of fiction. Names, characters, businesses, organizations, places, events and incidents either are the product of the author's imagination or are used fictitiously. Any resemblance to actual persons, living or dead, events, or locales is entirely coincidental.

The contents of this work are copyrighted and may not be used to train any AI model.

Contact: www.ranaschenke.com

Cover design: Rebecacovers
Editor: Ashley Wolfe
Formatting Template: Derek Murphy
ISBN: 979-8-9889166-1-1

First Edition: February 2024

10 9 8 7 6 5 4 3 2 1

ALWAYS A CHOICE

Daughter of Deception Book 1

Rana Schenke

To those who seek solace in stories.

* 1 *

IT'S BEEN THREE MINUTES, THIRTY-FIVE seconds since Jess left the dorms.

Too slow, she thinks to herself. No time to spare now.

She races down the basement hallway, the sound of the flickering fluorescents buzzing in her ears. They almost sound like the buzzing of tiny wings—*focus*. Jess shakes her head to clear the thought from her mind. They'll never catch her, not as long as she keeps to the time.

Three minutes, fifty seconds. She reaches the door she needs and stops. The handle doesn't budge when she tries it, but that doesn't dissuade her. She bends down and in thirty seconds, she's picked the lock and is inside. Her fingers touch cool concrete as she feels for the light switch, and once she finds it and flips it on, she sets off down the row of aisles.

The storage room smells musty, and the stillness of the air makes it obvious it hasn't been disturbed in a while. Exactly the way Jess likes it. She reaches the right aisle and heads down it, stopping just past the halfway point.

The shelves are full of identical plastic bins with handwritten labels, but Jess is only focused on one. Sitting squarely on the middle shelf, its tag reads "Gym Uniforms, 1932-1937" in neat block letters. Nothing about it marks it as special compared to the other bins, but appearances can be deceiving, as Jess well knows. She grabs the handle and pulls it out, then lifts the lid.

The old-fashioned clothes inside release the scent of chalk and mothballs as Jess digs through them. She reaches the bottom of the bin, and her fingers touch leather. She pulls the item out.

It's a small leather case, sized to hold a passport or maps. It bulges in the middle, and Jess knows it holds a stack of bills. She knows because she put it there.

She shoves the bin back into place and is about to tuck the case away when a voice stops her.

"Where do you think you're going with that?"

Jess freezes, then turns slowly to face the end of the aisle. A petite woman dressed like a 1950s schoolteacher stands there. Her face is in shadow at first, but then she steps forward and the light falls on her pursed red lips, cat-eye glasses, and the tips of her pointed ears.

"I won't ask again," Miss Colleen says, folding

her arms to display her perfectly manicured nails, so shiny and red they look plastic.

Jess knows the jig is up. She drops her shift, that of a generic-looking sophomore boy, and she's back to her own form, a look of defiance on her face. She's not going to try and pretend her intentions are anything other than they are.

"I'm leaving," she says. "You can't keep me here."

"Well, legally, I can," Miss Colleen says, "but that's beside the point." She tilts her head. "You are a curious one, Jessamine Richards. Hundreds of students in this school, and you're the only one who wants to leave."

"Then let me go," Jess says. "You've got hundreds of happy students; you don't need me. Just let me leave."

The headmistress shakes her head. "You know I can't do that."

"Then this place is no better than a prison."

Something like hurt flashes across Miss Colleen's face, so fast it's almost imperceptible, before her expression hardens into disappointment. "I'm sorry you feel that way," she says. "It has never been my intention to keep you here against your will. This place is intended to be an establishment of learning, yes, but also a home. All I want is for my students to feel safe and welcome."

Jess starts to feel bad for hurting Miss Colleen's feelings, but then realizes that's impossible. Fairies don't have feelings, at least not like humans and half-fae do. Miss Colleen is trying to manipulate her. Ironic, considering Miss Colleen knows perfectly well that Jess's abilities and training can help her detect lies and manipulation. Jess narrows her eyes.

"I don't have a home anymore."

Miss Colleen is silent. Jess waits for her to say something, to get angry, but she doesn't. She just stares. It feels like they stand there forever, student and teacher, eyes locked, waiting. Finally, Miss Colleen unfolds her arms and holds out her hand.

"Come with me."

Jess understands this is a test. She doesn't know what will happen if she takes Miss Colleen's hand, but if she refuses, she's not just rejecting the headmistress, but the Academy itself. They'll erase her from the records like she never existed, and everything she's worked for the past five years will have been for nothing.

Jess may have her issues with the place, but she's not quite ready to turn her back on it completely. She steps forward and grasps Miss Colleen's hand.

The air twists around them, and when it untwists, they're in Miss Colleen's office.

"Have a seat," Miss Colleen says.

Jess obliges, sitting in one of the cubelike leather chairs in front of a wooden desk that seems to take up half the office. She slides her backpack off her shoulder and lowers it to the floor, carefully slipping the money into a side pocket. It's all the cash she has left; she doesn't want it confiscated.

Miss Colleen sits on the other side of the desk, knitting her fingers together and leveling another piercing stare at Jess.

"I understand you're frustrated, Jess," Miss Colleen says, her voice calm. "I know things have not been easy for you since Joseph's accident—"

"That's not it!" Irritation flares, hot and sharp in Jess's chest. Will they never understand? "All of you are always making everything about—about what happened, and you're treating me like a child because of it. That was over three years ago, and I'm fine. Why can't you see that?"

She genuinely wants to know Miss Colleen's answer. The delicate treatment, the refusal to let her do anything important, and even the rigorous tests and challenges all originate here, with Miss Colleen. Nothing happens in this school without her knowing.

Miss Colleen tilts her head to the side, apparently thinking. After almost a minute, she speaks.

"I think I understand what you want."

Jess doubts that but decides to humor her. "What's that?"

Miss Colleen sits back in her chair, folding her hands in her lap. "You want an assignment."

This is such a gross simplification that Jess laughs out loud before she can help herself. As if giving her an assignment would fix everything that's happened in the past three years, make amends for the way they've treated her. It's actually insulting.

"It's going to take a lot more than a half-baked fake assignment that's two miles away to make me stay."

"I promise you, this assignment is very real," Miss Colleen says. "And you won't be two miles away; you'll be at McCreed's palace."

This catches Jess's attention.

Murdoch McCreed is the bane of the fairies' existence. He's neither fairy nor human—Jess doesn't know what he is, honestly—and he's made it his personal mission to create as much chaos for the fairies as possible, whether by tampering with their magic, sending his wichts to pillage and plunder their homes, cursing their crops, or worse.

Occasionally, he attempts more dangerous assaults on the fairies, but these are usually thwarted by the network of undercover intelligence officers the FIC, or Fairy Intelligence Commission, have planted in his palace.

Jess has been interested for years in becoming one of these officers after she graduates, but she knows it's a difficult placement to get. All her classmates who want to apply to the FIC will be using their assignments in their applications, so if she wants to stand out, she needs a good assignment. Anything to do with McCreed would fit the bill. She only needs it to succeed.

"So, what is the assignment?" she asks.

Miss Colleen purses her lips before she speaks. "What I'm about to tell you must not leave this room," she says. "If you do not accept the assignment, this conversation will be wiped from your mind, per FIC protocol. Do you understand?"

"I understand."

Jess is even more intrigued now. If this assignment is important enough that Miss Colleen is required to wipe it from her memory if she doesn't accept, that means it's big. It's not a shadowing assignment or something made up, like the dead drops Jess did in April that were definitely fabricated. This is the real deal.

Miss Colleen waves her hand, summoning a file from the cabinet in the corner of the office. It lands neatly on her desk and she opens it. Jess can see a stack of paperwork and, clipped to the top, a glossy photograph of a girl. She itches to know who the girl is and why she's important, but doesn't want to come across as desperate, so she waits for Miss Colleen to explain.

"McCreed has gone too far this time," Miss Colleen says. "As you know, he's made a habit of stealing from the fairies and attempting to cause us distress or even harm, but this time, he's directed his attention to our children."

She unclips the photograph and slides it across the desk for Jess to see. A young girl with dark hair, about twelve or thirteen, stares up at her with a serious expression. The photo is professional and looks like a headshot of some sort. The girl's hair is well-styled and she's wearing makeup. She could be a child actor, maybe, but if so, Jess doesn't recognize her.

"This is Della Easterly. Her mother is Harriet, the patron fairy of models. We've been in contact with her adoptive parents, but they've refused to send her to the Academy and her power index isn't high enough to require her to attend."

Jess wishes *her* power index was that low. If it was, Miss Colleen would have no standing to keep her here. She could walk straight out the front gate with no one stopping her instead of having to sneak out.

"I wish we'd pushed the matter further," Miss Colleen continues. "Della was kidnapped yesterday from her family's apartment in Chicago after arriving home from school, and McCreed is behind it."

"How do you know?" Jess thought McCreed wasn't allowed to leave his kingdom, let alone travel to the human world.

Miss Colleen lifts a few pages and pulls out another photograph, which she slides across the desk, next to Della's picture.

"This was found at the scene."

Jess picks up the photo to look at it closer. It shows what would be a nice living room, if it wasn't in complete disarray. Lamps were knocked over, cushions were strewn about, and the frames on the walls had fallen to the ground and shattered. To top it off, everything was coated in a thin layer of frost, McCreed's trademark. In the center of the photo, carved into the frost on the floor, were the words "COME AND GET HER."

Jess looks up at Miss Colleen, thoughts racing. She has so many questions, but one stands out over the others.

"If you know McCreed has her, then why haven't you gone to his palace and gotten her back already?"

Miss Colleen sighs in frustration. "First, we can't just barge into his palace to find her, as per the treaty we signed years ago. In fact, he technically hasn't violated anything in the treaty, since half-fae aren't protected under it to begin with."

Jess frowns, irritated. Of course the treaty only protects fairies, not their offspring.

"Second," Miss Colleen continues, "he's denying having any knowledge of or responsibility for the kidnapping. Our hands are pretty much tied, at least officially."

"But we have officers planted in his palace," Jess says. "One of them has to have heard or seen something."

Miss Colleen shakes her head. "Most of the officers we had there have been reassigned since McCreed ceased his direct attacks a few years back. Those who are left haven't been able to learn anything—we think he might have been secretly plotting against us this whole time and just kept it quiet. It would explain not only why he stopped acting against us, but also some of his behavior since."

All of this is news to Jess. She thought the FIC's McCreed operation was bigger. It's alarming that no one had detected anything suspicious until now. McCreed could be setting a plan into motion as they speak with no one the wiser.

"So, what the FIC needs from you is for you to infiltrate the palace undercover, find Della, and see if you can find any evidence of McCreed's larger plan," Miss Colleen says. "We need to get Della to safety, and we need to know what McCreed is planning next so we can stop him before he strikes."

Jess narrows her eyes. Miss Colleen hasn't offered her an assignment in over three years. Yet here she is, handing Jess a desirable assignment with high stakes, one she knows Jess couldn't refuse. There must be a catch.

"Those are two big objectives for one mission. Why is the FIC giving it to me?"

Miss Colleen smiles for the first time. "Smart girl. Why *would* the FIC want to send a half-fae high schooler on such an important and dangerous mission?"

Instantly, Jess knows the answer. "It's my mother, isn't it?"

"Of course," Miss Colleen says. "She's been pushing to put you on something big since the start of the semester. It's just a lucky coincidence that you decided to—ahem—conduct your prison break at the same time this developed."

Jess is furious. Of course her mother had a hand in it. Talia is not only the patron fairy of espionage and disguise, but also the director of the FIC. Her involvement isn't necessarily surprising, but Jess doesn't need her meddling like this.

Since she came into Jess's life, Jess's mom has kept trying to "help" her in an effort to—well, Jess doesn't even know what her end goal is. Fairies are all heartless and selfish, and she would be a fool to believe her mother is any different from the rest of them.

After all, she didn't help Jess when she really needed it, and nothing she does now will ever make up for that.

"Thanks for clearing that up," Jess says, "but I think I'm going to pass on this one." She stands, grabbing her backpack and heading toward the door.

"Jess."

The Call in Miss Colleen's voice is weak enough that Jess can dismiss it, but she turns back anyway. It doesn't end well to try to ignore a fairy using the Call, especially one who knows enough of your true name to be dangerous.

When Jess looks at Miss Colleen, she seems softer somehow. Less otherworldly. She's staring at Jess with large brown eyes and Jess feels, once again, that she is being evaluated.

"I know things are difficult with your mother," she says, "but this isn't about her. It isn't about McCreed, either, or you finally getting the important assignment you need. It's about Della."

The way Miss Colleen's eyes are boring into her makes Jess feel exposed, like her hopes, desires, and insecurities are laid out at a yard sale and Miss Colleen is sifting through them in search of something valuable.

"I'm not going to try to guilt you into anything by telling you to imagine what Della might be going through right now," Miss Colleen says. "I only want you to look at why you're declining this assignment and if it's for the right reasons. You're leaving a lot on the table if you say no, and I don't want you to regret it."

Jess knows Miss Colleen is right. If she says no, she's leaving an innocent girl in a dangerous situation just to get back at her mom. You can't get any pettier than that. And, though it's selfish, she does need this assignment, and she needs it to be a success.

She also knows she would feel awful if she didn't accept the mission, even though she's sure someone else—maybe even someone more qualified—would be sent in her place.

"Okay, I'll do it," Jess says. "When do I leave, now?"

"No, you'll be leaving tomorrow morning." Miss Colleen's manner is brisk and business-like as she spreads out the papers from the file on her desk. "Come here, I need you to sign a couple forms beforehand."

Jess crosses the room and sits back in front of the desk, setting her backpack down again.

"So, just to be clear, I'm supposed to infiltrate the palace, find Della first, and then focus on searching for evidence? How is that going to work? And do I have a time limit? What happens if something goes wrong while I'm inside?"

Miss Colleen waves her hand dismissively. "You'll be getting a full briefing tomorrow that will cover all the details. Here, sign here." She pushes a form across the desk and Jess signs the bottom. Miss Colleen waves her hand and the paper slides into a manila envelope that sets itself in the "Outgoing" tray at the corner of her desk.

"As far as the mission objectives," she continues, "you won't have to worry about getting both done. Here, sign this. You'll be a part of a small team, so you'll all be able to split up and search simultaneously. I should think that will make it much easier to complete both objectives."

Jess stops scanning the form and looks up at her. "What do you mean, a team? You didn't mention a team before."

"Well, you didn't think they would send you on your own, did you?" Miss Colleen laughs lightly. "Don't worry, it's just you and two others. They know what they're doing, so it'll be a good learning experience, too."

She mentions it off-handedly, like forgetting about the others was an accident, but Jess knows better. Miss Colleen's omission was entirely intentional.

Jess narrows her eyes in suspicion. "Who are the others?"

"Oh, one is a retired spy who spent thirty years undercover in McCreed's palace, so they'll be a real asset as far as helping you blend in and navigate," Miss Colleen says. "Their name is Lyle and they're also a child of Talia."

Up until now, Jess didn't even have confirmation that she had any adult half-siblings. Many of her classmates do, and their siblings have reached out to them or even come to campus. With the line of work Jess's siblings tend to go into, though, that's not exactly feasible.

She's interested to meet this sibling, especially with their experience undercover at McCreed's palace. But the other person...

"Who's the other person?"

"Well, good news, it's someone you already know!" Miss Colleen's voice is far too cheery for Jess's taste, and she doesn't like it at all.

"*Who?*"

Miss Colleen loses the smile and looks at Jess, her gaze a warning. "Keep in mind, I didn't have anything to do with this," she says, "so don't get mad at me. It's Penn."

Jess feels the sudden urge to break something, to knock the collection of "#1 Teacher!" mugs off Miss Colleen's desk and hear them shatter at her feet. But she resists, instead shoving the forms and pen back across the desk and standing up. Just her luck that the only assignment she's offered is the result of nepotism and requires her to work with the worst fairy in existence.

"Nope," she says. "You can go ahead and mind wipe me now. I'm not doing it if I have to work with him."

Miss Colleen raises an eyebrow. "So, first you were going to turn down this opportunity because of your mom, and now you're turning it down because of him? I'm beginning to think you don't want it at all."

The blatant attempt at manipulation makes

Jess even angrier. "Of course I want it! I know it's my mom's doing, I know you're trying to stop me from leaving, and I still want to take it. But I will NOT work with him!"

"You don't have a choice," Miss Colleen says. "The team's already been decided. You either take the mission with him or don't take it at all."

"How'd he even get on the mission, anyway? Isn't he still exiled?"

Penn had been exiled from the Realm, the world of the fairies, a few hundred years ago for reasons unknown to Jess. She's heard a few rumors as to why, but nothing concrete. She figured she would have heard if his exile had ended, though, since he works with the Academy so frequently.

"I assume special permission was granted by the Crown," Miss Colleen says, completely avoiding the topic of exile.

It's interesting that the king and queen would grant Penn special permission for this assignment when they would have been the ones to exile him, but Jess won't pretend to understand the complicated dynamics of fairy politics, which often span thousands of years.

"But why him? He's not an officer. Couldn't they get someone else?"

Jess is confident the FIC has better options than an exiled fairy with too much ego and not enough sense.

"You're not an officer, either," Miss Colleen points out coolly. "Your mother selected the team for this mission by hand, and she specifically chose you for it. She also chose him. The only way you'll find out why is by participating."

Miss Colleen is being purposely sharp, and Jess feels the urge to snap back in response, but she realizes that won't make things better. It's not Miss Colleen's fault this assignment comes with so much extra baggage. Too much extra baggage.

Although it pains her, Jess shakes her head. "I'm not going to do it."

"Are you sure?" One dark eyebrow edges up over the frame of Miss Colleen's glasses.

"Yes, I'm sure. Can you please wipe my mind now so I can go?"

Jess hates the idea of having her mind wiped, but it's better than the actual torture she'd experience if she took this mission and had to work with Penn.

"Jess," Miss Colleen says, and Jess recognizes her teacher tone, the one that means a lecture is imminent. Jess braces herself.

"I know you don't want to work with Penn, but think about it," she continues. "You're going to run into this situation the rest of your life. You should consider this a learning experience. Situations will come up in your career that will require you to work with people you don't get along with. It's better to learn how to deal with that now."

Jess doesn't understand why Miss Colleen is pushing her so hard to take this assignment. Is it just about needing to keep her at the Academy? Is it a favor to Jess's mom? It's certainly not because she's looking out for Jess's future. If that was the case, she would have let Jess take real assignments before now.

Although Jess is upset with Miss Colleen, she has to admit she's making a fair point. Jess will encounter situations like this in the future, hopefully as an FIC officer if she's accepted. She'll inevitably end up forced to work with people she doesn't like. Worst of all, she knows her dad would be telling her the same thing as Miss Colleen if he were here. He had a saying for situations like this: Sometimes you have to do things you don't want to do to get where you need to be.

"Fine, I'll do it," Jess says, sinking back down into the chair.

Miss Colleen smiles and clasps her hands together. "Excellent! I really hate doing mind wipes, anyway. You should be at the circle drive and ready to go by 8:00 a.m. tomorrow. He'll pick you up, then you'll drive to pick up Lyle in Iowa. I expect you'll be staying overnight and leaving for the Realm the following morning, so prepare accordingly."

"Wait, why aren't we going there tomorrow? Della's been kidnapped—shouldn't we go as soon as possible?"

Miss Colleen shrugs. "The FIC doesn't think McCreed is a threat to Della's safety. Torture or physical maiming isn't really his style; anyone or anything he's taken in the past has always been returned unharmed, and we haven't received any threats from him, either. Other than his choice of target, he's following his usual tactics of theft, so the FIC is confident she's not at risk of physical harm."

"All due respect, that's the most ridiculous thing I've ever heard," Jess says. "Either way, Della is probably terrified! And who's to say McCreed hasn't decided this is the time he changes tactics?"

Della's not a fairy. She could be hurt, or even killed. Her safety ought to be the top priority.

"And what about her parents?" she continues. "I don't envy the person who has to explain that they've waited a whole extra day to send someone in."

Miss Colleen's lips narrow into a thin line before she speaks. "I didn't say I agree with their rationale," she says. "However, you do have to take into account that a mission at this scale does take time and resources to execute. Not to mention, the FIC is walking a very fine line with the treaty. We only have one shot to get this right. A misstep could put us back at square one with McCreed, with nothing to show for it."

Jess gets it. This isn't her first assignment; she knows these things take a lot of planning and coordination to get right. Her last assignment took four months of planning, and it still...she pushes that thought away. She can't remind herself of that now.

"Okay, fine," she says. "But why are we wasting half a day driving? Can't we just teleport to Iowa? Or—he's got a magic car, hasn't he? Can't we just put it into magical hyperdrive or whatever and get there in fifteen minutes?"

Jess doesn't know where in Iowa they're heading, but it's got to be close to three hours from the Academy to the Illinois-Iowa border. That's a lot of time to spend trapped in a car with the world's most annoying magical being.

Miss Colleen shakes her head. "Magical Transport of Minors Act. Since you're under eighteen, you can't be magically transported over five miles by anyone other than a parent or guardian, and the special exception paperwork has to be filed five business days in advance."

"The joys of magical bureaucracy," Jess says, rolling her eyes.

"Speaking of paperwork, I have everything I need from you now, so you're free to go. I will give you this file to review; it has some background information on Della and some basic information about the palace. You can review it tonight or wait until the drive tomorrow, I'll leave that up to you."

"Thanks," Jess says, taking the file and slipping it in her backpack. She stands and heads toward the door.

"Don't forget, eight o'clock sharp," Miss Colleen says.

"Got it!" Jess gives her a thumbs up over her shoulder before pulling open the door.

"Oh, and Jess?"

Jess pauses in the doorway and looks back.

"Good luck," Miss Colleen says, lips upturned in a small smile.

* 2 *

THE FIRST THING JESS DOES IS GO FIND THE one person at the Academy who cares about her—her best (and only) friend, Cat.

When Jess started at the Academy, she knew absolutely no one. She was also a latecomer; most of the kids her age had already been there for two years or longer. Cat had been there for four years, which is why Miss Colleen had assigned her to be Jess's "buddy" for the first week and show her around. When Jess had found out that the bubbly, outgoing girl with the snow talent and bouncing braids was going to be her buddy, she'd instantly become nervous.

Cat seemed to know everyone; she was involved in a ton of activities and had a range of interests. Meanwhile, Jess had just come out of the worst two years of her life and was trying to find her footing again. Before she'd made it to the Academy, her top concerns had been where she was going to sleep and how she would find food, not learning a number for the musical or deciding which after-school club to join. She had no idea what she would even talk to Cat about.

Looking back, Jess wishes she could tell her younger self she had no reason to be worried. Cat is the nicest person Jess has ever met, and she made a real effort to make Jess feel welcome and become her friend. Since then, she's stuck with Jess through everything that's happened, good and bad. Jess would have left the Academy a lot sooner if it weren't for Cat.

She starts heading toward the forest, where the dorms are, before realizing Cat won't be in her dorm. It's Friday night—game night.

With a sigh of irritation, she turns back and takes the path to the football stadium. She's not a fan of football (she prefers watching basketball) and normally tries to avoid the games, but Cat is in the band, so if Jess wants to talk to her, that's where she'll have to go.

The sun has just set, but the air is still warm. As she approaches the game, she can smell popcorn and hear the dull roar of the crowd. Instead of going through the front gates, Jess takes a detour around the side. As she nears the gate where the band typically unloads, she takes off her backpack and holds it by the handle out in front of her.

When she feels it catch on something, she lets go and it vanishes, disappearing into the little pocket of the fairy world she refers to as her magic closet. She'll summon it back later, but for now, it's better to leave it there.

Free of the burden of her backpack, Jess shifts her clothing into a band uniform, mentally cringing. The school colors, bright blue and orange, always make her feel like a walking target. At least in this environment, she'll be one of a hundred dressed in the garish colors, not even including the spectators.

Now all she needs is an instrument—that's unfortunately something she can't create or summon.

Jess pauses and scans the area around her. There must be something—aha! She spots a long stick on the ground a few feet away and picks it up. Concentrating, she closes her eyes for a few seconds. When she opens them and looks down, she's holding a clarinet. At least, it looks like a clarinet; it still feels like a stick. It will work for what she needs, though.

She walks through the side gate and into the stadium. As she nears the steps to the stands, she picks up her pace, both to appear like a band kid in a rush and to avoid running into anyone she knows. She hasn't shifted her appearance, only her clothes, hoping it's enough to fool most people.

Once she's in the stands, it only takes her a minute to spot Cat in the band section, talking animatedly with one of the piccolos. For just a second, Jess feels a spot of envy for her friend, for how easy it is for her to get involved and engage with others, but she pushes it away. As soon as the band director's back is turned, she dashes up the stairs and maneuvers her way through the other clarinets until she's next to Cat.

Cat doesn't notice her at first—she's still talking to the piccolo player—so Jess taps her on the shoulder. Cat turns around.

"Hey," Jess says, giving an awkward smile.

A look of surprise crosses Cat's face, followed by confusion.

"What are you doing here? I thought you were leaving!"

"I got caught." It's embarrassing for Jess to admit, even to Cat.

Cat folds her arms and arches an eyebrow. "You got caught. Well, I'm not sure what you expected, but I for one am not surprised."

"Look, I know you're upset and I'm sorry, but—"

"You LEFT, Jess. Come on. It's senior year, we're going to graduate soon, and then you'll never have to come back here again. You couldn't hold out until then?"

"I *can't*," Jess says. She looks down at the fake clarinet, then back up at Cat. "You don't understand. The constant tests, the patronizing attitudes, the unending pressure—it's killing me to stay here." Her voice breaks a little on the last word. Deep breaths, deep breaths.

"If I don't go, I don't know who I'll be in eight

months. I don't know what will be left."

Cat's expression softens, and she's back to her normal, warm self, opening her arms for a hug, which Jess accepts.

"I'm sorry," Cat says, just for Jess to hear. "I know it's been hard for you, and I'm thankful you've stayed this long." She pulls back and looks at Jess, brown eyes wide and serious. "You're my best friend. You know that, right?"

Jess nods.

"Good." Cat smiles. "I'm not going to pretend I'm not glad you're still here, just so you know. I'd keep you with me forever if I could."

"Aww, getting sentimental?" Jess says, finally cracking a smile. She gives Cat a light punch on the shoulder. "Must be the senioritis talking."

Cat throws her head back in a laugh, the silver strands in her braids flashing. "Come on, you're going to miss this place too, just you watch. We're going to be back here for our ten-year reunion reminiscing with the rest of the saps, you'll see."

"Yeah, well, who's going to find me to deliver my invitation?" Jess asks. "I don't intend to be somewhere findable."

It's Cat's turn to punch Jess in the shoulder. "You think we're going to lose touch? Not on your life! I'll deliver your invitation. You might leave the Academy, but you'll never leave me."

That reminds Jess of why she actually came to talk to Cat. "Uh, yeah, so about the whole leaving thing..."

The smile drops from Cat's face. "You just said

you got caught. Are you trying to leave again? Seriously?"

"No, no," Jess says. "That would be ridiculous; they'd catch me again instantly. No, I got an assignment."

Cat's jaw drops. "An *assignment*? They finally gave you another assignment?"

Jess nods. "Yeah. It's just because of my mom and because Miss Colleen wants to keep me from leaving, but it's a real assignment."

"That's amazing! I'm so excited for you!" Cat says, hugging Jess again. "When do you leave, tonight?"

"Nope, tomorrow morning. *He's* picking me up."

The surprise is evident on Cat's face as she pulls back. "Hold up. You don't mean—"

Jess nods. "Yep, the one and only."

Jess has told Cat the full details of her history with Penn, so she doesn't need any further elaboration. She understands, without Jess saying anything else, exactly how Jess feels and why the situation is...undesirable, to say the least.

"If he's involved, it must be a big deal," Cat says, although Jess is not too sure that's the case. "I'm happy for you. You deserve this opportunity, and I know it's all going to work out."

"I really hope you're right." Jess doesn't tell Cat that she can't afford for it to go wrong, but Cat gets it. She always does.

* * * *

Ten minutes later, Jess is headed back to the forest again. She's shifted out of the band uniform and the stick she'd used as a prop has been discarded, the illusion gone.

As she enters the trees, Jess breathes in deeply, taking in the scent of pine and earth. She would never admit it, but she'll miss the forest when she leaves. Since it's a game night, it's peaceful and quiet, apart from the sounds of insects and Jess's own footsteps. Although it's fall and the weather is getting cooler, fireflies still dart between the trees, their lights blinking. They're a comforting sight, but not enough to calm her growing frustration.

She knows thinking about the assignment is only going to frustrate her further, but she can't help it. She hasn't had an assignment in so long. If only this one didn't have so many strings attached.

All of the strings have her riled up, from her mom's interference to the obvious attempt to placate her into staying, but none as much as being forced to work with Penn.

She may not know why Penn was kicked out of the fairy world, but there's no doubt he deserved it. For starters, he's incredibly self-absorbed, even by fairy standards. Second, the only thing bigger than his reputation is his ego, and third, Jess's experiences with him in the past—well, they don't reflect well on him and the less said about them, the better.

Which is why it's so annoying that literally every time she's around him, he has to bring them up.

Every. Single. Time.

On top of that, he tries to be NICE to her. Like that's going to fix anything.

Meanwhile, every time she sees him, she's thinking of how she would dearly love to punch him in his smug, scheming face for what he did. She allows herself a brief moment to indulge that fantasy, then shakes her head. He's a fairy. He could punch her through a wall if he felt like it, or end her puny mortal life in another, far more painful way. But he wouldn't.

She knows this because she knows him, and his biggest flaw—his biggest weakness—is his pride. And what he's most proud of? She knows that, too. His reputation.

One would think that being exiled from your homeland would annihilate your reputation, but looking at Penn, it almost seems the opposite is true. While many of the fairies dislike him and refuse to speak to him (which Jess only knows because she overheard Miss Colleen discussing it once), in the human world, he's almost a minor celebrity.

Jess has heard all the rumors: he has an apartment in every major city, he parties in LA every weekend, he's on a first-name basis with every A-lister you can think of—the usual. Like with the other rumors she's heard, there's a chance it isn't real. But what is real is the crowd of students who seem to swarm him every time he's on campus.

They could care less that he's an exile from the

Realm and many of their parents hate him; all they want is to see him, to hear his stories, to touch his car. And Penn indulges them, because the part of his reputation he prizes most is his image of being a nice guy.

The irony! Jess shakes her head. If they only knew.

She takes a deep breath, releasing the tension that's been building up in her body while she thought about him. It's no use dwelling on it right now. There are things she needs to do before she leaves in the morning.

She's reached the part of the forest where the path splits. She takes the path to the right, which leads to the dorms, but when she reaches the twisting wooden staircase to hers, she keeps walking. There's someone she needs to see first.

Luckily, the girl she needs also isn't one for football games, and she opens the door with a friendly smile when Jess knocks.

Five minutes later, Jess is crossing the rope bridge to her dorm with a small bottle tucked in her jacket pocket. When she reaches her room, she summons her backpack, tucks the bottle inside, then sends it back to where it came from.

She sits on her bed and flips through the file Miss Colleen gave her but isn't able to gain much from it. There are only basic details about Della and the information on McCreed's palace is woefully lacking. Even the page about the team, which she was hoping would give her some background on Lyle, only lists everyone's name, age, pronouns and status (fae or half-fae).

Realizing the file isn't going to yield anything useful, Jess sets it aside. She gets up and completes her nighttime routine, then falls into bed to sleep. It's only eight thirty.

* 3 *

THE AIR IS CRISP AND COOL WITH A HINT OF floral scent as Jess walks to Main Hall in the morning. Main Hall isn't the largest building on campus (that would be the Barn, despite its deceiving exterior), but it's the oldest and most impressive.

A classic Queen Anne-style house, Main Hall was originally the only building on campus. In the early days of the Academy, it held classrooms and lodging for students and faculty.

Jess has often imagined what it would have been like to be a student at the school's founding, living in Main Hall, taking every class with the same handful of fellow students. She imagines it's not unlike some of the novels she's read where the girls go to boarding or finishing school. It would probably be nice, but she thinks she'd prefer the Academy in the present day, faults and all. At least there are more course options, and not all of her classes are with the same people. And the treehouse dorms are a definite plus.

She enters the building through one of the back doors, making her way through the paneled hallways to the dining hall. Today, Main Hall only holds classrooms, faculty offices, and common areas such as the dining hall and library. Since it's the weekend, the hall is quiet, and even the dining hall is deserted.

Jess takes her time eating breakfast, but still reaches the circle drive by 7:50. She has a whole ten minutes until Penn is supposed to arrive, so she decides to wait in the atrium instead of sitting outside on the steps. She's brought a book to read and has just opened it when a group of other students enters from the hallway to the right of the main staircase. Jess recognizes them mostly as sophomores and juniors; she doesn't know most of them personally, but they are all children of nature fairies, judging by the color of their uniform ties.

"Jess!" calls one of the girls, waving enthusiastically. It's Sylvie, daughter of the rainforest fairy, and Jess immediately wishes her abilities included turning invisible.

Sylvie was her lab partner in biology last year and, while nice, seems to have made it her personal mission to elicit a conversation from Jess every time she sees her, which conveniently always seems to be when Jess is least in the mood or position to socialize.

"What are you doing here?" Sylvie continues, breaking away from the group and crossing the atrium toward Jess. Her long, dark hair sways as she walks, and her brown eyes are bright. "Are you coming with us?"

"No," Jess says. She has no idea where Sylvie's group is going, but judging from their sunhats and hiking boots, it's probably not to the frozen northern tip of the Realm where McCreed's palace is located.

"Oh," Sylvie says. Then, lowering her voice, "Do you have a mission?"

Jess despises the word "mission." It brings to mind every cheesy spy movie and unrealistic stereotype about intelligence work. It devalues everything she does, makes it sound like a child's pretend game. Yet everyone around her continues to use it.

"Maybe," she replies.

"Oooh, how exciting! What is it?" Sylvie claps her hands over her mouth. "Wait, forget I said that. You probably can't say, can you?"

Jess shakes her head, secretly grateful.

"That's so cool," Sylvie continues. "I'm totally jealous. We're just going to the Amazon again, for reforestation. Growing trees for three days! Not very exciting. But if we grow five hundred trees this time, we get to go to the palace to be recognized by the king and queen. Now that's exciting!" She giggles, and the sound grates on

Jess's nerves.

At that moment, the hairs on the back of her neck stand up, and she almost breathes a sigh of relief. He's arrived.

"I have to go," Jess says, putting her book away and standing up. "Good luck with the reforestation."

"Thanks! Good luck with your secret mission!" Sylvie says, and for a second, Jess is afraid Sylvie is about to hug her, but she doesn't, just smiles cheerfully.

"Thanks," Jess says, then hurries toward the door before Sylvie can get any ideas. She pauses before opening it, taking a deep breath to try to control her quickening heartbeat. It doesn't help much. She reaches behind her and pats the pocket of her bag. A comforting lump tells her the bottle is still there. It's okay. She's got this. With that thought, she pushes open the door.

To her surprise, Miss Colleen is standing on the steps, wearing a smart-looking navy blue sweater set and smiling. A red Porsche is just pulling into the circle drive.

Miss Colleen turns her smile toward Jess. "Excellent weather today. I'm sure the drive will be lovely."

The words are pleasant enough, but the tone of Miss Colleen's voice and the sharp edge to her smile make them sound more like a threat. Jess doesn't take kindly to threats.

She stares at Miss Colleen, a silent dare. "*Lovely*? Three hours in the car with him? No way.

This drive is going to be torture."

She is spared from Miss Colleen's reaction by a voice from below. "It doesn't have to be."

Jess turns.

Penn is standing next to the car, right arm casually slung over the open door, with an easy smile on his face that does nothing but irritate Jess. If he were anyone else, she would be embarrassed to have said something so rude, but he doesn't even look fazed by her insult.

"I mean, the car's pretty tricked out, and I've got a huge collection of audiobooks," he continues.

"Nerd," Jess mutters to herself, but Miss Colleen's enhanced hearing picks it up and she glares at Jess before turning back to face Penn.

"Penn, thank you so much for agreeing to help with this," she says, smoothly cutting him off in the middle of a description of the built-in mini fridge his car apparently has in limo mode. "You two had better hit the road if you want to arrive on time. Jess, do you want to put your bag in the trunk?"

Jess shakes her head. "Nope, I'm good."

Without another word, she hurries down the steps, passing Penn without a glance, and pulls open the door to slide into the passenger seat. The car currently doesn't have a backseat, so she is stuck sitting up front. With him. She shudders, thinking about the hours of suffering she is about to endure. She just has to focus on the assignment, on Della. It's only three hours. She can keep it together for three hours.

She looks around the interior of the car. It's

surprisingly devoid of anything personal, which, given its owner, she finds interesting. Jess's eyes wander before eventually fixing on the Porsche logo on the steering wheel, with its distinctive black horse and red and black stripes. The car is luxurious for sure, but it feels empty to Jess, like something's missing.

Penn is still talking with Miss Colleen. He's stepped away from the car and shut the door, so she can't hear what they're talking about. Jess assumes Miss Colleen is probably telling him the same stuff she told Jess last night. She notices, with minor irritation, that *he* doesn't have to sign any forms.

She watches as Miss Colleen smiles at something Penn says, and she wonders idly if there's something between the two of them. It would explain why he works with the school rather than, well, doing whatever it is the other fairies do. Jess hasn't met all that many fairies, but she knows Penn's lifestyle is not the norm.

Finally, the two finish talking. Penn opens the car door and slides into the driver's seat. The car starts automatically as he closes the door, and he buckles his seatbelt before looking over and smiling at her.

"Apologies for keeping you waiting," he says. "Did you find something you wanted to listen to?"

Jess stares straight ahead. Focus on Della. Focus on the mission. Don't mess this up. "No," she says, her tone cool.

"Suit yourself," Penn says, shifting the car into

drive and pulling out of the circle drive onto the road beyond the school.

Soon the trees start to thin out and they're driving through town, which Jess is surprised to see isn't very busy until she remembers it's a Saturday. No early morning traffic.

"I'm gonna make a quick detour," Penn says, glancing over at her as he changes lanes. "Hope you don't mind. I haven't had my coffee yet, and I'm no fun before coffee."

Jess shrugs, saying nothing. She does mind that this will delay them, but it's not like she can stop him. Maybe the coffee will make this trip—or rather, him—more bearable.

Penn turns at the next stoplight and navigates the Porsche into a Starbucks drive-through line. There are a few cars ahead of them, but the line moves quickly, and soon Penn is placing his order. Jess tunes him out, uninterested, until he asks her if she wants anything. Her response is a firm no. She's not taking anything from him.

He shrugs, then turns back to the order. "That's it!"

The barista reads back the order, and this time, Jess is paying attention. He's ordered two venti coffees, what sounds like half of the bakery menu, and a breakfast sandwich. Where he plans to put all this food is unclear, because the interior of the Porsche isn't very big.

Now they're at the window, and when the cashier, a girl not much older than Jess, opens the window to take Penn's card, she does a double take.

"Hi there!" Penn says, flashing her a giant smile as he holds out his card. "Saira, right? How's your day going?"

"I—uh—" The girl is at a loss for words. Between the car, Penn's megawatt smile, and the sunglasses he's rakishly tilted just enough to show off the startling green of his eyes, Jess would guess she probably thinks he's some kind of movie star.

Penn, of course, is eating up the attention like it's another scone he ordered. His smile has grown bigger, if that's even possible.

The girl blinks and shakes her head, as if to clear it. "Um, my day's going great," she says, eyes still locked on Penn. Jess doesn't think she's even aware there's someone else in the car. "How's yours?"

"Absolutely perfect," Penn says. "Beautiful weather, fabulous car, excellent coffee—what more could I ask for?"

"Right! Coffee," the girl says, finally seeming to notice the card in Penn's outstretched hand. She takes it and starts to process the order.

"So how long have you been working here?" Penn asks, resting his arm on the edge of the car window. Jess notices him leaning toward the girl, watches the careful way he holds his head to hit the right angle as he looks up at her. The movements are so precise Jess can only assume he practices in front of a mirror.

"I just started in July," the girl says as she runs his card.

"Well, congratulations!" Penn says. "What a

great place to work. I bet it's loads of fun."

"Yep!" the girl says, smiling at him as she hands back his card. "I love it." She looks back at the monitor for a second, then back at Penn, and Jess notices she's blushing a bit. "So, ah, do you come here often?"

"I wish!" Penn says. "No, I'm not from around here. But it's a lovely area, and the people are so friendly."

Jess cringes internally. He's laying it on so thick, but it's *working*. In barely over a minute, he's gotten this girl hanging off his every word. Jess would feel bad for her, but it seems like she's enjoying the experience as much as Penn is, judging by the way she appears to be devouring him with her eyes.

Jess has to look away. She knows Penn is conventionally attractive (being a fairy) and has basically weaponized charm and charisma, but she'll never understand how those two factors are an automatic kryptonite for everyone around him. They don't even know him.

Finally, the girl hands Penn his drinks and a bag of pastries. Penn asks Jess to hold the bag while he situates the drink carrier, and she takes it. The receipt is stapled to the bag, and she notices there's a phone number scribbled at the bottom in ballpoint pen, because of course there is. Jess rolls her eyes. She thought people only did that in movies.

Penn notices Jess noticing the number. "She was nice," he says, pulling the car forward and out of the parking lot. "You can take that if you want. I don't know what you're into, but she was giving off major bi energy to me."

She has to take a moment to register the sheer absurdity of the situation. He flirted with this girl to the point where she gave him her number, and now he's trying to offer it to Jess?

If he was anyone else, she'd let him know she's asexual and texting a random girl from Starbucks is about the last thing she would ever do, but the less he thinks he knows about her, the better. Instead, she just says "I'm good" and leaves it at that.

While they're waiting for the light, she sees Penn twist an odd sort of knob just to the right of the gauges and suddenly, the car is shifting.

Jess knew the car could change forms, just like she knows it really isn't a car at all, but a living, breathing magical being. Knowing this and actually being inside it as it shifts, however, are two different things.

Despite being able to shift herself, it's disorienting and almost dizzying to feel the car changing shape beneath her—even her seat changes shape and texture, going from black leather to fuzzy gray fabric. The dashboard morphs into a heavy gray plastic and the digital touchscreen display disappears, replaced by a radio and CD player. Jess even notices a slot for a cassette.

"Camo mode," Penn says by way of explanation. He puts one coffee in the cup holder, takes a swig of the second, and puts it in another cup holder that has popped out of the dashboard to the left of the steering wheel. Then he takes the bag from Jess, opens it, and starts eating the breakfast sandwich.

The light changes, and as the car turns, Jess notices it even drives differently now. She's not sure what he means by "camo mode," but isn't going to ask and give him the satisfaction of knowing she's curious. With annoyance, she notices the car now has a backseat, and she looks enviously at it in the mirror for a few seconds before turning to stare out the window.

They are just reaching the highway now, and Penn merges seamlessly into the flow of cars. Traffic is a little denser on the highway, but still not bad, and it only takes a few minutes before Penn attempts to start a conversation again.

"So how was your summer? Do anything fun?"

"No," Jess says, keeping her eyes fixated on the landscape flashing by her window.

This is a lie; she and Cat went to Cancun for a week with Cat's dad. The trip was for Cat's birthday and they had a lot of fun. She stayed with them for the rest of the summer at their house in Arizona, too, and overall, it was one of the best summers she's had since her dad died. But she's not about to tell Penn that.

Penn seems caught off guard by her curt response, but he doesn't give up.

"What classes are you taking this semester? You're a senior, you probably get to take just fun ones now, right?"

"No," Jess says, not elaborating. She really does not want to engage in conversation with him, and the more he talks, the more he tries to pretend to be her friend, the more irritated she gets. She has to remind herself to breathe. Focus on Della. Stay calm and don't react. She wonders if he's going to go for a third try or cut his losses now.

She only has to wait about thirty seconds to find out.

"Did you see the new Marvel movie?" he tries, a hopeful but almost pleading note in his voice.

Surely this will be his last attempt. Surely he'll get the message now. "No."

"Okay then."

They drive in silence for a few minutes. Naturally, Penn can only stand it for so long, and he turns the radio on.

For a split second while he was reaching for the dial, Jess had hope; maybe he would put on NPR or some eighties rock and they could spend the rest of the drive ignoring each other. But the radio bursts to life with a jazzy big band number, and worse, Penn turns it up.

A tidal wave of memory hits Jess, more vivid than she's felt in years. She *knows* this song. Suddenly she's five years old again, dancing around the living room, the sharp notes of the horn section punctuated by her dad's warm laugh. The feel of the carpet under her bare toes, the distinctive warm smell that means home—NO.

With tremendous effort, Jess yanks herself out of the memory, shutting it down. She takes a breath and is scared to feel how shaky it is. This can't happen. Not here, not now, not in front of him.

She turns away from the window, gives Penn a disgusted look, and says, "Can you turn that off?"

Penn looks startled—exactly as she expected—and says "Okay, fine." He switches it off and Jess settles back into staring out the window.

Without the music, the memory fades away completely and Jess's breathing stabilizes. She feels a sense of relief until she realizes he's looking at her, probably hoping she'll explain or apologize.

Anger sparks, sudden and unexpected, in Jess's chest. She doesn't owe him anything, least of all an apology. She wishes he would focus on why they're here and leave her alone. That's all she's trying to do.

But of course, he can't. It's not even fifteen minutes before he starts to fidget. Jess can tell something's coming. Penn won't stay silent forever; he can't.

She's starting to hear other sounds now, short, irritated breaths and sighs, and she can tell he's looking over in her direction every couple of minutes or so. She continues to stare out the window. She's trying to remember the assignment, to remember that Della's counting on her, but a little part of her can't help but feel satisfied that Penn is as irritated and uncomfortable on this drive as she is.

Surprisingly, he holds out for another thirty minutes. There were a couple times where she could tell he was about to say something before stopping himself, and she has started to amuse herself by trying to predict what he's most likely to say. She's whittled her guesses down to two options (a question about school or a statement about her being rude) when he finally speaks.

"Why do you hate me?" he asks, his words sharp and pointed.

She should have figured he would cut to the heart of it. Or at least what he assumes the heart is. It's not that he's far off—she does hate him, in a way—but that, after everything he did, he *still* has to ask. That's what touches a nerve.

She unfurls herself from where she's been curled up on the seat and looks at him, eyes wide. If he's going to play innocent, she will, too.

"What makes you think I hate you?"

Penn throws his hands in the air. "Oh, I don't know! Maybe when you snapped at me to turn off the music? Or when you very loudly slammed the car door getting in? Or maybe it's the fact that you've refused to speak more than a syllable to me this entire drive!" He slaps his hands down on the steering wheel. "Seems pretty clear that you've got a problem with me, but correct me if I'm wrong."

She shouldn't say it, she *knows* she shouldn't say it, but the fact that he has the audacity to go off on her, to pretend he DOESN'T KNOW, has set her off. Two can play this game.

"You are wrong," Jess says. She crosses her arms and looks out at the road ahead. "I didn't slam the door. You were parked on a hill. It was gravity."

Such a bad idea, but it felt so good to say. A little voice in the back of her head tells Jess that she's going to get herself kicked off the assignment, but the harder, angrier side pushes it away. She's been holding in this anger for so long, and it feels good to finally let her feelings loose. Let him suffer the way he made her suffer.

"Great, now you're arguing with me," he snaps. He turns to look at her, and she's glad the car is self-driving or they'd be in trouble. Irritation and anger are clear on his face. "Are you always like this? What did I ever do to you?"

There it is, plain as day. He doesn't know. Well, he's about to.

"Are you serious right now?" Jess whips her head around to glare at him. "What did you ever do to me? YOU STALKED ME FOR TWO YEARS! *TWO YEARS!*"

"I wasn't stalking—" Penn starts, but Jess cuts him off.

"Oh yeah? Then what do you call it, huh? 'Following?' 'Tracking?' 'Closely observing for special purposes?'"

"I was doing *my job*," he snaps.

"Doing your job?" Jess laughs, then mimics his voice, shifting her vocal cords for maximum accuracy. "'Hi, my name is Penn, I'm a professional stalker and my job is to stalk little girls!'" She drops the voice and points at him. "If you weren't a fairy, you'd be in prison right now."

"You know it wasn't like that," Penn says. His cheeks are tinged pink. "I wasn't stalking you. I was trying to HELP you."

"Oh, of course, you were trying to *help* me. How could I have missed it? All those times I was lost or hungry or didn't have a place to sleep, and you were there, and you helped me...except, funny thing, I don't actually remember that. Really, I don't remember you there at all!"

"That's because I was too busy trying to find you!" It's no longer irritation on Penn's face, but something else, something Jess doesn't expect—pain? "You think I didn't know what you were facing? You think I wanted you to suffer? All I was trying to do was help you get somewhere safe—I didn't want you in those situations, I was trying to get you out of them! Not like you made it easy, oh no." He crosses his arms and narrows his eyes. "You think *I* put you through a lot? You led me on a wild goose chase across the country! You played games with me for fun, you made me look like a—"

"THAT'S NOT THE SAME THING!" Jess yells, and Penn falls silent.

Jess turns away. She feels hollow. Now that she's released the anger, she realizes she doesn't know how it even got to this point, and it scares her. Her one chance for a big assignment and she's blown it before it's even started. What's wrong with her?

"I was terrified," she says quietly by way of explanation, eyes focused on the road. "I was ten, I was alone, a stranger was following my every move, and I was terrified."

Out of the corner of her eye, she sees Penn

look away, too, down at his lap. There's a long pause before he speaks, as if he's weighing his words, or debating them internally.

"So was I," he says finally. He raises his head and looks at her. "I thought you died, multiple times. If I went more than a few days without spotting you or finding some trace of you, I worried you were dead. And if you died—well, it would have been my fault."

Jess looks over at him. His words don't register as blatantly false, but she has a hard time believing he had cared about her safety, outside of what her death would do to his reputation. "Yeah, it would have," she says.

She expects him to go off again, but there's no trace of anger on his face, only acceptance and disappointment. He looks away, back at the road.

"The other fairies—they made out like it was some sort of game. Placing bets, stuff like that. They acted like it was one big joke that I couldn't find you, and meanwhile I was scared out of my mind that I would find you too late. I just wanted you to be safe."

Again, no lies. Jess doesn't know what to make of this.

She'd always assumed that whatever his initial motive had been had morphed into something else as he failed to catch her over and over again. She assumed he hated her in the end, wanted her to suffer, to be punished.

She assumed he felt the same way about her as she did about him.

His tone holds no anger, though. No resentment. Even when he snapped at her before, Jess is surprised to realize she didn't feel anger or hatred from him; more frustration than anything.

Penn breaks the stifling, heavy silence with a soft laugh.

"We certainly are top-notch picks to partner on this mission, aren't we? Almost makes me wonder if the FIC is just hoping we'll finish each other off so they don't have to deal with us anymore."

He stays facing the road, but Jess sees his eyes slide over to look at her. She doesn't respond, but she does allow her lips to creep up in a small smile.

Wordlessly, Penn reaches out and turns on the radio. This time, she doesn't say anything.

* 4 *

A COUPLE HOURS LATER, THEY ARRIVE AT the house. Jess gets out and immediately stretches her legs. They had stopped once during the drive—just for a break, because the car doesn't need fuel—but Jess is glad they have finally arrived.

When they had stopped, at one of the chain gas stations right off the highway, Jess got out and looked at the car. She had been curious when it shifted but hadn't wanted to show it. What she saw surprised her.

The car was a far cry from the Porsche—bulky, painted in a strange not-quite-silver color, and, most surprising of all, *old*. Millennium-era, if she had to guess. She wasn't sure what she had expected, but it definitely wasn't that.

"What *is* this?" she asked Penn as he got out of the car. He shut the door and came around the front, patting the hood.

"This is a '98 Oldsmobile Cutlass," he said, a hint of pride in his voice.

Jess didn't think the car seemed like something to be proud of. "It looks like an old person car."

Penn shrugged. "I see it more as 'broke college student.' It's good camouflage."

"And you're supposed to be the broke college student?"

"Naturally."

Jess looked him up and down, eyes landing on his fitted dark wash jeans, pressed shirt, and fancy watch. "Yeah, no one's going to buy that."

Penn lifted an eyebrow. "Why not? Am I too handsome to be broke?"

Gross. Jess rolled her eyes. "Too full of yourself is more like it."

Penn laughed. "Well, nobody's perfect. Except this beautiful vehicle here." He patted the hood of the car.

Perfect and beautiful were not terms Jess would attribute to the car, but to each their own. She wasn't about to start a fight with him over his choice of vehicle.

Now, looking at the car, Jess feels like she had been somewhat harsh and judgemental earlier. She was surprised that Penn would drive a nondescript car like this, but she has to admit that it's definitely not noticeable. Not that she thinks anyone is keeping tabs on them besides the FIC, but it never hurts to try and blend in.

Speaking of blending in, the house they are approaching is definitely doing just that. All the houses on the street look similar: one-story ranch houses with two-car garages and blacktop driveways. This one, however, looks even blander than the others.

It's painted a light gray, the kind where you can't tell if it was originally a different color and faded, or someone actually chose to paint it that way. There are no yard decorations, and the doormat is plain and worn. Jess wipes her shoes on it even though they're barely dirty; she doesn't want to make a bad impression by tracking dust into the house.

She lets Penn ring the doorbell; it seems fitting since, as a fairy, he has seniority. Plus, she doesn't want to be the one to explain why they're there, or introduce him.

It feels like they are standing on the stoop for a good five minutes, but in reality, it's probably no longer than a minute and a half. Finally, the door creaks open to reveal an elderly individual with neatly-tied gray hair, tanned skin, and sharp, dark brown eyes. This must be Lyle.

"You're with the FIC?" they say, their voice gravelly.

"Yes, we are," Penn says, a little too chipper in Jess's opinion. "May we come in?"

"Make yourselves at home," they say, stepping back from the screen door.

Penn opens the door and Jess follows him

inside, careful to pull the door closed behind her so it doesn't slam. They follow Lyle further into the house and she starts to feel disoriented. She's not sure where the feeling is coming from at first, but she quickly realizes it as soon as they walk into the living room. The layout of the house is completely different on the inside from how it appears on the outside.

From the front of the house, it appears as though the living room is at the front right and a bedroom is on the left, but the living room is actually in the back of the house, the kitchen is in the front on the left, and an office seems to be on the right. It's incredibly confusing and Jess has no idea why someone would design their house this way.

Penn looks as confused as Jess feels, and Lyle seems to notice this when they all sit.

"It's magic," they say. "I had one of Angelo's kids rig it up for me. It makes it so intruders don't know where to go. Gives me the element of surprise."

"That's very clever," Penn says, although his face shows he's clearly thinking something very different. In a second, that expression is gone, and he is reaching his hand out for Lyle to shake. "I'm Penn, by the way. The fairy of—"

"Yes, we've met," Lyle says. They turn to look at Jess, sizing her up. "I'm more interested in her. We're half-siblings, aren't we?"

"Yes," Jess says. "I'm Jess. It's nice to meet you."

"Lyle." She can't tell from the look on their face

whether she's passed the visual evaluation or not. It's weird for her to meet an adult sibling. Sure, she knew she had to have at least a few, but she hasn't knowingly met any before. She thinks Lyle is likely finding this as strange as she is.

Penn breaks the silence first. "Colleen said you would have a message for us from the FIC?"

Jess hasn't heard about a message. She's a little irritated that in over three hours, Penn hadn't mentioned anything about it, but she tries to brush it off. She's only moderately successful.

Lyle is rummaging through a bin of what looks like cat toys, and Jess is not sure what they are looking for until they pull out a small, black, saucer-shaped object. They set it down on the coffee table.

"You have to touch it," they say when Penn and Jess don't react. "Haven't you used one of these before?"

They both hurry to put their hands on it. Jess feels like whatever evaluation she's being subjected to, she's already failed.

As soon as they all touch the object, it vibrates with a loud buzzing noise, and they pull their hands back. A holographic image appears, and Jess recognizes her mother.

Talia is wearing a black zip-up jacket with the FIC logo on the breast, and her hair is dark, like Jess's, and pulled back into a ponytail. Her tone is all business as she starts the prerecorded message.

"Hello, team. I trust you all have read the background briefing already. As you know, a girl named Della has been kidnapped by Murdoch McCreed, and we believe she is being held prisoner in his palace. We have no reason to believe McCreed has harmed her or has any plans to do so, however, rest assured, there will be formidable consequences in store for him if he does."

Jess's lips tighten at the casual disregard for Della's safety. After experiencing her mother's disregard for her own daughter's safety, though, it really isn't that surprising.

"For this mission, you have two objectives," the Talia hologram continues. "The first is to find Della and safely extract her from McCreed's palace. The second is to investigate for any evidence of McCreed's current and future plans. We are almost entirely in the dark here, so we are counting on you to find solid evidence we can use to counter his plans.

"Of course, it is imperative that you are not discovered. You will be disguising yourselves as wichts to prevent this from happening."

Jess assumed as much; McCreed's palace is entirely staffed by wichts, small humanoid creatures native to the northern reaches of the Realm. Besides the wichts, McCreed lives alone, so it would be near impossible to infiltrate his palace in any other disguise.

"If your cover is compromised," the message continues, "you must not reveal your teammates. Instead, use the diverters enclosed in the bottom of this device. They will cause a loud noise or other diversion to allow you to escape to safety.

"This device also will serve as your transport to the Realm, since Jess is a minor. I have set it for tomorrow morning at eight, so be sure you are all holding it at that time so no one is left behind."

She goes on for a bit more about how close they will be to McCreed's palace, the route they should take to get there, and more instructions on blending in and seeking out information. Jess is paying attention but feels like most of this could have been put in the file, saving them all a lot of time.

Finally, mercifully, the speech ends and the hologram shuts off. Jess wonders if Lyle is going to put the device back in the box of cat toys, but they don't.

"I'm too old for this," they growl. "This business about plots, special technology, kidnapping—this mission is not going to be easy."

"What do you mean?" Penn asks.

Lyle sighs like Penn has asked a really dumb question, but Jess is curious, too. It's not that she thinks the mission will be easy—she doesn't—but it sounds like they have their own reasons for thinking it won't be, and she wants to know what they are.

"Look at the objectives," Lyle says. "They're slapped together. Rescue the girl and find the evidence. Those should be two separate missions, not one mission with a team."

Jess agrees with this. While sending a team to cover both objectives seems more efficient, two separate missions with one or two people would likely yield better results.

"Speaking of teams," Lyle continues, "on something like this, we've got no room for error. The team needs to be like a well-oiled machine, and it's only as strong as its weakest member. We need to be sure we're all bringing our best skills and experience to the table."

They are looking pointedly at Jess, and she feels a wave of anger rise up at the indignity. Just because she's still a student doesn't mean she's inexperienced.

Penn has started yammering about stuff he's helped the FIC with, but Lyle cuts him off.

"I'm not talking about you, I'm talking about her," they say, nodding in Jess's direction.

Penn looks at her in surprise. "Jess is the best shifter at the Academy," he says. "You can ask anyone there and they'll tell you. No one else even comes close."

Jess suddenly feels like she's taken a wrong turn and her brain is recalculating. Penn is talking up her abilities? The same abilities she used against him for two years? It makes no sense.

And where did he come up with the idea that she's the best shifter at the Academy? To her knowledge, he's never seen any of her classmates' skills; it's not like they do public showcases or anything. Maybe Miss Colleen said something to him, but if so, in what context?

"Be that as it may, I still want to know what I'm working with," Lyle says.

Jess's confusion is replaced by anger, slow and

simmering this time. "What do you want from me?" she says.

"A test of your abilities," they say. "Memory shifts, original shifts, touch shifts—assuming you can do touch shifts—"

"I can do touch shifts," Jess snaps.

"Good. It shouldn't take too long, and if you're as good as they say you are, it shouldn't be a big deal for you."

Hot anger courses through Jess's body, swift and volatile. "I am as good as they say I am, and I don't need to jump through hoops to prove it," she snaps, whirling around before she can say something she'll regret. She's halfway down the hallway toward the front door before she even realizes it.

"Jess, wait!" Penn calls, but she doesn't listen.

In a few seconds, she's outside sitting on the front stoop, her body shaking with anger and adrenaline. She doesn't know what's happening to her. The anger came on so fast and unexpectedly, just like earlier in the car, and she feels like she lost control. The feeling scares her.

She takes a deep breath, shaky at first, but she holds it for a few seconds before letting it go. Her exhale is steady, and that fact alone helps to calm her a little. Maybe she's not as broken as she thought.

The screen door squeaks open, then shuts with a bang. Now Penn is sitting beside her, concern written on his face.

"Hey, um, are you all right?"

"I'm fine," Jess says, hoping he'll go away. His presence, as usual, is making things worse.

"You don't seem fine," he notes.

"Oh, sorry, let me put on my 'I'm fine' face." She plasters on a fake smile, eyes a little too wide and teeth a little too many. "Is that better?"

Penn shrinks back. "That's creepy. You look possessed."

Jess smiles, for real this time. "Thanks! I try."

Penn laughs at that, and though Jess would never admit it, it makes her happy to have made someone laugh. Even if it's him.

"Seriously, though," he says, looking at her, "you seemed pretty upset back there. If you want to talk about it—"

Penn is the LAST person Jess would want to talk to about what she's feeling. He's a fairy; he could never understand. He's just not capable.

"I'm fine," Jess repeats. "Just—it's been a rough day. I'll be fine."

"Oh," Penn says, looking away. "I'm sorry."

It occurs to Jess that he may have assumed she was referring to their argument in the car earlier. Her instinct is to correct him, to say it wasn't his fault, but wouldn't it be? She had used "rough day" as an excuse for behavior she doesn't even fully understand, but if it was true, wouldn't it be his fault?

She leans forward, putting her head in her hands. It's all so confusing, and it's really hard to think with him right there. She wishes he would just go back inside and let her sit for a minute to figure things out.

"It's pointless," Penn says, "what Lyle's asking you to do. I mean, I get where they're coming from, but Talia wouldn't have chosen you if you weren't the best option."

Jess raises her head. "She wouldn't have chosen me if I wasn't her daughter."

Penn looks at her. "Does it matter? Sure, you were born with her magic in your blood, but it was up to you to develop it and hone your abilities. She didn't do that for you."

"She didn't do anything for me." At least, not when Jess needed her.

Penn's lips tighten before he speaks. "I wouldn't judge her too harshly."

"Whose side are you on here?"

Penn holds up his hands in defense. "Hey! No sides. We're all on the same team, aren't we? We all want to help Della and stop McCreed's plan, whatever it is. We have to work together."

Della. Jess has been so wrapped up in her anger, she's forgotten what they're here for. Shame floods through her. Della's all that matters. Not Jess's anger at her mom, not Lyle's dumb test, not the annoying fairy sitting next to her. She's here for Della.

"I get where you're coming from, though," Penn continues. Jess doubts that but is interested to see what he'll say. "It's frustrating, having your abilities questioned all the time. You work so hard, and..." He waves his hand, like a bird flying away. "For some people, it's never enough."

Jess is fairly certain Penn has never worked a day in his life, especially on his abilities. Still, he's actually managed to correctly nail down some of what Jess is experiencing. For a fairy, that's mildly impressive.

"It's not just being questioned," she says, "it's the tests. Do you know how much they test you at the Academy? It's constant. They test you when you start, to gauge your power index. They test you in class. They test you outside of class. Practical tests, written tests, field tests, you name it. It's exhausting."

"Isn't that what school is?"

"Yeah. School. This isn't school," Jess points out. "I passed all those tests just to prove I'm good enough to be here, and now they want to test me again? What's the point?"

Penn shrugs. "You don't have to do it, you know. The test. We can leave, find a way to complete the mission ourselves. We don't have to stay here."

This takes Jess by surprise. She'd expected Penn would try and talk her into it; suggesting they ditch the mission guidelines and go it alone is the last thing she thought she would hear from him. But here he is, casually suggesting outright insubordination just because she doesn't want to play Lyle's games. She feels a grudging sort of appreciation for the suggestion, even though it isn't feasible.

She shakes her head. "We don't know our way around McCreed's castle like they do. And without that device, I can't travel to the fairy realm. Not to mention, it would take a lot of time and planning to successfully pull something off by ourselves, and we don't have time."

Penn looks away toward the deserted street. "So you're going to do it, then?"

Jess unfurls her legs and lets her feet rest on the step. "Della's in danger. I don't have much choice, do I?"

"There's always a choice," Penn says. He stands up and heads to the door, pausing before he opens it. "Coming?"

"You go on, I'll be there in a minute," she says.

"Suit yourself." The screen door opens, then shuts with a bang.

Jess spends another minute breathing in the warm air and feeling the sun on her face before she too gets up and heads inside.

She hears low voices coming from the living room. It sounds like they are arguing, which seems odd. When she enters the room, Penn and Lyle stop talking. Penn looks agitated and Lyle just looks vaguely bored.

"Glad you could rejoin us," they drawl. Penn retreats from the couch and stands off to the side of the room by the armchair, his arms crossed and a frown on his face. Lyle sets some photographs facedown on the table.

"I'm going to start you off easy with half-shifts," they say. "Then we'll move onto full shifts. You can use stored shifts for those. A couple of times, I'm going to call out the name of a celebrity—don't worry, they're ones you would know—and you'll do a half or full shift into them. Then we'll do some image shifts, by sight and by touch. Do you understand?"

"Yes," Jess says, her voice flat and emotionless.

"Good. Let's do it."

And so it begins.

* 5 *

AS MUCH AS JESS HATES BEING TESTED, SHE actually loves shifting. She loves the process of taking on another appearance: capturing it in her mind, analyzing and replicating tiny details, and figuring out movement and expressions to make it as authentic as possible. When she was first learning, it took her forever to master each step; now it's second nature.

Above all, she loves continuous shifting. It doesn't have much practical application, so Jess only ever does it for tests, but she loves the fluidity of it. The smooth flow between forms is exhilarating.

It takes a couple shifts for Jess to warm up, but from there, she gets into the rhythm and lets it take her away. It's almost like a dance, one shift flowing into the next like moves in a sequence, each held just long enough to be distinct before the next one starts.

The half-shifts are easy, frames of film that flit by on the screen that is her body. Since they're only illusions, they take minimal energy or effort to maintain and melt smoothly into one another. Jess's body is a blank canvas and they are her decoration.

Full shifts are next, and she has fun with these, twisting and morphing her body into different forms. Full shifts are more difficult to learn and can be painful at first, but Jess has been practicing for so many years that her muscles, bones and body are used to it now. The energy expenditure is much higher than the half-shifts, but that's to be expected. Full shifts are much more demanding, and the effort to switch between them isn't minimal.

A few times during the full shifts, Lyle calls out celebrity names, and Jess easily switches mid-shift to capture them. It's not even a conscious effort at this point; her ears hear and her body becomes.

Next it's on to photo shifts, which Jess breezes through—first by sight, switching quick as the snap of a camera shutter, then by touch, closing her eyes and downloading the data into her body with a tap of her finger. The dichotomy between the two types is evident when she does them back-to-back; sight shifts are the easiest to learn and how most shifters start, while blind image shifts are the most difficult. It wasn't until Jess came to the Academy that she realized they were even possible, and it took a not-insignificant amount of time and effort to master them.

To finish things off, Lyle instructs her to go through some of her original shifts, ones she's created herself. She keeps her eyes closed and starts shifting through some of the more complex ones, the ones she's most proud of. She's aware she's showing off, but right now, she doesn't care. It feels good to let loose, to let her talents fully envelop her, surrounding her, protecting her. She's fully in the zone now; nothing can touch her. Not the demands of her teachers, the callous remarks of her classmates, nor any unexpected or unwanted bursts of emotion.

Her form may be shifting, but her mind and soul are made of stone. Nothing can touch her and nothing will break her.

Fabric rustles as something moves in the room, and Jess opens her eyes to see Penn, still standing off to the side, but his arms are uncrossed now. An expression crosses his face, so quickly she doesn't recognize it, and it seems like he's mouthing something, but she's so in the zone that what he's saying doesn't register. She's looking to Lyle to see what their reaction is when something speeds toward her, so fast she can't even tell what's happening.

A shooting pain erupts in her abdomen and she crumples forward, the wind knocked out of her. She feels a hand on her shoulder and Penn is at her side, muttering something faintly that she can't decipher because she's too focused on trying to breathe and the PAIN, what happened? And suddenly it's gone and she can breathe again and she can hear Penn saying "I'm sorry I'm sorry I'm sorry are you okay? I'm really sorry" and she realizes he was mouthing "I'm sorry" before the pain hit, right before he punched her in the stomach.

"What the frost was that for?" she yells. She's still in the form she had been shifting into, but now she shifts back.

"To test if you can hold a shift under pressure," Lyle says matter-of-factly. "I have to say, you've performed quite admirably. You've passed the test. Well done."

Jess doesn't care about the test. She's reeling from the shock of being hit. She had thought she and Penn were getting along now—how could he do something like that?

He says "I'm sorry" again and offers a hand to help her up, but she swats it away and stands on her own.

"Any more 'pressure tests' you want to inflict on me?" she snaps. "Maybe hold me underwater for a bit, see if I can hold a shift while drowning? Or get Penn to break a bone next time, that would be a real test."

"If it's any consolation, he didn't want to do it," Lyle says.

"Like I care what he wants," Jess snaps. "Where's my room? I want to be alone."

Lyle tells her, and without another word, she turns and leaves the living room. As she heads down the hall to the room she'll be staying in, she rages internally at both of them. At Lyle, for being cruel and unyielding and for making someone else do their dirty work, and at Penn for actually doing it. Once inside the room, she closes the door and sinks down against it.

This whole assignment isn't what she expected. She thought it would be straightforward; it seemed that way when Miss Colleen had explained it, and since she already knew one of the other members of the team, she thought she had some idea of how this was going to go.

But she hadn't accounted for Lyle, or Penn's strange behavior, or being tested on an essential part of herself. She feels like the mission is spiraling out of control already, and it's barely even started.

There's something wet on her cheek, and the sensation makes her pause. Is she bleeding? She wipes her cheek with the palm of her hand, then looks at it, expecting to see a smear of red. But there is none, just water. Is she *crying*?

The realization scares Jess more than if she'd been bleeding. She never cries, not since her dad died. What is wrong with her?

She wills herself to stop. She needs to pull it together; this assignment can't go wrong, it just can't. If something happens—to Della or anyone else—she'll be done for. Neither Miss Colleen nor her mother will write her recommendations, and she'll end up an infomercial actor, or worse, a teacher at the Academy. And that's assuming she would ever recover from the mission. She doesn't know if she can take another loss.

Great. Now, on top of her haywire emotions, she's reopening old wounds again. After she had been doing so well. She tries to shut out the negative thoughts, but she can't help thinking that today's events don't bode well for the success of the mission. She thinks of how Penn had seemed concerned for her, even presented himself as an ally, then immediately turned around and punched her in the gut right after.

She had thought maybe, after their fight in the car, some of the tension had eased and they might be able to get through this assignment without killing each other. It had certainly seemed that way outside on the steps. But she had thought wrong, apparently, and Penn's betrayal hurt more than the punch itself. She was wrong to think she might find any allies on this mission. The only real ally she has is Cat, but she can only do so much. No, Jess is just going to have to go it alone, like she always does.

Her resolve hardens and she gets to her feet, unsteady at first but quickly regaining her bearings. She looks around the rest of the room. It's plain, with a nondescript nightstand, lamp, desk and chair as the only other furniture besides the bed. A window looks out into the backyard, and Jess goes over to it.

The backyard is as plain and unassuming as the rest of the house. The yard backs up to a wooded area, and Jess does a double take when she notices a small path partially hidden by trees, running behind the houses.

It looks like freedom.

Without pausing to consider, she opens the window and climbs out. No sooner do her feet touch the ground than she is across the yard and into the trees. She hesitates on the path, debating on which way to go, before deciding on the left, which looks to lead to a less populated area. She takes off at a run.

It's glorious. The mid-afternoon sun peers through the foliage, the air hums with the calls of birds and cicadas, and a light breeze plays with her hair as she runs. All her troubles seem to melt away until all she can feel is her heartbeat and her feet hitting the ground.

After about fifteen minutes, she reaches a bridge spanning a small creek. Just over the bridge and to the left is a small clearing on the bank of the creek, and in the clearing is a large flat-topped rock, about a foot taller than Jess and as wide as a dinner table.

Jess crosses the bridge and heads over to the rock. The edges are rough, and she's able to find foot and handholds, which she uses to climb it.

Once atop the rock, Jess looks out over the creek and the path. Standing, it's like she's in the trees themselves, and it reminds her of the dorms at the Academy. A pang of homesickness hits her out of nowhere, and for a second, she wishes she was back at school.

Just as quickly, she pushes the thought away. Only yesterday, all she wanted to do was leave the Academy. Now she's wishing she could go back? She takes a second to remind herself of all the things she doesn't miss—the high expectations, the "handle with care" treatment, the feeling of being trapped and locked into a destiny not of her choosing—and it helps her banish the sentimental feelings. Good. She doesn't need any more distractions.

She takes a deep breath, then lies down on the rock and closes her eyes. The sunlight is warm and it feels good to be able to relax, at least a little bit. The warmth, the fresh air, and the distance help her thoughts become clearer, although they don't totally relieve the tension she feels.

She still doesn't know what to make of Lyle. She didn't know what to expect from meeting a grown sibling; maybe some kindness? Curiosity? But Lyle doesn't seem to have any interest in her outside of what she brings to the assignment. It scares Jess a little to know they're related. Lyle's existence seems so lonely; all alone in their weird house with no one to keep them company except their own paranoia. Jess hopes she doesn't end up like them in the future.

Then there's Penn. He told her out on the steps that they're all on the same side, but it certainly doesn't feel that way to Jess. It's pretty clear he, Lyle, and Jess's mom are on one side, and she is on the other, alone like usual. Of course, it was ridiculous for her to even imagine he might be on her side. She's a nobody, or worse than a nobody; she, a mortal child, embarrassed him and made him look like a fool. There's no way he would ever pick her side; his pride wouldn't allow it.

Jess turns over the day's happenings in her mind, analyzing them in the context of this latest event. It makes sense to her why Penn would go along with Lyle's plan, but what's tripping her up is why he was trying to be nice to her, particularly out on the steps. What does he have to gain? And, more broadly, what does he have to gain by participating in this assignment at all?

Miss Colleen said Talia hand-picked each of them for this assignment...maybe he wants something from her? A position at the FIC, perhaps? It would explain why he was trying to be nice to Jess; maybe he thinks that will help him win Talia's approval. Jess doubts that. But punching her in the gut doesn't align with that theory...

She exhales in frustration. There are so many layers to this assignment, so many more than she expected. If she sits here trying to analyze everyone's motives, she's going to drive herself crazy, getting nowhere in the process.

She takes a breath, listening to the trickle of water in the creek below. What would it be like to not go back? She could follow this creek, see where it takes her, and never have to go back to any of it. She could be free.

But that's the easy route, a voice says in the back of her mind. It sounds an awful lot like her dad. *The easy route will take you away, but it will never take you farther. It's a distraction, not a solution.*

Jess sighs. She knows what she needs to do. It was just wishful thinking, imagining she could disappear without a care. She has a job to do, and she needs to see it through to the end. After the day she's had so far, though, she thinks she's earned this little break.

An hour later, Jess emerges from the trees and crosses the backyard to the open window. She climbs through and closes it, only looking back briefly at the path. With a sigh, she summons her suitcase and backpack, though she doesn't unpack. There really isn't a point if they'll be gone tomorrow. She gets out her book and reads until she senses Penn in the hallway. Sure enough, there's a knock on the door a second later.

"Dinner's ready," he says.

She wants to wait until he leaves to come out, but she's too hungry to care about being petty right now. She passes him without a second glance.

Dinner is spaghetti with meatballs and garlic bread. Simple but very good. Penn tries to engage her in conversation a couple times, but she doesn't join in. Just because he apologized doesn't mean she can forgive him.

Instead, she listens to Penn and Lyle swap stories. For every story of a perilous escapade Lyle shares, Penn has a story of meeting a historical figure or being at a famous event. Their stories are actually quite interesting and entertaining, although Jess would never admit it. She does feel a bit left out, though, because even if she did join the conversation, what could she offer? Everything interesting that's happened in her life has been bookended with misery. She doesn't want sympathy.

Eventually, dinner ends. Silently, Jess helps clear away the dishes, avoiding Penn. After that, she goes to her room and calls Cat.

"So how's it going so far?" Cat asks as soon as she picks up. "Tell me everything."

Jess can't lie to her. "It's kind of awful." She gives Cat a brief recap of the day's events, and Cat responds with appropriate shock or agreement.

When she gets to the part with the test and Penn punching her, Cat freaks out.

"He PUNCHED you? For a test? That's so messed up," she says. "Who do these people think they are? First off, that's like, child abuse, since you're a minor, and second off, this isn't some top-secret government thing where anyone would need to do that kind of testing."

"Well, they're sure acting like it is," Jess said. "I wish I could tell you what we're actually doing, but it's serious stuff." She sinks to the floor and leans against the bed. "That's part of why it's so awful. If I mess up, or anything goes wrong, there are serious consequences. This isn't some field practice for class. Not to mention, I've already been on one failed operation. I can't afford to have another one."

"Jess, no one blames you for what happened before," Cat says.

"I know that!" Jess takes a deep breath. "I just...I

need this one not to go wrong. I need those recommendation letters from my mom and Miss Colleen. If this mission isn't successful, I'm not going to get another chance. And it already seems like it's off to a bad start."

"Hmm," Cat says. "I wouldn't make a call based only on what happened today. Tomorrow's a new day and a fresh start. I'm sure things will look better in the morning."

"I hope you're right," Jess says.

After ending the call, Jess reads a bit more before gathering up her toiletries and heading to the bathroom to get ready for bed. She's in the middle of brushing her teeth when she senses Penn in the hallway. He stops by the bathroom door and stays there.

Jess fumes. Only hours ago he was claiming he's not a stalker, and what's he doing now? Creep. She doesn't feel threatened by him—incredibly, he never seems to intend to harm anyone, with the exception of punching her earlier—she just feels annoyed.

Like all fairies, he seems to have no concept of personal space, or that people might not actually want to talk to him. Fairies all have grandiose opinions of themselves and how others see them, so it's inconceivable to most of them that someone might dislike them or want to avoid them.

Just to mess with him, Jess draws out her routine as long as possible, since she knows he has next to zero patience. It's petty, but she doesn't care. He made her life a living hell for two years;

she can irritate him for twenty minutes.

Finally, she leaves the bathroom, and sure enough, there he is.

"Look, Jess, I'm sorry. I can explain—"

"I don't want your explanation. Leave me alone."

Jess turns and goes into her room, shutting the door firmly behind her. He doesn't move at first, but then she senses him head down the hall to his room.

She opens her backpack and pulls out the small bottle she got from Celia. There's enough in the bottle for three nights, but thankfully she'll only need it for one. She sets her alarm, then sits on the bed and pours out a capful of the purple liquid. She swallows it down quickly. It tastes like lavender and flowers. Carefully, she screws the lid back on and puts the bottle away in her backpack. She turns off the light and lies down.

Within a few minutes, she starts to notice the difference. For the first time since eight this morning, the tension in her body is completely gone. Her heartbeat slows to a resting rhythm and she breathes a sigh of relief.

She doesn't like that she has to take a potion to be able to sleep, but that's the only safe way she knows how to quiet that unwanted sixth sense. If she could get rid of it, she would, but she doesn't even know how to explain it to someone, let alone figure out how one might get rid of it. So she will be stuck the rest of her life knowing when Penn is within a mile radius of her. Such a helpful ability.

She drifts off to sleep and dreams peacefully and uninterrupted. It's the best sleep she's had in months.

* 6 *

JESS WAKES TO THE SOUND OF HER ALARM, which is currently set to "relaxing bird call," because anything louder, more annoying, or more grating would not be tolerated by her dormmates. She doesn't mind it, though. It reminds her of a toy her dad gave her as a kid—a nest of stuffed birds that chirped when she squeezed their tummies.

She doesn't know what happened to that toy. For all she knows, it's gathering dust in her old bedroom, along with the rest of her childhood belongings. Or her grandmother could have gotten rid of everything and sold the house. She doesn't know. She never went back after she ran away.

She gets up and shifts her outfit, changing into clean jeans, a T-shirt, and a lightweight but warm jacket. She puts her boots on and stows her suitcase and backpack. It's much easier and safer to be able to stow them magically than haul them out to the car and leave them there.

She leaves her room and heads to the kitchen, where she can already hear Penn and Lyle moving about.

When she enters, Penn eyes her over the rim of his coffee mug but says nothing. Jess is secretly satisfied. It seems he's received the message.

Lyle looks up from rinsing a cup in the sink and says, "Good, you're up." They turn off the water, wipe their hands on a towel, and pass Jess a bowl from the counter. It's full of raisin bran. "Milk's in the fridge," they say. "Eat fast."

Jess doesn't understand why she needs to rush when they still have forty minutes before they leave, but she doesn't argue and eats the cereal. When she finishes, she makes a quick stop by the restroom, and when she returns, she heads to the living room, where she finds Penn and Lyle waiting, discussing shifting into wicht forms as Lyle packs a small black backpack.

"As with any shift, the face is the most important," Lyle is saying as they tuck a flashlight into a side pocket. "If you get the face right, people will ignore most other discrepancies. But if something's off with the face, it gives that uncanny valley effect and puts people on edge. You don't want them on edge around you."

Jess is on edge around Penn all the time, but that has less to do with any uncanny valley effect and more to do with the radar sense he triggers.

Penn is nodding along eagerly as Lyle talks. Jess is surprised he isn't diligently taking notes like a schoolboy, but it's likely fairies have some sort of enhanced memory abilities she isn't aware of.

"With wichts, the hands are important, too," Lyle continues. "You need to get the finger shape right, and you always have to do a full shift on the hands because the shape is different from ours. If you do a half-shift and try to pick something up, it won't look right because the way they hold things is strongly affected by the anatomy of their hands."

Jess finds this all very fascinating and is interested to hear more, but Lyle is interrupted by a loud beeping noise emitting from the FIC device, which is sitting on the coffee table.

"Ten minutes to go," they say, sliding a slim black case into the backpack and zipping it up. "I recommend taking this time to do some mental preparation. Things might move very quickly when we get there."

They swing the backpack over their shoulder, then close their eyes. Penn glances over at Jess, then does the same. Finally, Jess closes her eyes.

She isn't sure how she should be "mentally preparing." She guesses it might help to try and clear her mind, but she's never been good at meditation. Instead, she thinks of a few calming songs and runs through them in her head. Whatever benefit that might have, though, is negated by Penn's presence.

The last of the potion's effects dissipated when

she woke up, and the radar sense is back in full force. Honestly, if the sense did anything besides alert her to Penn's presence, she wouldn't mind it so much, but no, it only works on him.

Another alarm blares from the device, this one louder and more urgent. The noise startles Jess, and she attributes the involuntary reaction to the effects of the unwanted sense. The sense keeps her body on constant high alert against her will, and Jess knows heightened anxiety is the main cause of jumpiness.

There's a reason a class on relaxation techniques is part of the standard curriculum—the last thing you want is an intelligence officer who jumps at the drop of a hat—but the lessons never covered how to counteract an inexplicable, magical fight-or-flight response. If Jess ever figures it out, she'll offer to do a guest lecture.

The device shows they have two minutes remaining, and Lyle has them place their hands on it early as a precaution.

"Not always reliable," they grumble by way of explanation.

It's very awkward to be crammed so close together, everyone holding onto the device with both hands. (Another precaution, to prevent anyone from being left behind.) Jess is trying to avoid both touching anyone else's hand and looking at Penn, so she stares at their hands instead.

She tries to pay attention to the details, as if she was planning to do a sight shift into either one of their forms. Lyle's hands have a square shape to them, and their fingers aren't much longer than hers. They have the weathered appearance that comes with age, but are solid and steady.

She knows what to expect when she looks at Penn's hands; he's a fairy and can modify his appearance at will like she can, so they'll look inhumanly perfect, like hands cut from a marble statue and brought to life.

She could do the same thing with shifting—make herself look like an airbrushed model from a magazine cover, hide every freckle or hair out of place—but she doesn't. That's a trap she doesn't want to lose herself in. Fairies are different, though. They aren't human and they want you to know it.

Jess looks at Penn's hands anyway, just as a mental exercise. She's thinking of the marble statues again, but...they're just regular hands. Fingers, knuckles, wrists—there's nothing "magical" about them. Weird.

She wonders if this is his "human" disguise. Many fairies take more subtle forms when in the human world, although what fairies think is "subtle" and what the rest of the world thinks are two different things. Penn's lived in the human world for a long time, though, so it would make sense that his human form would fit in better.

The device buzzes again, and now it's counting down. Fifty-nine...fifty-eight...fifty-seven...

Jess's anticipation rises as the numbers go down. She's finally going to get to see McCreed's palace. She's finally on a proper mission at last. She feels the rush of energy she always gets when she's about to use her powers, and it excites her.

Three...two...one...

It feels like she's being pulled inward and she's afraid she's going to collide with the others, but that doesn't happen. Everything twists around them for an instant, then rights itself, and they all fall away from the device into a fresh dusting of snow.

Jess looks around, her breath forming a cloud in front of her. They must be in the forest near McCreed's palace. Tall pine trees, their branches encrusted in snow and ice, rise up to meet the gray sky. Jess has never been to this part of the Realm before, but that familiar rush of new energy, like the air itself is charging her up, lets her know she's once again in the homeland of the fairies.

Around them, everything is still; there is no sign of wildlife or any sort of activity other than the three of them. They all stand up and brush the snow off. Lyle stoops down and picks up the device where it had fallen when they arrived and puts it in their coat pocket.

"Right then," they say. "One of us needs to scout ahead and see how far out we are from the palace, and get a read on the activity there. If there are a lot of guards on duty, we're going to have to come up with a better strategy."

Jess opens her mouth to say she'll go when Penn beats her to it.

"I should do it," he says. "That'll be safest, and I'll be quick, too."

So this is how it's going to be. Penn and Lyle will do all the important stuff, while Jess is left on the sidelines. Just like at the Academy.

And Penn's smug face—he's so SURE of himself, so sure that he's the best choice, the most important one on the team. Jess sees his face, sees that proud posture, and all she can see are her classmates, basking in their pride as they were chosen over and over again for assignments she would never get. She sees their faces and she laughs; at them, at Penn, at herself for thinking this was her chance. None of it means anything.

"A brilliant plan," Jess says, before she can think twice. "We'll send you bumbling through the woods, alerting McCreed and all his wichts that we're here. Then they can kidnap us, too, and we'll easily find Della's location as they lock us up in the cells next to hers. Truly a strategy to be proud of."

As soon as she's said it, Jess knows it was a bad idea. Sure, he's a selfish, double-crossing creep, but she doesn't need to deliberately make him angry.

It's too late now, though. She's poked the bear—or, rather, horse—and he's not going to take it lying down.

"We could send you," he says, words sharp and eyes flashing, "except you'd probably run off and we'd never see you again."

A low blow, and one that hits a little too close to home.

"Well, you've got one thing right at least," Jess snaps. "If I did run off, I can guarantee you'll never see me again. You could barely track me when I was ten; you don't stand a chance now."

Penn opens his mouth to respond, then pauses, like he's heard someone call his name in the distance. Lyle takes the opportunity to step between them.

"That's enough," they say. "Here's what's going to happen. I'm going to scout ahead, and while I'm doing that, you two are going to sort out whatever's got you at each other's throats so you can settle down and focus on this mission. Remember I said you need to be at the top of your game? This isn't a cage match. So whatever's got you two up in arms, sort it out now. You need to have each other's backs when we go in, or we're not going in at all. Clear?"

Jess and Penn both nod, properly chastised.

"Good," Lyle says. "While you're at it, please don't alert the whole forest we're here. I didn't put in thirty years in deep cover only to get compromised in retirement by you two."

With that, they turn and head toward the palace, leaving Jess and Penn to work things out—or, more likely, fight to the death.

Once Lyle is out of sight, Jess turns away from Penn. Lyle's remarks have yanked her out of her haze of anger and now she feels hollow again. Something's wrong with her. What was she thinking, provoking Penn like that? It doesn't even feel like her. She's been a master at keeping her emotions in check since she was young, but ever since she was put on this assignment, something's been different. She feels like she's slowly losing control and it scares her. She needs to keep it together, for Della and for the sake of the mission.

There's a large rock nearby; she brushes the snow off the top and sits down, her back to Penn.

There's a soft crunching sound as he digs his toe into the snow a couple times, then a deep sigh.

"I'm sorry," he says. "I shouldn't have said that, about you running off. That was completely uncalled for."

There's a long pause, and she's not sure if he's waiting for her to respond or trying to figure out what to say next. She's not sure if she cares.

"Look," he says finally, "I know you don't want to talk to me, and I'm not asking you to. But would you be willing to listen?"

Jess doesn't move for a minute. She's sick of excuses. She's sick of being hurt. But she also knows they have to work something out so they can complete this mission. Della is counting on them. So she nods.

"Thank you," he says. She hears him sit down on something as well, probably a tree stump.

"I didn't want to hurt you, I promise I didn't. I argued with Lyle; I said it was a bad idea and I wouldn't go along with it, but they said it had to be done for the mission. They said they would send you back to the Academy and you wouldn't be on the mission if I didn't do it."

Jess turns around at this. "They were going to send me back?"

Penn nods, and she can see the truth in his expression. "That's what they said."

He looks down at his hands, which, strangely,

look exactly the same as before they left. Jess wonders briefly why he hasn't taken on his fairy form now that they're in the Realm.

"I know this mission is really important," he continues, "not just for Della, but for you, too. I didn't want to be the one to take the opportunity away from you." He looks back up at her. "I tried not to put too much force into it. I hope it didn't hurt too badly."

"You knocked the wind out of me and it felt like I got hit by a train."

Penn looks shocked. He puts a hand over his mouth and looks away from her for a few seconds, as if collecting himself. Then he looks back up, visibly upset.

"I'm so sorry. I didn't mean—I wasn't trying—"

His voice trails off and he looks lost for a second. Jess almost pities him. Almost.

"Never again," he says. "I will not raise a hand against you again, I swear it on the Crown."

Jess wants to ask how he can swear on the Crown if the Crown exiled him, but now doesn't seem like a good time. And it seems the Crown doesn't care that he's an outcast, because a golden light flares briefly around him after he makes the oath, then fades.

"I can't change what happened, but I won't make the same mistake again," he says, his face solemn. "I won't hurt you."

Jess doesn't know how to tell him there are many ways to hurt someone beyond the physical, so she says nothing.

Footsteps sound and they both turn to see Lyle returning.

"So," they say, brushing snow off their sleeves, "you two get yourselves figured out?"

Penn glances over at Jess and she nods. "Everything's fine," he says.

"Good. Palace is about a quarter of a mile away. Guard looks pretty light; we shouldn't have an issue getting in around back. Let's get a little closer and then we'll stop and do shifts."

Lyle turns back the way they came, and Jess and Penn follow. They hike through the trees for a little bit until they reach the edge of the forest. The ground slopes gently in front of them and, for the first time, Jess sees McCreed's palace.

The entire palace is made of ice, like a sculpture at a fancy party, but bigger and harsher. The architecture isn't like that of the fairies, which has an organic, flowing quality to it, while still feeling intentional. McCreed's palace feels wilder, the geometric patterns and lines descending gradually from order into chaos. Having visited the fairies' palace, Jess can say this one is the more interesting of the two.

"All right, you can look while we're walking," Lyle grumbles. "Let's do the shifts. I'll do mine first, then you two copy it, but modify it. Make the nose a different shape, the ears a little bigger, you get the picture. Ready?"

Jess and Penn both nod, and Lyle shifts. Jess steps forward and touches their shoulder to grab the shift. She steps back and closes her eyes, focusing on the parts she wants to change. She can hear Penn stepping away as well, and a rustling noise as Lyle removes something from their pack. When she opens her eyes, she sees they have a pair of binoculars and are fixing them on the palace walls, where a few wichts can be seen standing watch. Thankfully, they are still under the cover of the trees, so they aren't visible from the palace.

Penn says, "Well? How did I do?"

Jess turns to look. He's gotten some parts right—the diminutive stature, the grayish-blue tint to the skin, the thin, bony limbs—but the rest looks wrong. The proportions are off and everything looks kind of squished, like a child tried to mold a wicht out of Play-Doh and gave up.

"You look horrible," she says.

"Gee, thanks," he says with a grin, which makes his shift look even more grotesque. "You don't look too pleasant yourself."

"No, like that's not a good shift."

Lyle puts the binoculars down and looks at Penn. "That is a truly terrible shift. Jess, help him out with that, please." They go back to scanning the palace walls with the binoculars.

Jess sighs and goes over to where Penn is standing. "Don't move," she says.

"I won't."

She starts to work her magic, reshaping the form of the illusion to make it more realistic. It's been a while since she's edited someone else's shift—it's not something they spend a lot of time on in her classes—but the process is not that different from editing her own. Penn closes his eyes as she works, which she's grateful for because this is awkward enough already.

"I hope you're making me an attractive wicht," he says.

"Sure. The handsomest wicht that ever lived. The lady wichts will swoon at your ear hair and massive feet."

"You're giving me ear hair?" he says.

"All the male wichts have ear hair. It's a point of pride, I hear."

Penn opens his eyes and glares at her while she fixes his jawline. "You better not be pulling my leg."

"She's not," Lyle says. "Ear hair is considered a desirable trait among wichts. The bushier, the better."

"Wonderful," Penn says.

Jess finishes her work and steps back. "There. You're ready."

Penn opens his eyes. "What do I look like?"

Jess touches his arm and assumes the shift, holding it for a couple seconds before returning to her wicht shift.

"That's...disturbing," Penn says, and she's not sure if he means the wicht form or her shifting.

"If you two are done messing around, we should start heading down there," Lyle says. "Penn, you can cloak us, right?"

"Of course."

"Good. I'll take the lead, you take up the rear. Make sure to erase our tracks as we go. Once we get inside, we'll be in the back room, which is typically empty. We'll take a minute to regroup, then split up for the search." They take one last look through the binoculars, then wave Jess and Penn forward. "All looks good. Let's put up the cloak and head out."

With a wave of his hand, Penn puts up a cloaking spell. The three of them are inside it, so they can see each other, but outsiders won't be able to. They can't really see the spell either, but Jess can tell it's working because the edges of her vision blur as they move.

The closer they get to the palace, the more Jess's anticipation grows. She's only been waiting for this moment since she decided she wanted to become an FIC officer years ago. If she'd imagined as a tiny freshman that she would be here right now, it would have made the years between so much more bearable.

As they draw near to the palace walls, Lyle leads them around the back, where they find a loading dock. They climb the stairs, and Lyle tries the smaller door next to the huge dock door. It's locked, so Lyle waves Jess forward. She summons the pouch where she keeps her lockpicks, a gift from her mother.

While most lockpicks leave marks or scratches on the lock mechanism, making it clear the lock has been picked, these lockpicks are enchanted to leave no trace. They also make no noise and automatically size-adjust for whatever lock she uses them on. They were a surprisingly thoughtful gift from someone who wanted no part in Jess's life until she was twelve.

Jess picks the lock quickly, and they're inside in less than a minute. The dock is connected to a warehouse-like storage area, and Lyle leads them up a set of metal stairs to the upper level, where they weave their way through rows of shelves to find a discreet spot to confer before they each go their separate ways.

"Okay," Lyle whispers when they stop. "As you saw from the map, this place is huge. We don't have time to search everything, so we need to prioritize. Based on my experience with McCreed, it's most likely he's holding Della in the dungeons. If I had to hazard a guess, I'd say he's probably got one guard down there, maybe two if he's got more than one prisoner."

"Who else would he have down there?" Jess asks.

Lyle shrugs. "Likely no one. Maybe a wicht if he's in a foul mood. He never used the dungeons much when I was here, but we should be prepared for anything."

"I can take the dungeons," Penn says. "I can cloak myself and sneak up on the guards, and if Della's hurt or sick, I can help heal her. It makes the most sense."

He glances at Jess as he says it; whether on purpose or reflexively, she doesn't know. She isn't going to argue with him this time, though. Even she can admit his reasoning is valid.

Lyle nods. "I agree. You take the dungeons. You must remember this, though—if I'm wrong and McCreed has anyone besides Della down there, you must leave them there."

Confusion crosses Penn's face. "Why? Shouldn't we rescue them, too?"

"No." Lyle turns to look at Jess. "Jess, why would that be a bad idea?"

Jess was not expecting to be put on the spot like that, but she thinks quickly. "Because it could be a trap. The other people could be wichts McCreed's disguised, or illusions. If you try to help them, not only would it be a waste of time, but it would immediately alert McCreed that we're here."

"Good," Lyle says. "And if you were Penn, what would you do if there were multiple captives?"

Jess has done thought exercises like this in class; a teacher will give them a scenario and a hypothetical team, and each student has to come up with a strategy to accomplish the objective. This is her first time doing one with potential real-world consequences, though.

"The first thing I'd do is weave a spell to make everyone in the vicinity drowsy." It's not a spell she's capable of, but it's a standard piece of general magic that would be no problem for a fairy. "It doesn't need to be strong enough for them to fall asleep, just to see who reacts. An illusion wouldn't react, but people and wichts would.

"Once I knew who was real, if it's not clear which one is Della, I'd approach each cell carefully while still cloaked and use my abilities to pinpoint which individual has magic levels that align with Della's. He could have her on drugs to disguise her magic"—a tactic Jess knows is used by undercover officers stationed in McCreed's palace—"but it's very unlikely he'd take it that far. Once I knew which one was Della, I'd put everyone else to sleep, unlock the door with the guard's key, and rescue her. If I had the time, I might even leave a brief illusion in her place to confuse the guards when they wake up, so no one realizes immediately that she's missing."

When she finishes, Penn is staring at her, surprise evident on his face.

"Not bad," Lyle says. The corner of their mouth just barely quirks upward. "Straightforward, easy to follow, no mess. A solid plan."

Jess doesn't react, but inside she's elated. Lyle may be gruff and a little cruel, but they're still the most experienced person in the field Jess has ever met, apart from her mom, so their approval carries undeniable weight.

"Okay," Penn says, "if there's more than one person, I'll follow that. What if the others are real captives, though?"

"In that unlikely event, you still have to leave them," Lyle says. "Our objectives are clear: rescue Della and uncover evidence of McCreed's larger plan. Anything else is a distraction and will endanger the mission."

Jess agrees with Lyle; what they're saying aligns with what was drilled into her in class. The objective takes priority, no exceptions. Penn doesn't look happy with it, but he doesn't argue.

Lyle turns to Jess. "You should take McCreed's

study. If he's working on any plans, that's where the evidence would be. I'll head to the kitchens and see if I can pick up on any gossip from the other wichts. They might have some insights on what he's up to."

Lyle holds up their wrist, where a watch appears briefly before disappearing just as quickly. "It's 8:35 now. Jess, you and I will leave first, to get a head start. Penn, wait here for ten minutes, then head to the dungeons. That should give Jess and I enough time to find something before we have to get out of here. We'll assume another ten minutes for you to extract the girl, and all plan to meet back here by nine. Got it?"

Jess and Penn nod.

"Good. Now let's go find the girl and get out of this overgrown freezer."

They quietly head back down the stairs, although the dock seems to be empty. There are a couple doors leading out into the hallway. Penn drops the cloaking spell, and Lyle exits through the far door. Jess waits a minute, then heads out the closer door, leaving Penn to wait in the frigid dock alone.

As she heads toward McCreed's living quarters, Jess is grateful not to be the one going to the dungeons, for a few reasons. The first is she's scared of what she might find. She's not sure what she could do or say to comfort the girl if she found her, and she doesn't have Penn's healing abilities to help Della if she's injured or sick.

Second, the most important and dangerous

part of the mission is getting Della out. If something happened or went wrong, Jess wouldn't be able to live with herself. Third, she's actually curious to see what McCreed's palace is like, and the dungeons (or the kitchens, for that matter) wouldn't give her a very good idea.

She travels the hallways quickly but carefully—she can't turn invisible, so she has to avoid the other wichts as much as possible to prevent them from noticing she doesn't belong. She is forced to duck into hallways several times to hide from them before stumbling across an abandoned cleaning cart, which she commandeers to use as a further disguise. With any luck, anyone else she passes will only see the cart and ignore her. It also gives her a "purpose" for being in certain areas of the palace where she otherwise might be questioned.

The wing housing McCreed's living quarters is empty; McCreed must be in the throne room, which Lyle said is where he spends most of his time. Jess finds the study door easily (she memorized the map they had been given) and, after checking the hall in both directions, ducks down behind the cleaning cart and picks the lock.

The first thing that surprises her about the study is its size. The map didn't reflect how large it is, or maybe it's enchanted to be bigger on the inside, Jess isn't sure. It's as much a study as it is a laboratory, library, and studio, all rolled into one.

It's also a mess; clutter covers every surface and collects in the corners, and there seems to be no rhyme or reason to the placement of any objects.

The second thing that surprises Jess is that the study seems to be abandoned. Everything is covered in a thick layer of dust. Bottles only hold dried and congealed remains of their original contents, and the air is musty and still. Jess doesn't think anyone has used this room in a long time.

She searches it anyway; after all, that's what she's here for. She does her best not to disturb the dust, but it's unavoidable and she knows it will be obvious someone has been in the room—if anyone checks it within the next year or so.

She searches the drawers and shelves, but she doesn't find anything pointing to an active plot or scheme against the fairies. A couple documents detail inventions or spells that *could* be used against the fairies, and she takes pictures of them for the FIC, but if McCreed has an overarching plan for world domination or the like, there's no sign of it in his study.

In a last ditch attempt, she summons the basic magic detector ring her mom gave her for her thirteenth birthday and tries to use it. It's not very strong, but it can pick up concealment spells and a few other types of magic as well. Fairies can use spells to detect even small traces of magic, and even half-fae can learn to do so with training, but Jess doesn't practice general magic beyond basic spells, so she has to use the ring.

She walks around the room once again, waving it at any place she suspects something could be concealed, but doesn't find anything until she passes the wall behind the desk. When she waves her hand over the rightmost portion, the detector pulses with a blue light, indicating a concealing spell is present.

Jess at least knows how to reverse a basic concealing spell, and she hopes that's all it is. She whispers the incantation and, with a wave of her hand, the paneling on the wall vanishes, revealing a map. Pins are stuck in it in various locations, although none of them are labeled, so she has no idea what they mean. Something seems odd about the map, but she can't quite put a finger on what it is.

Tacked next to the map is a grainy photograph of a baby. Jess looks at it closely, but there's nothing particularly interesting about it, and no features that could be used to identify who the baby is or where the photo was taken. It's definitely not a photo of Della, so it's unlikely to be connected to the mission, but Jess snaps photos of it and the map anyway, then restores the concealing spell. At least she'll have something to show for their efforts, although, based on the state of the study, it doesn't appear that the concealed map has anything to do with current events.

Jess leaves the office, checking to make sure the door is closed and locked behind her. When she looks up again, she sees, to her horror, that another wicht is standing about ten feet away, staring at her. Fear rises in her stomach before she recognizes her own handiwork.

"What are you doing up here?" she whispers.

"Della wasn't down there," Penn says, walking

over to where she's standing. "I came to let you know. I figured I'd get you first and then we can find Lyle."

Jess grabs her cart and starts pushing it toward the main part of the palace. Penn follows. "How about you?" he asks. "Did you find anything?"

Jess spots the room she is looking for—a linen closet. She looks around and, seeing no one else, opens the door and waves Penn inside, following him and shutting the door. He waves a hand and a ball of light appears, glowing over their heads.

"Are you trying to jeopardize this assignment?" Jess hisses.

Penn recoils. "What? No, of course not!"

"Then why are you up here? You could have blown both our covers just now. If anyone heard you—"

Penn's face pales. "I'm sorry, I wasn't thinking."

That much is obvious. "You should be. If this goes wrong—"

"I know!" Penn moves like he's going to run his hand through his hair, but tugs on his ear instead. "It's just...does this seem a little off to you? Everything feels kind of weird. Have you noticed there are barely any other wichts around? It doesn't feel like McCreed is prepping for some grand scheme. Have you found anything?"

Jess's initial anger fades a little as she contemplates his words. He's not wrong; she had the same feeling in McCreed's abandoned study. Something isn't right here.

"I found a map and a picture of a baby," Jess

says. She shows Penn the photos. He's interested in the one of the baby, but when she asks him if he recognizes it, he says no.

"Were there any other clues? Anything that stood out?"

Jess shakes her head. "The place was full of junk. Really dusty junk."

"Like no one uses it?"

"Exactly."

"It was like that downstairs, too. I was expecting a dungeon with holding cells, guards, captives—but it wasn't like that at all."

"What do you mean? What's down there?"

"It wasn't even a dungeon, it was like a regular basement. And it was weird; the stuff that was in it—well, it's not relevant. Nothing helpful." His brow furrows. "I really don't know what to make of all of this. It doesn't make any sense. If McCreed kidnapped Della to start a conflict with the fairies, why is this place so dead? And where is Della?"

"Maybe he has a secret bunker for war planning or something," Jess suggests.

"I doubt it," Penn says. "Not much about McCreed is secret. I suppose he could have her hidden in a different part of the palace to throw us off, but we don't have time to search the whole place before we have to meet up with Lyle again."

Jess thinks for a moment before the idea strikes her. "We don't have to search the whole place. We just need to find McCreed. I bet if we observed him for a bit, he'd do or say something that would point us in the right direction."

Penn hesitates. "I'm not sure that's a good—"
"Do you have a better plan?"
Penn says nothing.
"Let's go find him, then."

* 7 *

IT'S NOT A DIFFICULT TASK. MCCREED IS where he normally is—seated on his ice throne in the throne room, surrounded by groveling wichts. Jess and Penn sneak in through the back and stand behind the curtains that serve as a backdrop for the throne. They can hear every word McCreed says, and Penn casts a quick spell so they can see through the curtain, although McCreed is blocked from view by the back of the throne.

"These are all hideous," McCreed says, and Jess and Penn can see he's referring to fabric samples supplied by the wichts. "Are these stolen cleaning rags from the fairies? Because that's what they look like." He lets out an exasperated sigh. "Why do we need new dining room curtains again?"

"The old ones were destroyed, sir," one wicht says.

"Destroyed? I liked those ones!"

"But, sir, you said you *didn't* like those ones, so you ripped them down and tore them to shreds," says another wicht. The other wichts glare at him, clearly certain they are about to be berated for his error.

But McCreed just sighs. "That's right, I did shred them. I remember now." Another sigh, this one longer. "It doesn't matter anyway; it's not like I ever have any guests. If I'd known when the fairies confined me here that I would be spending my days reviewing curtain samples, I would have begged them to kill me instead."

The wichts all look at one another. They don't know how to respond to this.

"Enough of that doom and gloom, though," McCreed says, clapping his hands. "We need some excitement around here. Something to spice things up a bit. A party, perhaps, or maybe a performance. Why don't you all come up with some ideas, and we'll reconvene at four to discuss."

The wichts practically fall over themselves in their haste to give their bows and "yessirs." As they scramble to exit, Jess pulls Penn out of the throne room into the hallway behind.

After checking to make sure it's clear, she whispers, "I think we have this all wrong."

"What do you mean?"

"I'll explain when we get back to the dock," Jess

says. "Lyle needs to know, too."

But when they arrive at the dock, Lyle isn't there yet. They go to the upper level to wait. Jess does a quick shift to check her watch; they're on time, but Lyle is late. A few minutes pass and Jess is starting to get concerned when they hear the dock door open. Penn gives Jess a look of relief. They hear footsteps coming up the stairs and Penn is moving toward them when a voice rings out from below.

"Make sure they're SALTINE crackers," a wicht shouts. It's not Lyle, and neither is the wicht who responds.

Penn looks back at Jess, fear bright in his eyes.

"Cloak us," Jess mouths, making a gesture like a cloaking spell. Penn understands and performs the spell. They're no sooner cloaked than the wicht rounds the corner and heads down the aisle they're standing in. Jess fits herself into an empty space on the bottom shelf, but Penn doesn't have the same luxury on his side of the aisle. He flattens himself against the shelving so the wicht won't run into him.

The wicht, who is dressed in pressed black pants and a white shirt like a waiter, stops in front of the shelf Penn is blocking. To Jess's horror, she realizes the boxes behind Penn's right shoulder are saltine crackers. If the wicht tries to grab them, he'll hit Penn's shoulder, and Penn can't move without alerting the wicht to his presence. He's trapped and, from the looks of it, panicking.

Jess quickly scans the shelves around her.

There has to be something she can do. She looks beside her, then behind. The shelves are open, so she can see through to the next aisle. Without pausing to think, she pushes the items stacked next to her into the other aisle. The heavy paper bags hit the frozen floor and burst, filling the air and covering the aisle in fine white dust—flour.

The wicht whips around, looking toward the other aisle. "What was that? Bez, was that you?"

"Was what me?" yells the other wicht from below.

"That noise!" The first wicht is moving away from Penn's shelf now, and Penn takes the opportunity to inch to his right, away from the wicht.

"Whatever it is, I didn't do it," Bez yells.

"You better come up here and help me check it out. If another one of those frost possums got in here, I'm not dealing with it alone."

Jess doesn't know what a frost possum is, but it doesn't sound pleasant.

"Fine," Bez snaps. Footsteps clang up the steps, and the wicht in their aisle heads to meet his comrade.

Jess takes the opportunity to grab Penn and pull him to the end of the aisle, where they stand with their backs pressed against the cold wall. They can hear the wichts bemoaning the mess in the next aisle.

"That was close," Penn whispers. "Thanks for saving me."

Jess turns her head to look at him. "No offense,

but why didn't you just shrink down and fly away? It would have been an easy escape."

Jess knows the popular myth of fairies as tiny, winged creatures didn't come from nowhere; some say it was even their original form way back when the first fairies came into existence, before they evolved and took on more human-like forms. Regardless, it's something every fairy can do, so Jess is surprised it wasn't Penn's first reaction.

Penn's cheeks color, and he bows his head. Even disguised as a wicht, his face is easy to read. "I didn't think of it. It's been a long time since I've done that. I guess it isn't my first instinct anymore."

His face may be easy to read, but the rest of him is still a puzzle to Jess. She's starting to realize, for all her assumptions and the rumors she's heard, there's a lot about this fairy that she doesn't know.

"It all worked out," she says. She can hear the wichts sweeping up the flour in the next aisle. "This is why my mom sent a team of us. So we can help each other in tough situations."

Penn lifts his head. "Speaking of teams, where's Lyle?"

Jess had almost forgotten about their third member. "I don't know. Maybe they saw the other wichts and they're waiting for them to leave?"

"Maybe," Penn says. "I hope they had better luck than us."

A few minutes later, the two wichts finish cleaning up the flour and head down the stairs. The door bangs shut behind them as they leave the dock, and Jess and Penn step away from the wall. Jess's back is freezing, and she moves her arms and shoulders to get the blood flowing again. Penn copies her movements, even though she's pretty sure he's not cold. One of the many perks of being an immortal fairy.

The door opens again below them, and they both freeze. This time it's Lyle, though, whom Jess recognizes from their clothes as they come up the stairs. Penn drops the cloaking spell.

"Where were you?" he asks. "We were almost caught by a couple wichts just now, waiting up here."

"Got held up," Lyle says, rather evasively in Jess's opinion. "Where's the girl?"

"I didn't find her. She wasn't in the dungeons, which, by the way, aren't dungeons at all—"

"What?" Lyle looks genuinely confused. "What's he got down there, then?"

"Nothing important. Point is, Della wasn't there, and Jess didn't find her, either. She did find something else, though, and I think she has a theory about what's going on."

They both look at Jess expectantly.

Jess starts by explaining what she found (and didn't find) in McCreed's office, then recaps what she overheard.

"So what's the theory?" Lyle asks when she finishes.

She takes a deep breath. She doesn't know how either of them are going to take this, but she has to get it out there.

"I don't think McCreed took Della at all."

The reaction is immediate. Lyle looks skeptical, like they think the idea of McCreed not having taken Della is highly unlikely. Penn looks confused and a little outraged. Jess forges on.

"It doesn't make sense," she says. "Why is he picking out curtain samples and complaining about being bored if he's holding a hostage and about to start a war with the fairies? Unless you found evidence to the contrary, it seems unlikely that he's taken her."

Lyle shakes their head. "I tried to get in on the gossip and none of the wichts said a thing about captives or an upcoming war. In fact, I didn't get anything useful from them at all. It seemed suspicious to me, too."

Jess is proud that she picked up on it and glad they are all in agreement at last, although she's not sure yet what they're going to do about it. Then Penn voices a more important concern.

"If McCreed didn't take Della, then who did? And where is she now?"

They are all silent for a minute.

"We need to find that out," Lyle says.

"How?" Penn sounds more agitated now. "We have no idea where she could be if McCreed doesn't have her, and we have absolutely nothing to go on. How would we ever find her?"

Lyle shrugs. "We can't. We just report our findings back to the FIC, and they'll have to figure it out. We've done our part; it's out of our hands now."

"So we do nothing? We're just going to give up?" Penn's voice is rising, and Jess is nervous they are going to be overheard if he doesn't pipe down.

"Keep your voice down," Lyle hisses. "We're not giving up, we're following the directive. There's nothing more we can do here."

"Yes, there is," Jess says, and Penn and Lyle look at her like they have just remembered she's there. Lyle looks unimpressed but Penn looks almost hopeful, which she figures she must be interpreting wrong because it makes no sense.

"We can ask McCreed to help us," she says.

A beat of silence, then Lyle bursts out laughing. "McCreed, help us find a missing girl? Mister Master Thief himself? The fairies' greatest enemy? You've got to be joking."

Jess is perfectly serious. "I think it could work."

Penn looks at her. He's not laughing. "How would you do it?"

Jess explains her plan. When she finishes, Penn looks thoughtful and Lyle looks skeptical, but at least they're not laughing anymore.

"We might be able to pull it off," Penn says.

Lyle shakes their head. "Too risky. We can't do it. Besides, McCreed will lock us up immediately for violating the treaty. Even Mom couldn't get us out, I bet."

It's weird for Jess to be reminded in this moment that she and Lyle share a parent.

"If we play it right at the gate, we can make him want to see us," she says. "Do you want to find Della or not?"

Penn sighs. "I don't like this plan much, but Jess is right. Time is of the essence, and we need all the help we can get." He tugs on his ear. "I don't seriously think McCreed will help us, but he might be able to give us an idea of who might have taken her. As for the risk, well, I am a fairy. He'd be hard-pressed to capture us. I've got a few tricks up my sleeve yet."

He looks at Jess as he says it, and she can tell he still feels bad about freezing in front of the wicht. She just hopes that if it comes to it, he's prepared this time.

"I don't like this at all," Lyle grumbles. "I didn't spend thirty years safely in deep cover in this dump *and* make it out only to get caught by some high schooler's hare-brained scheme."

Rage rises hot and sharp inside Jess, and she opens her mouth to respond, but Penn is faster.

"You can stay behind if you want," he says sharply, "but I, for one, am going to do what I can to help Della, even at risk of capture. She deserves to have at least one person with the FIC who actually cares that she needs help."

Lyle rolls their eyes, but finally concedes. "If this goes wrong, though, remember that you're the one who convinced me, not the other way around," they say to Penn.

As they trudge back around to the front of the palace, Jess pulls Penn aside. "You don't need to stick up for me, you know. I can stand up for myself."

"What?"

"Back at the palace. When Lyle insulted my plan, you interrupted and took care of it before I could even say anything. I don't need you to fight my battles for me."

Penn looks surprised. "I didn't even realize I was doing that," he says. "Sorry. I talk a lot when I don't always need to. I'll try and do better."

"Thanks," Jess says. She doesn't think he'll remember—he's a fairy, after all—but at least he acknowledged he was wrong.

* 8 *

WHEN THEY REACH THE FRONT GATES, LYLE lets Jess take the lead. At her signal, Penn drops the cloaking spell and they approach. The wicht guards are not paying attention, so Jess has to pull a rope to ring the bell and announce their presence.

"Who goes there?" shouts one of the wichts. He shoulders a crossbow and aims it at their group.

"We're representatives from the FIC," Jess says, holding up her hands. They had agreed it would be best not to misrepresent themselves. "We've come for an audience with Murdoch McCreed."

"That's Erlkönig McCreed to you," the wicht snaps, "and if this is about the missing girl, the Erlkönig has nothing to say to you."

"He's using that title again?" Penn mutters. "He

hasn't used that for at least a century."

Jess isn't familiar with the title, but she doubts it's relevant, so she doesn't respond.

"Yeah, he already told the wings he doesn't have her," another wicht chimes in. "So shove off!" This one is armed with what appears to be a spear gun, which he waves threateningly at them.

Penn looks at Jess uncomfortably and Lyle mutters, "I knew this was a bad idea."

Jess thinks the situation can still be salvaged. She takes a breath to calm herself, then looks back up at the wichts.

"We're not here to get information from him," she says. "We're here because we have information for him."

The first wicht's eyes narrow. "What kind of information?"

"The kind we think he'll want to hear."

"Tell me what it is and I'll give him the message. He doesn't want to see you."

Jess shakes her head. "No can do. Our orders are to give the message to the Erlkönig himself. If we can't get an audience, we're leaving."

"Well then, leave!" the second wicht says. "He doesn't want to talk to you anyway."

Jess tilts her head. "How do you know? Did you ask him?"

"I don't have to. He told us he doesn't want to talk to wings, and especially not spook wings. So go away before we make you!"

"All right, let's go," Jess says to Penn and Lyle, turning away from the palace.

"What are you doing?" Penn hisses. "I thought we were trying to get in to see him. Why would we leave?"

"I told you this wouldn't work," Lyle grumbles. "At least they haven't locked us up."

"We're not leaving," Jess whispers. "Watch." She raises her voice so the wichts can hear her. "Boy, I sure wouldn't want to be in the room with McCreed when he finds out FIC representatives were here to tell him something and got turned away!"

The wichts, who had been laughing and fist-bumping each other, fall silent.

"I bet he'll be absolutely furious!" Jess continues. A slow smile blooms on Penn's face as he realizes what she's doing.

"Oh yeah, I hear he's really big on punishment," he says loudly. "He'll probably make everyone responsible do some really horrible chore, like scrubbing the whole exterior of the palace with toothbrushes!"

"You are both insane," Lyle mutters. "You're going to get us shot."

Jess is fairly confident that the wichts won't risk attacking them and slightly more confident that Penn would be able to deflect any shots that might come their way. Regardless, if they back down now, they'll have nothing to show for the mission and nothing to help Della. It will all have been a waste.

"Or he could make them serenade him at dinner every night for a month!" Jess calls.

The wichts are muttering amongst themselves

now. Jess thinks they've almost got them.

"Or maybe they'll have to feed bird livers to the ice wolves!" Penn adds. "By hand!"

"They probably wouldn't have hands after that," Jess responds.

"WAIT!" The three of them turn to see the first wicht, a panicked look in his eyes. He's lowered his weapon and no longer looks remotely intimidating. "Fine. We'll go tell him you want an audience. But quit saying all those awful things! You're going to give him ideas!"

"Okay," Jess says. "Go tell him. We'll wait. But if you take too long, who knows? We might come up with some more ideas."

The second wicht turns to the first. His weapon is still aimed at them, but his hand isn't on the trigger. "Are you sure about this? The boss was pretty clear. He said absolutely no spook wings. They are definitely spook wings." He gestures at Jess's group with the spear gun.

"There are exceptions to every rule," the first wicht says. He grabs the second wicht by the front of the shirt and shoves him toward a small door behind them. "Go tell him about the spooks. See what he wants to do. He's in a good mood today; I'm sure he won't turn you into a lemming this time. But hurry up!"

The second wicht leaves, and the first one turns around, crossing his arms to try and appear tough.

"No funny business from you three down there!" he snaps. "You'll wait quietly or you won't get your audience!"

Penn smiles and gives him a thumbs up. "Got it!"

"QUIETLY!" the wicht roars. Jess tries not to laugh.

A few minutes later, the second wicht returns. He confers quietly with the first wicht, who turns back to look down at Jess and the others.

"Erlkönig McCreed has granted you an audience," he says, lips puckered in distaste. He pulls the lever to open the gates. Jess and the others walk inside, where they are met after a moment by the second wicht, who is out of breath from having run down the spiral staircase to the left of the doors to get to them.

"This way," the wicht says, taking the lead.

They cross a small courtyard before entering the palace itself. Jess looks around with interest as they pass through the corridors to get to the throne room. She hadn't been in this part of the palace when they were searching for Della and the evidence. It's clearly the more formal part, with high, vaulted ceilings and angular pillars stretching up to meet them.

The lighting is natural, coming from skylights up above, and it makes the pillars, which are covered in a fine layer of frost, glitter like diamonds. Jess finds this interesting, since none of the other hallways or rooms she'd been in earlier had used frost as decoration. It's very cold but pretty at the same time.

When they arrive at the doors to the throne room, the two wichts guarding it stare at them openly. Jess supposes not many fairies make it into the palace. The guards open the doors, and the wicht leading them strides into the room.

When Jess and Penn had been in here earlier, concealed by the curtains at the end of the room, Jess had been focused on McCreed and hadn't really noticed the rest of the chamber. Now she does, and it's even more formal and impressive than the hallway.

The same glittering columns rise to meet a far more elaborate ceiling, which is tiled with beautiful concentric geometric patterns in shades of blue, purple and white. A large chandelier hangs down from the center of the circle, but it isn't like any chandelier Jess has seen before. It looks rather like a bare tree sculpted out of ice and turned upside down. At the ends of the twisted branches, tiny white flames glow steadily.

Jess tears her eyes away from the chandelier to look at the rest of the room. It's almost as minimally decorated as the hallway, but the walls are covered in embroidered hangings. Each one depicts a different winter landscape design, some featuring wildlife like snow-white foxes and ice wolves. All are embroidered in white and silver on a deep blue background, and Jess can't help but admire their craftsmanship.

Finally, her eyes land on the throne and the figure seated in it.

McCreed is tall and lean, and his skin is a pale blue, almost translucent. His face is angular and his dark hair appears frozen in place. He looks like he could be any age from late twenties to mid-forties, but Jess knows he's much older than that.

The most striking part of his appearance is his eyes, which are a bright, piercing blue. They are ringed in shadows, giving him a sickly look while also making his eyes stand out even more. He is wearing a cobalt blue three-piece suit and lounging on his throne, but when the group stops in front of him, he sits up with interest.

"Well, well. What do we have here? Wait! Don't tell me; I want to guess." His piercing eyes analyze each of them in turn. "Hmm. Half-fae, fairy, another half-fae. An interesting mix." His eyes scan over them all again, then snap back to Penn. "I know you. I don't know them."

Jess can hear distaste in his voice. She doesn't know what his history is with Penn, but it doesn't sound like it's positive. She steps forward. "I'm Jess, and this is Lyle. We're from the FIC."

"Come to harass me about that girl again? I already gave my response to the FIC, and I refuse—"

"We know you don't have Della," Jess interrupts. "You never did."

McCreed pauses, surprised, then a smile blooms on his face and he throws his hands in the air.

"Finally! They've sent someone with a bit of sense! No, I don't have her. What would I want with a half-fae girl, anyway? But of course, the fairies always have to blame me for every little misfortune that happens to them."

"That's because they're usually your fault," Penn says. Jess wants to elbow him so he'll shut up, but Lyle is between them, preventing her from reaching him.

McCreed's expression sours as he looks at Penn. "Which fairy are you again? I know we've met, but it seems I've blocked that unfortunate memory and I can't recall which one you are. I don't like your attitude, though."

"Look," Jess interrupts, trying to get the conversation back on track. "I know you don't have Della. But someone's doing a pretty neat job of framing you. I just want to figure out who it is so I can find her. Do you know anything that could help?"

McCreed looks back at Jess, suddenly more interested.

"Find her, you say? Do you find people often?"

"I've been trained in advanced-level tracking and investigation techniques," Jess says. This is true—she took those classes last year and received top grades in both. This will be her first time using them in the real world, though.

McCreed leans forward with a gleam in his eye. "Do you think you will actually find her?"

Jess has no idea. She doesn't know what the scope of this assignment even looks like now that they know McCreed doesn't have Della. But she doesn't think that's the answer McCreed is looking for, and she feels it's important to project confidence.

"I believe so, yes."

The room is so silent, Jess thinks Penn and Lyle must be holding their breath like she is. A drop of water could fall from one of the icicles decorating McCreed's throne, and Jess would be able to hear it.

"Hmm," McCreed says, leaning back on the throne. He appears to be thinking deeply, then snaps back to reality and looks at the others. "You two, out. I want to speak with her alone."

Penn looks outraged. "Absolutely not! We are not leaving her alone with you."

Jess wants to scream in frustration. They made it this far, and now McCreed is going to throw them out because Penn can't keep his mouth shut.

To Jess's surprise, though, McCreed doesn't get angry. Instead, a slow smile appears on the Erlkönig's face.

"Oho! I do remember you now! You're *that* fairy!" He laughs to himself. "I thought it was odd you weren't wearing your wings. Now it makes sense! Why don't you, by the way? I've always been curious."

"None of your business," Penn snaps.

Jess had wondered why he doesn't wear his wings, too, but she's never asked, and it seems like it's a touchy subject. She turns to him. "You can go. I'll be fine."

"That's *Murdoch McCreed*," Penn hisses, as though McCreed's not sitting twenty feet away listening to every word they say. "He's the fairies' worst enemy. If we leave you alone with him, you might be the next one we have to search for!"

McCreed has started cleaning his fingernails with a chip of ice. "Hurry up and go before I change my mind! You don't want me to get angry."

"I'll be fine," Jess repeats. She looks to Lyle, pleading with her eyes. If anyone would understand how important this conversation could be, it would be them. They need to get Penn to back down before McCreed gets angry and kicks them all out.

Lyle grabs Penn's arm.

"She'll be fine," they say. "Come on, let's go."

They lead Penn toward the doors, and he looks back, the question in his eyes. Jess mouths "Go" and finally they both leave, with the wichts following close behind and pulling the great doors shut. Jess turns back to McCreed, who smiles.

"Glad we got that taken care of. I really do hate fairies. You *are* half-fae, right?"

Jess nods.

"Good." McCreed drops the piece of ice. "That means you're half-something-else, which makes you automatically better than a fairy in my book. Do you know how annoying they are? Always coming here accusing me of this or that, or telling me what I can and can't do. It's actually quite refreshing to have someone come and accuse me of *not* doing something. Finally! Some variety!"

"I know you didn't take her, sir," Jess says carefully, "but do you have any idea who did?"

She should feel nervous, alone with him with Lyle and Penn gone, but she feels strangely calm instead. She can do this.

"No. I'm mightily ticked off that they're framing me for it, though." He sighs. "I wouldn't be surprised if it was the fairies themselves again."

Jess spots her opportunity. "Whoever it is must want to cause a fight between you and the fairies. I mean, think about it. They did a pretty thorough job of making it look like you took her, and they probably figured the fairies would think you're lying. It's the perfect storm."

McCreed leans back on his throne. "It certainly is. Girl goes missing. Fairies blame me as usual. Fairies think I'm lying because they always think I'm lying. Fairies attack." He shakes his head. "I hate war more than I hate fairies, and I *really* hate fairies."

"We have the same goal, then," Jess says. "Prevent a war in the Realm."

"Well, I wouldn't mind a nice little apology from the fairies for wrongly accusing me. But yes, I suppose our goals are in alignment." He stares off into the distance over Jess's head, clearly thinking. The corner of his mouth starts to creep upward; whether that's a good sign or bad, Jess doesn't know.

"I can't promise an apology from the fairies, but if we find Della, that will clear your name and prevent a war," Jess says. "You can avoid fighting and avoid the fairies. All you have to do is help us find her."

McCreed snaps out of his musings and looks taken aback. "Me, help you? What would I do that for?"

His immediate negative response surprises Jess. She'd thought the ramifications of not finding Della were pretty obvious.

"Um, war? Angry fairies? Needless conflict and bloodshed?" She takes a more serious tone. "Look, sir, my team—we don't have anything to go on right now. We can go and look for evidence, but by the time we find anything useful, it could be too late. If you can help at all, we will be able to find Della and clear your name that much sooner."

"Too late for what? It sounds like the fairies, as usual, have no clue what's going on. How do you even know she's been taken? What if she's run away? She could be perfectly fine, off with one of her little friends."

"She's not," Jess says. "The kidnappers left a message in her family's apartment, carved in frost. It said 'Come and get her.' That's not something a runaway does."

"Oh, I see how it is," McCreed says. "The fairies see a little bit of frost and they immediately think I'm responsible." He rolls his eyes. "Whoever did this has a good understanding of how fairies think, then. Tell me, are they running an internal investigation, too? Checking to make sure it wasn't one of their own?"

It hadn't occurred to Jess that a fairy could be responsible. She doesn't think that's likely, but she's curious to hear what he thinks.

"Why would a fairy do this?"

"For exactly the reasons you stated before. To have an excuse to start a war with me. I know they're still furious they didn't finish me off the first time; I wouldn't be surprised if they're ready to try again."

Jess is unsure what "the first time" refers to; it's been a while since she took the "Introduction to Fairy History" class, but she thinks she'd remember learning about a previous war between McCreed and the fairies.

"Sir, all due respect, but I don't think the fairies are looking to instigate a war," Jess says.

"Okay, say I believe that. I don't, but for argument's sake, say that I do." McCreed leans forward, an elbow resting on the armrest of his throne. "That doesn't mean it's not a fairy. Just because the fairies as a whole don't want a war doesn't mean there aren't a few dissatisfied ones who would love to watch the world burn." His eyes slide to Jess as he says this. Did he somehow pick up on her dissatisfaction with the fairies, or is he just being dramatic?

"That's a possibility," Jess says cautiously, "but it seems unlikely. The fairies tend to follow the Crown to a T. There isn't a lot of deviance from the norm."

It's one of the things that annoys her about fairies—how they always have similar opinions on everything.

McCreed gives a wry smile. "Oh really? You're telling me that every fairy is satisfied with how the Crown is running things over there? That not one of them would be angry enough at the Crown to do something about it?" He leans back, folding his arms and tilting his chin up smugly.

"What about your fairy friend out there? I remember his story now. Didn't follow the rules, didn't fit in, now he's exiled. He would have had a home there, a life, and that was taken from him. You don't think he'd be mad enough to do something about it?"

Jess hadn't considered that before. Of course there was a reason Penn had been exiled, and although she doesn't know what it is, it's safe to assume it was because the king and queen were displeased with him. She hadn't considered that he might resent them for it, that he might even want revenge. But even if that was the case, she can't see him taking it this far. She might not like him, but she can pretty confidently say kidnapping a girl to start a war is way out of character.

"Penn didn't do this," she says. "If the FIC even suspected him in the slightest, he wouldn't be helping on the case. And anyway, he's too soft. He could never go through with it."

McCreed smirks. "I don't think there's a fairy in this world that can be classified as 'soft,'" he says. "You of all people should know that, working with the FIC."

Jess doesn't officially work with the FIC, at least not yet, but she's not going to correct him.

"That may be true, but it doesn't matter. Someone took Della, they're framing you, and you can help us find her."

"How would I do that? I don't have any special insights to give you, and if you haven't noticed, I'm stuck here. I can't leave." His voice is bitter. "Besides, not my kid, not my problem."

"Not your problem? You're being framed to start a war. Like it or not, you're involved," Jess says. "And what if it is a fairy? Wouldn't you like to catch them in the act?"

McCreed looks down at her, eyes narrowed. "Who did you say your fairy parent was again?"

"I didn't." The sudden change in subject is off-putting. Jess doesn't know where he's going with this, but it's probably not good.

Another smirk crosses McCreed's face. "Ah, let me guess, then. The FIC tends to be a family business, so it must be someone there. That limits my choices."

He stands up and steps off the dais, coming over to Jess and looking at her closely. He circles her once, an icy breeze following in his wake, then pauses, stepping back and holding his hand to his chin as if pondering.

"Hmm...a tricky one," he says. "It's all so familiar; the way you talk, the way you carry yourself, and all that magic just radiating off of you...must be someone pretty powerful."

Jess still doesn't know where he's going with this. His face is unreadable, as is his tone. She starts to wonder if maybe Penn was right to be concerned.

"It's her, isn't it?" McCreed says. "The leader. Shapeshifter, intense gaze, kind of scary."

"Talia," Jess says. She's not heard her mother described as "kind of scary" before, but it fits.

McCreed's smirk widens into a grin that reminds Jess of a wolf baring its teeth. "So, Talia sends her daughter into my territory to ask for help. My, my, she must be desperate!" He clasps his hands together and bounces on the balls of his feet. "This is good. Very good. A daughter of Talia...you must be very talented."

His words and gaze are unnerving. Jess starts running through escape plans in her mind just in case things go south.

"I'm not that talented," she tells him. "Very average, really."

McCreed laughs. "Don't be modest. With that amount of power, there's no way you're average. I know how they train you at that little school, and the FIC is even better. Flawless little espionage machines, every one of you. It's perfect!"

Jess gets the bad feeling she's miscalculated. Clearly McCreed has a plan of his own, and she's walked right into it of her own accord. "What do you want from me?"

"Oh, you misunderstand me, young Jess," he says, turning and walking back toward his throne. When he reaches the dais, he turns to face Jess as he steps onto it. "I don't want anything from you now. No, all I want is to know how I can help you with your mission to find this missing girl."

Jess's mouth almost drops open in surprise. A minute ago, she was afraid he was going to kidnap her, and now he's offering to help? His behavior makes no sense, but Jess isn't going to let his change of heart go to waste.

"Well, we're at a bit of a standstill right now," she says. "Since you don't have her, our focus will be on finding who actually took her and where they're keeping her. If you have any way to help with that..."

McCreed sits back on his throne with a thoughtful expression. "I'm not sure..." He ponders for a moment, then stands up. "Wait a second. There is one thing. Or things." His demeanor brightens and he seems almost excited. "I created them a while back but haven't found a use for them yet. Maybe you can figure one out. Follow me!"

* 9 *

JESS FOLLOWS MCCREED DOWN WINDING hallways until they reach a nondescript door. From her best guess, they are not too far from the dock, but she doesn't recall passing this way before.

McCreed pulls a set of keys out of his pocket and uses one to unlock the door. Jess follows him inside and he switches on the lights.

They are standing on a balcony overlooking what appears to be a small warehouse. Jess is not sure how this fits into the architecture or where it was on the plans she saw, but that's not the part that shocks her. That would be what fills the warehouse—rows and rows of what look like humanoid ice statues. They remind Jess of the terracotta soldiers found in the tombs of some

Chinese emperors, and she is afraid of what they might be used for.

"What are those?" she asks.

"They're a clever little invention of mine, really," McCreed says. "They're essentially magical ice automatons. They'll mimic the motions of the person controlling them, and with a pretty significant distance range, too."

"Are they meant for fighting?" Jess asks.

"Pssh, no," McCreed says, waving a hand dismissively. "They'd be useless in a fight with the fairies. Made of ice, see. One heat blast and poof, they're puddles!"

"Why did you make so many, then?"

McCreed shrugs. "I thought I might be able to replace some of the staff, guards and such. But they aren't autonomous and I couldn't find a way to get them to do what I needed them to do. Maybe you could use some, though."

Jess has absolutely no idea how ice automatons might be used to find a missing girl. Maybe they could be used to intimidate the kidnappers? But that would require finding the kidnappers first. Even then, having a few ice automatons who could only mimic motions doesn't seem that helpful.

McCreed is watching her and apparently interprets her silence correctly. He shrugs and says, "I knew it was a long shot, but I figured I'd offer. I'll probably end up melting them at some point when I need this space for something else."

Jess is not sure she wants to know what else McCreed would need a giant warehouse for.

"They're cool, but I don't think we can really use them for this. Not unless they have some magical tracking abilities or something."

"No," McCreed says, tapping a finger to his chin, "but that gives me a different idea."

Before Jess can even blink, he's out the door and halfway down the corridor. She has to run to catch up.

"It'll take some arranging," McCreed says, "but I think this might do the trick."

Jess follows him back to the throne room, where he presses a button on the throne's armrest to call one of his attendants. Within seconds, a thin wicht with abundant ear hair enters through a side door.

"Yes, your majesty?"

"Bring Noe'or to me immediately," McCreed says. "And one of the roomcases from my workshop. That should do nicely."

"Yes, sir." The wicht salutes McCreed, turns on his heel, and hurries back through the door he came from.

Jess doesn't know what Noe'or is, or what a roomcase is, either. If they're inventions, she hopes they're less creepy than the lifeless statues filling McCreed's warehouse.

McCreed has surprised her. He's a little unnerving and she still isn't sure why he changed his mind on helping, but the energy he exudes seems more "mad scientist" than malicious. The way the fairies talk about him makes him seem like the most heinous villain imaginable, but from what she's seen, he seems more sarcastic and quirky than outright evil.

"So Talia is your mom," McCreed says, interrupting her train of thought. "Bet that's fun. Who's your dad?"

"My dad was in the Secret Service," Jess says. Practiced, unemotional. Just the facts. "He died when I was ten. Shot on the job."

McCreed looks at her like he's seeing her in a new light. "Stars. That's horrible. I'm sorry for your loss."

This catches Jess off guard. She shouldn't be surprised; it's a common response. Not one she would have expected from Public Fairy Enemy No. 1, though.

McCreed sits back and stares into the distance like he's recalling something. "My parents are dead, too," he says. "I never knew them, so I guess that's supposed to make it easier. But being alone still sucks."

Jess didn't think McCreed had parents. The fairies don't—they sort of spontaneously form from a buildup of energy—but McCreed isn't a fairy. There's a good chance he's lying just to gain sympathy, but her instincts are telling her that's not the case, and she has a pretty good internal lie detector. She doesn't know what to think.

She's saved from having to respond to McCreed's revelation by the return of the attendant wicht. He's carrying what looks like a pet carrier and is followed by a small wicht with a cartoonishly large nose. Jess looks closer at him and realizes he must be a child. She turns to McCreed.

"I don't understand. What's going on?"

"This is Noe'or," McCreed says, waving a hand at the wicht child. "He's got an incredible sense of smell. Specializes in sniffing out magic, but he's not too bad at tracking fairy blood, either. If you take him to the scene of the crime, maybe he'll be able to pick up the girl's trail."

Jess blinks in confusion. "So you want me to take a child with me in a dog carrier?"

McCreed waves a hand dismissively. "He's not as young as he looks. Wichts age faster than humans, and he's small for his age. And that's not a dog carrier, it's a roomcase."

"What's a roomcase?"

McCreed smiles and Jess realizes she is about to get another invention spiel.

"Well, let me show you!" he says, tapping on the roof of the carrier. It grows until it's almost as tall as Jess's shoulders, and McCreed opens the wire door and steps inside until she can no longer see him. "Come on in and take a look!" he calls.

After a moment of hesitation, Jess ducks inside. When she straightens up, her jaw drops.

The interior of the roomcase looks nothing like a pet carrier. It looks more like a luxury camping tent, with canvas walls and all the amenities one would expect to use when traveling. Jess can even see a small washroom behind a curtain in the corner. She turns to McCreed.

"Isn't it amazing?" he asks before she can say anything. "This is one of my favorite inventions.

Practical yet fun at the same time!"

Jess looks around. A full-size bed, made up with crisp white sheets, is to her left, while a small table with two wooden folding chairs is set up on her right. Behind the table is a little wood stove. The floor is made of sturdy, weathered planks like a deck, and a striped woven rug covers most of it. In the corner next to the washroom, there's even a loveseat, with two big pillows and a blanket thrown across the top as a final touch.

Jess turns to McCreed. "This is really cool. How did you make it?"

"A lot of effort and some advanced spellwork, too. The toilet was a nightmare to set up. Had to figure out a spell to automatically empty it, and then a place for the waste to end up! That was probably the trickiest part, along with supplying the water."

"Where does the waste end up?"

McCreed lets out an undignified giggle. "Ooh, it's fun! Guess."

Jess has no idea. "In the human world?"

"Nope! It's the front lawn of the fairy royal palace!" McCreed lets out a peal of laughter. "I've been dying to have someone test it out; can you imagine the king and queen trying to figure out why there's random poop appearing on the lawn?" He's laughing so hard now that he's practically crying. "Ah, to be a fly on the wall when that happens."

Jess can't help it; she lets out a small giggle as well. The king and queen are so uptight that she can hardly imagine how they might react.

"You're almost doing me a favor, taking it with you," McCreed says. "I haven't had a chance to test it properly yet."

"Why not?"

McCreed shrugs. "Can't leave. That inane treaty the wings forced me to sign keeps me here on threat of death and dismemberment, practically. Really puts a damper on my plans for conscripting an army of humans to do my bidding." He gives an exaggerated frown. "Although I hear they have too much free will to make that plan remotely feasible, so I suppose I'll have to scrap it anyway."

Jess can understand why the fairies would want to keep McCreed away from the human world, but she can't help but think it seems a little cruel, especially since the fairies pop back and forth all the time with no restrictions.

"So, the features," McCreed says, apparently done with the previous subject. "It can obviously change size, as you saw, but there's also a spell on it to maintain equilibrium as it's moved, so things won't knock over as you carry it." He walks over to the wood stove and slaps the side of it. "This bad boy controls the climate in here. See, it's not actually a wood-burning stove, it's powered by magic! So, no fire risk, plus it keeps you nice and toasty in the winter and cool in the summer.

"Anyway, you'll have to tell me how it works and if you have any ideas for improvement," McCreed continues. "Or Noe'or will, at any rate."

He turns and exits the roomcase, and Jess follows.

"It should be very simple," McCreed says when they are both outside. "Just take Noe'or to the girl's last known location, give him an item of hers, and he should be able to guide you to where they've taken her, as long as it's in the human world and they haven't used any enchantments to block her scent."

Jess is still unsure about the prospect of being responsible for the wicht. "What about food and stuff? Is there anything I should know about?"

McCreed shrugs. "Nope, I don't think so. Whatever you eat is fine for him, and everything he would need besides food should be in the roomcase. Just make sure to bring him back when you're done."

Jess notices he doesn't say "when you've found her," and this gives her a sense of foreboding. What if they don't find Della? What if she's dead?

"Oh, and don't feed him after midnight," McCreed adds.

"Why not?"

He waves his hand dismissively, a smile on his face. "Because he'll turn into a gremlin, obviously!"

Jess has to roll her eyes at that. "Got it. Don't feed after midnight, make sure to bring him back. Not a problem."

"Oh, and I wouldn't mind a formal letter of apology from the FIC, too, while you're at it," McCreed says with a sly-looking grin. "Just thought I'd throw that in there."

He turns to the wicht and addresses him.

"Noe'or, you will be going with Jess to the human world. You must listen to and obey her as you would me, and you must aid her in her quest to find the missing girl. Do you understand?"

The wicht nods. "Yes, sir," he says in a quiet voice.

"Good. I want this girl found so the fairies will leave me alone, and you play an important role in that. Don't screw up or mess around, or I will be most displeased." He fixes the wicht with a ferocious glare. "You don't want me displeased."

Just as quickly, he's turned around and is smiling at Jess. "That should cover it. I'd recommend not letting him out of the roomcase unless he's tracking, because he's likely to cause mischief. Force of habit. Other than that, I don't think you'll have any problems with him."

The attendant wicht ushers Noe'or into the roomcase. Once he's inside, it shrinks down to pet carrier-size and the other wicht holds it out to Jess. She takes it carefully, trying not to jostle it too much. She looks back to McCreed.

"Thank you for offering your help," she says. "You've been most accommodating and I'm sure we'll be able to take care of this quickly due to your assistance."

As expected, McCreed looks flattered. "Pssh, it was nothing. And I assure you my motivations were purely selfish. Now let's get you back to your unfortunate acquaintances. Come on, now." He motions her toward the door, following behind.

They walk back through the palace toward the

entrance, tailed by a couple of wicht guards. They find Penn and Lyle sitting on a bench in the courtyard with another pair of wichts standing over them. The two look cold and annoyed, but otherwise unharmed. When Penn sees them, he jumps up and starts toward them before the wichts move together to stop him.

"No need for any of that," McCreed says with a slight edge to his voice, and it's unclear if he's talking to Penn or the wichts. None of them move and Penn looks like he might fight someone. Behind him on the bench, Lyle just looks bored.

Jess adjusts her grip on the roomcase. "We can leave now. We have what we need."

"Yes, exactly," says McCreed. "You are all invited to leave and preferably not come back, with the exception of Jess when she returns my small friend, and possibly by my future invitation."

He gives them all an unnervingly wide smile. Jess isn't sure why she might receive a future invitation from McCreed, but it's likely he's saying that just to irritate the other two.

"What the frost are you even talking about?" Penn demands.

McCreed ignores him. "I'll let my guards see you out," he says cheerily. "Good luck on your mission; I'm sure you'll need it!"

With that, he turns and strides away. The wichts direct them to the entrance and watch as they trek back up the hill to the forest.

* 10 *

"WHAT'S IN THE CAGE?" LYLE ASKS ONCE they are out of earshot.

Jess explains about the wicht. When she's finished, Penn glares at the carrier like it's personally offended him. "I don't like this."

"Neither do I," Lyle says, their eyes narrowed. "Sounds to me like McCreed gave in too easily. He didn't ask you for any favors?"

"No," Jess says. "I just pointed out that he needs Della found just as much, if not more, than we do, and he came around after that."

She doesn't know how to explain his reaction to her parentage and subsequent change of heart, so she leaves it at that.

Lyle shakes their head. "Nothing's ever that

easy with McCreed. He's going to want something from you in return, mark my words."

"I hate that guy," Penn grumbles.

Jess doesn't know what McCreed would want from her, and she's not sure she wants to. Maybe if she understood him better, his behavior would make more sense.

"What's McCreed's deal?" she asks. "How come he lives all the way out here and, you know, does what he does?"

Penn sighs, then reaches out with two fingers and taps the carrier twice.

"What was that for?" Jess asks.

"Temporary muffling spell. He doesn't need to know everything we're saying." He's silent for a few seconds before answering Jess's original question.

"Many millennia ago, there were more like McCreed. I guess the closest term for them in English would be elves, although the loose translation from Old Faerie is 'the cold wingless ones.' This area was their kingdom. But then they decided that wasn't enough and they wanted to rule over the entire Realm, so they went to war with the fairies.

"The fairies were able to hold them back, but they would not surrender. So the fairies drove them into the human world and set up the barrier so they wouldn't be able to attack them again. Trapped in the human world, their magic diminished until they eventually faded away. The only one who remains is McCreed, who was hidden away with wichts when he was born so he wouldn't be discovered.

"McCreed has gone by many names over the centuries, but his goal has remained the same: to get revenge on the fairies for pushing his people out, even though the fairies were just trying to defend themselves and keep the peace after the elves attacked them."

"Makes sense," Jess says. Penn shoots her a look, eyes narrowed.

"Obviously there are a lot more layers and nuances to it," he says. "All of that was before my time, but he's done a lot of things to the fairies since then that are unforgivable. The fairy attitude toward him is rightfully earned."

"Things like what?"

"He used to send groups of wichts to attack fairy houses or set up ambushes, and when the fairies started putting up defensive spells and fighting back, he started attacking their domains in the human world. The fairies blocked him and the wichts from traveling between worlds, which has solved most of the problem, although they occasionally do find ways to sneak through," he says, glaring at the carrier. "McCreed is manipulative and evil and always playing his own agenda. I wouldn't be surprised if he does have an overarching plot for world domination or the like."

Jess purses her lips. "He didn't come across as evil and manipulative. More lonely, I thought."

Penn gives her a sideways glare. "That's how he gets you," he says. "He wants you to feel bad for him and open up so he can prey on your weaknesses and use you. I hope you didn't tell him anything important."

An angry heat rises in Jess's cheeks. "I think I can tell for myself if someone's trying to manipulate me, thanks. Maybe you've forgotten my talents extend beyond shapeshifting?"

That's a jab and they both know it, but to his credit, Penn takes it with surprisingly little fight.

"I haven't," he says, his voice cool but otherwise impassive.

Lyle is the one to break the frigid silence that follows. "You know, I spied on McCreed for thirty years and he never did seem to be as horrid as the FIC made him out to be. It was a pretty easy gig, actually, other than the hard labor I had to do as a wicht. He made a lot of mischief, and the fairies always blew it way out of proportion, but he wasn't the worst to work for."

"What do you mean, blew it out of proportion?" Jess asks.

Lyle shrugs. "They'd take little things and turn them into these elaborate plots that they convinced themselves he was executing. 'Course, this was the eighties and everyone was paranoid, but they were taking it to the extreme. Say, if he'd turn someone's sugar stash into salt, they accidentally drink salty tea, and suddenly it's an attempt on their life. Stuff like that."

Penn rolls his eyes. "It wasn't that extreme. And he did way worse stuff than that."

Lyle shoots him a piercing glare. "And what would you know? You weren't around. Off enjoying your many dalliances, I suppose."

"Just because I didn't live in the Realm twenty-four seven doesn't mean I wasn't involved," Penn says hotly. "Also, my personal life is none of your business, and I'd rather you not discuss it, in front of kids or otherwise."

Kids? He's lumping Jess in with the wicht and calling them *kids*? This ignites her anger again. "I'm almost eighteen," she interjects. "I am not a kid!"

"I'm clipping immortal, Jess," he says, shoving a hand roughly through his hair. "You're all kids to me. Or were. Are." His brows knit in confusion and frustration. "I don't know. Never mind."

He picks up his pace, moving ahead of Jess, which is fine by her. She doesn't know what to make of whatever that was, and she doesn't particularly want to keep talking to someone who thinks of her as an immature child.

When they reach their original landing point, they all stop.

"What do we do now?" Penn asks.

"We have to let the FIC know Della isn't there," Jess says, not looking at him. "We have to tell them they're chasing the wrong trail."

"That's gonna be a fun conversation," Lyle mutters. "Still, Jess is right. We need to take this to the FIC. They'll be able to take it from here."

"You mean they're going to take us off the mission?" Penn voices the exact thought running through Jess's mind. After everything they've done, the FIC would just send them home?

Lyle shrugs. "We had a job and we did it.

Technically, they don't need us anymore. The parameters have changed."

"But—McCreed. And the wicht," Jess says. "What is the FIC supposed to do with that? He didn't agree to help them, he agreed to help us."

"He agreed to help *you*," Penn corrects, and Jess can tell from the way he bends the last word that he's still mad about it.

"Why does it matter?" Jess demands, turning on him. "I know you think he manipulated me because I'm a gullible child, but you can't ignore the facts, and the facts are he agreed to help, he sent the wicht with me, and he wants Della found too, if only for selfish reasons. We got a lot more out of that encounter than he did. So why does it matter that I was the one who convinced him?"

"Because it's weird and creepy and it doesn't make SENSE!" As he says it, Penn shoves both hands forcefully into his hair, and turns away like he can't stand to look at her. He starts pacing, gesturing as he speaks, as if that might help him get his point across.

"He's literally the fairies' worst enemy. He's been tormenting them *for millennia*. He's never had a pure motive in his life—"

"I *just said* it was for selfish reasons!"

"—and he's a conniving, lying, soulless bastard!" Penn finishes, ignoring Jess's interruption entirely. He turns to them both. "Don't you see what he's doing? He's playing with us! Misleading us! Now I'm not saying he has Della—"

"He doesn't." Lyle's turn to interject.

"—but that doesn't mean he isn't misdirecting us. I mean, think about it! He hates the FIC as much as they hate him. You don't think he'd get a kick out of sending us on a wild goose chase for some sort of petty revenge?"

Penn's words bring Jess back to McCreed's palace for a moment as she recalls him saying something eerily similar about Penn. Could *Penn* be trying to mislead them? Is he trying to keep himself on the assignment so he can lead them astray?

The idea is so foreign, so contradictory to Penn's personality, but who's to say his personality isn't an intentionally crafted hollow shell? After all, it's one thing to believe you're a good person and another to actually be one, and Penn's not a person at all. He's a fairy, and everyone knows fairies are manipulative. Even Miss Colleen is. How does Jess know Penn's whole "I'm a good guy" routine isn't just a front to cover his lust for vengeance against the fairy throne?

All these competing theories are making Jess's head spin. She doesn't know McCreed's motives. She doesn't know Penn's, either. All she knows for sure is that a girl is missing and she needs help. She raises her head to meet Penn's eyes.

"It doesn't matter," she says. "Della is missing and she needs to be found. Whether you like McCreed or not, he gave us help. Help that we desperately need. Don't you see? We have nothing to go on. So unless you would rather work your way down a list of anyone with a grievance against the fairies"—she might have imagined it, but she thinks she sees Penn's lips tighten at this—"we should accept his help."

"I agree with Jess on this," Lyle says. "I know McCreed just about as well as you can, and if he was really trying to sabotage us, he wouldn't have sent Jess with one of his living servants and one of his beloved inventions. Did he make you sign a nondisclosure agreement when he gave it to you?"

Jess shakes her head.

"That's a surprise. It doesn't matter, though. My point is, he did offer us valid assistance. Not sure yet how we'll get Mom on board with it, but we'll figure it out. It's not like they have any better leads."

"You're making a terrible mistake, both of you," Penn says, shaking his head. "This is McCreed we're talking about. What does he have to gain from this arrangement? Where's the value for him? Mark my words, he sees this as an IOU and someday he's going to come knocking for his dues." He locks eyes with Jess, the warning clear in his gaze. "I just hope you're ready to pay."

Jess wants to reply, to say something sarcastic that will shut him up, but nothing comes to mind. Worse, he's probably right. She can't forget the way McCreed said he doesn't want anything from her "now"—as though that might change in the near future. She doesn't know what McCreed would want from her, and she's afraid to guess. He may not be the evil villain she was always told he was, but she still doesn't trust him.

A clap from Lyle startles her back to the present. "Right then," they say, "we should get going. Mom will be expecting us, and the sooner we get back, the sooner we can get everyone on the right path to finding Della."

Jess sneaks a glance at Penn to see if he has any reaction to this, but his expression is blank. Lyle pulls the transporter out of their pocket and fiddles with a couple of buttons before setting it on a nearby rock. "All right, I've got it calibrated. Should take us directly to headquarters. You both ready?"

Jess nods and steps over to the rock, placing her hand on the transporter. Lyle places their hand, and finally, Penn steps over and touches the transporter with the tips of his fingers. A few seconds later, they've landed on a sidewalk in front of the building. Jess feels a tingle of excitement and anticipation. She's always wanted to visit FIC headquarters.

From the first glance, the building does not disappoint. Its size alone sets it apart from other fairy structures; it's the closest thing the Realm has to a skyscraper. Tall and paneled with black glass, the building is imposing and impressive. The impossibly clean glass of the windows—at least, Jess assumes they're windows—reflects the blue skies and rolling green hills of the surrounding landscape back in cool, monochrome tones of gray.

The major thing that sets the building apart from human-made buildings, that makes it clearly fairy, is its shape. Each wall slopes ever so gently inward until they meet at the top, forming an elongated pyramid. The top is flat, as though the tip of the pyramid has been removed, and Jess knows she would find a landing pad (both vehicle and fairy friendly) if she were to travel up there.

The carrier shifts in her hand, bringing her back to reality. She can't bring a wicht into FIC headquarters, and she also can't leave him alone outside.

Lyle realizes this at the same time she does, and they look back at her. "He's going to have to stay out here," they say.

"I know," Jess says, resigned. "I'll wait with him."

"No, I'll do it," Penn says from behind her, and Jess turns. "I shouldn't go in anyway. Some of them probably wouldn't take too kindly to me being here."

Jess cannot get a good read on him. Not even ten minutes ago, he was calling her a kid and implying McCreed had manipulated her, and now he's trying to be nice? If it can even be called that. There's something going on here that she hasn't figured out yet, but whatever it is, it's working in her favor right now, so she's not going to complain.

"Okay," she says. "Don't let anything happen to him."

Penn rolls his eyes. "He'll be fine. Go on."

Jess sets the carrier down and turns toward the doors, but she's barely made it five steps before a screeching sound erupts behind her. She whirls around to see Penn staring in shock at the carrier, where the sound is coming from.

"What did you do?" She has to yell to be heard over the sound.

"Nothing!" Penn looks offended. "I didn't even move!"

"Then why is he shrieking?"

"I don't know!"

Jess walks back over to the carrier and bends down. She taps the side. Looking inside, it looks like the wicht is in a pet carrier, and although she knows that isn't actually the case, it still makes her uncomfortable.

"Hey," she says. "What's the matter?"

Noe'or stops shrieking and glares at her. "Don't wanna be left with that rotten wing," he says. "McCreed said to stay with you, listen to you. Not him."

"Okay," Jess says. "I won't leave you with him." She stands up. "You'll have to go without me."

"You're giving up your chance to visit FIC headquarters for a *wicht*?" Penn asks, incredulous.

"Clip you, wing!" the wicht shrieks.

Penn wrinkles his nose. "A foul-mouthed wicht, too."

"Well, I don't have much of a choice, do I?" Jess says. "And we're not here for me, we're here for Della. So you two need to go and give the update so we can help her."

Lyle shifts their weight. "Penn, you made a good point. It's probably best if you don't go in. If we're going to be able to help Della, I'm going to have to do some hard negotiating, and it's best we don't do anything that might make them upset."

Penn shoves his hand roughly through his hair. "Yeah, seems like I make everyone upset. You go on, then. May luck favor you."

Lyle nods, then turns and heads inside the building. Jess watches the doors slide shut behind them. She can see her longing reflected in the black glass, and it unsettles her. She sits down on one of the benches, moving the carrier so it's next to her, beside the bench. She doesn't know how long they'll be there and she thinks about retrieving her book, then talks herself out of it. There are definitely cameras watching them, and she doesn't need her mom spying on her choice of reading material.

Penn paces for a bit, then drops onto the bench across the path with a sigh. He starts fidgeting almost immediately, first with the strap of his watch, then with his keys, to the point where the jingling noise starts getting on Jess's nerves.

Yesterday, or even earlier today, she would have snapped at him to stop. But he did offer to stay with the wicht to let her see the FIC, so she supposes she can cut him a little slack for that. The noise needs to stop, though. She decides to employ her top distraction strategy: asking him a question.

"What did you mean earlier when you said the McCreed stuff was before your time?"

As expected, Penn stops fidgeting with the keys and looks up at her. "What?"

"When we were walking back to the forest. You said the war with the elves and McCreed being hidden away were before your time. What did you mean by that?"

Penn shrugs. "Exactly what I said. I wasn't in existence, or born, or whatever you want to call it, when all that happened."

Jess's brows furrow in confusion. "I thought you were immortal."

"I am and I'm not," Penn replies, "but I think what you mean is, haven't I been around forever? And the answer is no."

Jess really wants to ask how old he is, but thinks that's probably considered rude even for fairies, so she phrases it a little more carefully. "How long have you been around?"

Penn gives another shrug. "I actually don't know for sure. I mean, you know how fairies originated, right? Embodiments of the forces behind nature, springing forth fully formed from buildups of energy, all that fun stuff."

Jess knows what he's talking about; unlike the war he'd mentioned, this was actually covered in her fairy history class.

"Then, when humans started becoming a dominant force on Earth," Penn continues, "the fate and the domains of new fairies started becoming intertwined with human actions. So, as far as I can tell, I appeared around six thousand years ago when humans began domesticating horses."

Jess knew some of the fairies were very old, but it's still hard to grasp that Penn, who looks college-aged at most, is not only six thousand years old but is also too young to have experienced the war with the elves. The thought makes her head spin.

"It's kind of unclear because I spent a while kicking around as a horse before the fairies found me," Penn explains. "I don't know how long that was. Time is hard as a horse."

"Wait, so you started as a horse?"

"Yes," Penn says, then clarifies: "a magic horse."

Jess tries to imagine Penn as a horse. Knowing him, his horse form is probably tall, with a pure white coat that inexplicably glows. She remembers old myths she read as a child where gods turned into glowing animals to seduce unsuspecting mortal women; she wouldn't be surprised if Penn was the inspiration behind some of those stories.

"So, let me get this straight. The fairies found you as a magical horse, but you were actually a fairy, and now you own a magic horse, which is also a car? Is your horse a fairy, too?"

Penn laughs. "No, no, Natoi isn't a fairy. In a way, I would say she's a physical manifestation of my power, but with a mind of her own. Most animal fairies have a familiar or companion that represents their abilities and domain, although most are not as, um, free-willed as Natoi."

Jess senses an opportunity to ask something she's been curious about. "Speaking of domains, how come you have two?"

She's never understood why he is the patron fairy of both cars and horses. Most fairies have one primary domain, but Penn has two, and not only that, but the two he has are wildly different.

Penn runs his hand through his hair; it's clear he has to think about his response. Which, naturally, makes Jess even more curious.

"It's complicated," he says finally. "It's not easy for fairies to take on another domain; you don't just say 'I want to be the fairy of cars now' and it magically happens. There's a whole process you're supposed to follow, and then, even if you do it, it might not take. That's why most fairies don't add to their domains, and those who do usually take on ones that are related, like your mom did."

Jess knows her mom's domain encompasses disguise, espionage, and even some forms of acting, but she didn't realize there was a process to it. She'd assumed her mom had always had the exact same power and abilities.

"It was a little different for me," Penn says. "All this happened right when automobiles were on the rise and starting to replace the horse and carriage. I should have seen them as a threat, but I didn't—I thought they were amazing. When I took my first automobile ride, it was like I'd found something I'd been missing without even knowing, you know?"

Jess nods. That's how she'd felt when she and Cat bonded for the first time, all the way back in her early days at the Academy—like she'd found a missing piece of herself. It was a wonderful feeling. She realizes with a pang that she misses Cat. She has to remember to call her tonight, wherever they might end up.

"I knew that I needed cars in my domain," Penn continues, and Jess focuses back on what he's saying. "I had to complete the ritual process, and I did, following it to the letter. I didn't really know what I was doing, but I expected it to take simply because I felt so strongly about it, and it did. Sort of."

"'Sort of?'" Jess asks.

"Well, what they don't tell you as a fairy is you don't control the domain. Fairies, half-fae, we're all just conduits through which the domain's power and energy are channeled."

Jess isn't sure she likes the thought of being a conduit. It makes her feel like a tool wielded by powers beyond her control, instead of a living person with her own feelings and dreams. She hates feeling used.

Penn's tone changes, suddenly more serious. "The energy of automobiles? It's not the same as the energy of horses. They can't both go through the same conduit at the same time."

He stares off into the distance, face grim as though remembering something painful. "I didn't know this. So when I completed the ritual and the domain took, it literally ripped my psyche in half to form two conduits."

Jess is caught off-guard. "Wait, what?"

Penn's attention returns to her, and he smiles sympathetically, as though he relates to her confusion.

"Don't worry about it; it was only horrifically painful in the moment. Afterward, we were both fine."

"*Both?*" Jess is even more confused now.

Penn nods. "Yep. The force of the domain taking split one mind, or one soul, if you will, into two fully formed ones. Two aspects, two conduits, two beings in one form. That's me and Nell."

Jess knows many of the fairies have other aspects, and has even met a few of them. Usually they'll have a male and a female aspect, or some other combination of expressions of self. They're still the same being, though. What Penn's describing—sharing a body with another person—sounds confusing and even uncomfortable. It makes his behavior a lot more understandable, though.

"Have I ever met Nell?" she asks.

"I don't think so, but let me check." He tilts his head, gaze unfocused like he's thinking, before snapping back to reality. "Nope, Nell says you two have never met. I think she'd like to meet you someday, though. You'd probably get along."

Jess doesn't know what he's basing this on, seeing as she can't get along with him, but maybe Nell is different. Maybe when the split happened, Nell got the good personality traits and Penn got stuck with the leftovers. It would certainly explain a lot. Jess would be interested to meet her, if only to see if her theory is true.

Penn seems to interpret her silence as a need to process everything he's told her.

"Sorry," he says with a laugh. He looks away and rubs the back of his neck absentmindedly. "Didn't mean to offload all that onto you. I know it's a lot. I just—this is the first time someone's asked me about my domains and I've actually wanted to answer. The fairies ask me all the time, but I know they're just morbidly curious about the whole thing, so I've never told any of them."

Jess stares at him. "You realize you just told the story in front of FIC headquarters. The whole Realm is going to know by tomorrow."

Penn looks up at her and laughs. "It was never about who knew. It was only about who asked."

He holds her gaze for a couple seconds, then looks at his watch. "I get the feeling Lyle is going to be a bit. What do you say we go meet a friend of mine? She's very wise, knows a little about everything. If anyone can give us some guidance for the next part of the mission, it would be her."

"Provided there is a next part of the mission for us," Jess says.

"Touché." Penn stands up and Jess follows suit. "It's a little ways away. Probably faster if we drive."

Jess is not sure how they're going to do that at first, but Penn takes his keys back out of his pocket, unclips a keychain with a toy car on it, and sets it on the ground. He presses his thumb to the hood of the tiny car and steps back as it grows into a full-size, bright red Maserati.

Penn grins at Jess across the roof of the car. "We're riding in style now!"

Like something from a movie, the doors open upward with a slight hiss. The trunk pops open and Penn comes around the back of the car. He holds out his hand to take the carrier. Jess gives it to him hesitantly, half expecting Noe'or to start shrieking again, but the wicht is silent. Penn places the carrier in the trunk and secures it, then shuts the trunk.

"Don't worry, there's plenty of air circulation," he says, heading back around the side of the car and sliding into the driver's seat. He looks up at her. "Well, what are you waiting for? Get in!"

She slides into the passenger seat, feeling like she's in a race car. The interior is even more minimalistic than the Porsche, with solely digital displays and minimal buttons and controls. It's also an automatic transmission, whereas the Porsche was manual. The Cutlass was automatic, too, but that's about the only similarity between the two cars. This car puts the Cutlass at an even sharper contrast, making Jess question the "camo" car choice even more.

Penn opens a compartment in the armrest, pulls out a pair of dark sunglasses, and puts them on. With a snap of his fingers, a second pair appears in his hand. He holds them out to Jess, but she doesn't take them.

"I'm not wearing those."

Penn looks at her from behind his shades. "You have to. Car rules."

Jess shakes her head. "That's ridiculous. I'm not putting them on."

Penn shrugs. "Guess we're stuck here, then..."

He lets his voice trail off and Jess can hear the laugh in it. She knows he's messing with her, but she also knows he's stubborn and won't back down, and this isn't a battle she particularly wants to fight.

"Fine," she says, taking them and shoving them on. "Can we go now?"

Penn smiles. "Your wish is my command."

With a rev of the engine, the car darts forward and they're off, driving down the winding road that Jess knows leads to the middle of the fairy town. She looks over at Penn.

"You going to explain why the car rules now include wearing sunglasses?"

Penn gives her a side glance. "We're on a mission," he says, as if it's obvious.

When he doesn't elaborate, Jess follows up with, "Yeah, and?"

"We're on a mission...*from God*." He emphasizes the last two words, and Jess thinks he's finally lost it. Since when are fairies religious?

"Sorry, what?"

"You know, 'They're not gonna catch us, we're on a mission from God?'" Now he's looking at her like she's the crazy one.

She shakes her head. "I have no idea what you're talking about."

"*The Blues Brothers*!" Penn says, throwing his hands in the air. "It's a quote from *The Blues Brothers*! They're trying to save the orphanage, and they say they're on a mission from God, because it's a Catholic orphanage. And they wear sunglasses throughout almost the entire movie, even at night." He looks over at her. "It's a classic movie. Haven't you seen it?"

"No."

There are a lot of supposedly "classic" movies

Jess hasn't seen. Her life since her dad died hasn't really been conducive to watching movies.

Penn shakes his head. "You're missing out. It's hilarious, has incredible music, and the car chases are epic. It's so good."

"I'll add it to my list," Jess says, planning to do the exact opposite.

"I'll do you one better," Penn says. "I'll organize a screening for students at the Academy and you can come to that. Ooh, and maybe if a lot of people come, Colleen will let me run a movie club..."

Jess suddenly has a horrible vision of Penn running a movie club, complete with his own scholarly lectures on each film and a running commentary while they watch it. She hopes Miss Colleen shuts the idea down so they can avoid any students being bored to death.

They reach the outskirts of the town, and Penn blows past the welcome sign at close to fifty miles per hour. He slows down a bit as the streets grow narrower, lined with little houses and shops.

Jess has visited the town before, but it's been a few years now. It hasn't changed much in that time. The houses and buildings are still perfectly painted and arranged, looking as bright and appealing as cupcakes in a bakery case. The sun is out, casting everything in a warm glow. Jess is secretly glad she put on Penn's sunglasses.

The town is achingly pretty, but it also unsettles Jess. It's too perfect, like a movie set or something from a theme park. Every tree is perfectly formed, every sidewalk meticulously clean. The colors are all so bright they may have been painted yesterday, and nothing is out of place—no trash bins, no electrical wires, no squirrels, birds or stray cats.

Fairies bustle up and down the sidewalk, but theirs is the only vehicle on the streets, and Jess notices the way the other fairies turn to watch them. Their reactions to the car range from irritated to downright hostile. It gives Jess an uncomfortable feeling in the pit of her stomach, and she feels more on edge than her "Penn radar" senses normally make her feel.

She tells herself it's silly, that the other fairies would never try to attack or harm them, but then realizes she doesn't know if that's true. She doesn't know why Penn was banished or what he did to make the other fairies hate him. It's entirely possible it was bad enough to spur someone into violence.

"Are you sure we're supposed to be driving here?" Jess asks cautiously.

Penn laughs. "Definitely not."

He revs the car's engine, scaring a pair of fairies at a fruit stand on the sidewalk. One of them drops a crate of oranges, and Jess sees him shake a fist at them in the rearview mirror.

"Technically, I'm not supposed to be here at all," Penn says, his voice smooth. Jess looks away from the mirror to see him also looking at it, a smile of satisfaction playing on his lips. He's enjoying this.

"What happens if you get caught?" Something

Jess thinks is inevitable, considering they are driving a very fast, very expensive, very flashy sports car right through the center of the fairy town.

Penn looks over, and his demeanor softens a bit. "Don't worry about it, it's not a big deal. Besides, they're not gonna catch us." He lowers his sunglasses so Jess can see his eyes, which are twinkling with laughter. "We're on a mission from God, remember?"

He winks at her before pushing the sunglasses up his nose again and turning his eyes to the road.

* 11 *

IT DOESN'T TAKE LONG FOR THEM TO REACH their destination, a small cottage with a vibrant and well-tended garden. When Jess gets out of the car, she takes a deep breath and smells a variety of flowers and herbs. She has zero talent for caring for plants—she once managed to kill a mini cactus Cat brought her from Arizona—but she has great admiration for people who can tend to amazing gardens like this.

She moves around to the back of the car and opens the trunk to get the wicht out. Hopefully they'll be able to actually start tracking Della today, because keeping Noe'or trapped makes her uncomfortable, even if the roomcase is pretty nice.

The house and garden are bordered by a little

picket fence with a gate, which Penn holds open for her. Inside the fence, the garden is even prettier. Jess recognizes the standard roses, irises, and daisies, but there are stranger plants, too—hanging flowers on trellises that tinkle like windchimes, huge yellow roses with clusters of diamonds in their centers, and a bush with transparent, glasslike leaves dotted with tiny, bloodred berries.

The flowering plants only make up half the garden, though; the other half is dominated by rows of fragrant herbs, carefully labeled with small, handwritten signs. Above it all, fuzzy bumblebees hum as they fly lazily from flower to flower. Jess feels like she is walking through a storybook.

When they reach the door, Penn uses the wooden knocker, elaborately carved in the shape of a crescent moon, to announce their presence.

Within a minute, they hear noise from inside the house and the door opens to reveal a fairy wearing a long dress with a changing pattern of colors and shapes. Her thick, waist-length hair is braided, and her iridescent wings feature a unique swirled pattern that seems to change as she moves. She is smiling when she answers the door, but the smile quickly falls and her wings drop when she sees Penn.

"Nope," she says, and tries to shut the door. Penn sticks his foot in before she can shut it fully.

"C'mon, please, Aster? We could really use your guidance," he says.

Aster scoffs from behind the door. "Since when have you ever listened to my guidance? You come to me, ask for my services, and then you don't like what you hear and pitch a fit."

"I do not!"

"I seem to remember a certain incident after I told you the *Back to the Future II* writers were wrong and the Cubs would not win the World Series in 2015."

"Okay, maybe I did raise my voice a little then, but in my defense, I had just left the theater after seeing the movie and was a bit overexcited. This is different."

"I already told you no. Now get your foot out of my door before I cut it off."

Penn finally relents and pulls his foot back. Aster slams the door and they hear it lock.

"That went well," Penn says.

"I thought you said you were friends," Jess says.

Penn rubs the back of his neck. "I may have underestimated her ability to hold grudges."

"All that over *Back to the Future II*?"

"Eh, among other stuff. You might have noticed I'm not exactly VIP status around here."

"You don't say."

Penn laughs. "They're not very subtle about it, are they?"

"'Subtle' is never a word I would use to describe a fairy, no."

Penn gasps and puts his hand to his chest. "I'm insulted! Subtlety is one of my greatest attributes."

Jess laughs before she can stop herself. "That's a good one. You're about as subtle as, well, a Maserati!"

Instead of getting offended by Jess's crack or laughing it off, Penn hams it up in response.

"Ah! You've killed me!" he says, clutching his chest and falling back against the porch post. "You've stabbed me with your quick wit, and now I'm bleeding out and will surely die!"

With a groan, he sinks dramatically to the ground. Jess can't help but laugh, which only serves to encourage him.

"Oh, the misery! Look how she laughs at my plight!" he says, as though speaking to an imaginary audience. "See the joy she takes in my pain! I would curse her, but I fear it is too late for me! I can only hope my dear friends will avenge my senseless murder!"

It's cold, but Jess has to say it. She can't let this opportunity go to waste.

"What friends?"

Penn gasps and flails dramatically. "She's dealt the final blow! I shall die now, alone and friendless, with no one to mourn me! Goodbye, cruel world!"

With a final gasp, he closes his eyes and goes still as though dead, but only for a second before he opens one eye to look at Jess. "How was that?"

"Most subtle," Jess says, and now they're both laughing.

Usually, Penn's antics would be annoying, but right now, Jess finds them hilarious. She reasons it's her brain's way of releasing the pent-up stress from yesterday and earlier today, and it seems to be working.

They'll be back to business soon, if they do

continue on the mission, but for now it's nice just to smile, laugh a little, and take in the fresh air and sunshine.

"All right, that's enough," says a voice behind her.

Penn scrambles to his feet and Jess turns to see Aster standing in the doorway. She must have opened the door while they were busy laughing.

"You're making me want to tell you what I can so you'll stop laughing," she says. "You're ruining my vibes. Come on." She waves them inside.

The interior of the cottage looks much like Jess expected from the exterior. Cute, cozy decor and lots of floral motifs. They pass a kitchen where a boy and girl, probably about nine or ten years old, are arranging dried herbs in bundles. The children look up as they pass, but show no surprise. Jess guesses they must be Aster's half-fae children—some fairies choose to educate their kids themselves in the Realm—and they are probably used to random people coming to Aster with their problems.

Aster leads them into a sitting room and gestures for them to pick a seat. They each select a chair, and Jess sets the roomcase down next to hers when she sits.

Aster sits across from them on the loveseat. "I presume you've come about the girl," she says.

Penn leans forward. "Yes. We thought McCreed had her, but we went to his palace—"

Aster waves a hand dismissively. "Yes, I'm aware. She isn't there."

Penn sits back, his gaze appraising the other fairy. "Perhaps we should've come to see you first."

"Perhaps," Aster says, reaching over to the side table and picking up a delicate teacup with a star pattern. She raises it to her lips, blows lightly on the contents, then takes a sip. When she's done, she raises her eyes to Penn over the rim of the cup. "Isn't it fascinating how patterns tend to repeat themselves?"

Confusion crosses Penn's face. "Patterns? I don't follow."

Jess doesn't, either, but she's not about to admit it.

Aster sighs and sets the teacup back on its saucer. "I don't expect you to," she says. "At least, not yet. The threads of the universe take skilled hands to untangle."

Somehow, despite never having met any of Aster's children or knowing anything about the psychic fairy, Jess feels this experience is shaping up to her expectations. An eccentric fairy feeding them cryptic words while saying nothing. Jess side-eyes Penn. He seemed to have a lot of respect for Aster and her abilities earlier, but so far, she's not seeing why.

He leans forward and Jess can sense what's about to happen. He'll turn on the charm and Aster will melt in his words, just like the barista yesterday morning. So predictable.

But when he speaks, his voice isn't the smooth tone he used at Starbucks. "Enough with the mumbo-jumbo, Aster," he says, each word short and crisp like a snap of the fingers. "Can you tell us anything helpful or not?"

Jess expects Aster to snap back, but instead she smiles, one corner of her mouth tilting up more than the other. "There it is! That famous temper. Please try not to break anything this time."

Penn's brow furrows. "I never broke anything."

Aster tilts her head, evaluating him. "Right. My mistake. Of course you didn't break anything." But Jess can tell from her voice and the way she's still sizing Penn up that she doesn't believe what she's saying.

"Aster, please," Penn says, his voice gentler this time. "Della is in danger. If you can give us any insight, it could help us with the rescue. It may even save her life."

Aster's face softens. "Of course. Harriet is a friend of mine. I would not see her daughter suffer longer, if I can help it. Let me see what I can do." She closes her eyes and leans back in her seat.

Jess watches intently, although she's not sure what's going on. She doesn't have any idea how the whole psychic thing is supposed to work.

Aster continues to sit. And sit. And sit some more. Finally, just as Jess starts to feel restless, Aster's eyes snap open.

"Your friend is making a strong case for you with the FIC," she says. "The future holds many possibilities, but I can see that if your friend is successful, it is likely the girl will be found within the next few days."

"Can you tell us how to find her?" Jess asks,

surprising herself. It's the first thing she's said since they've entered the house. It's not that she had decided not to talk; she just didn't feel she had anything to add until now.

Aster looks at Jess and shakes her head. "I cannot tell you the exact location, no. I see relevant glimpses of potential futures, and I'm afraid none of them contain enough detail on location to be of any help."

"Well, what can you tell us, then?" Penn asks.

"Careful." There's a note of warning in Aster's voice that reminds Jess of her comment about Penn's temper.

"Sorry," Penn says, apparently reminded of the same.

"As I was going to say, Jess was right when she realized this has nothing to do with McCreed. As far as who is behind this, I'm afraid I don't know. That itself is valuable information, though. Whoever is responsible is one not known to the fairies."

Jess looks at Penn. He looks just as wary of this information as she feels.

"When you find the girl, you will find a great deal more as well," Aster continues. "I caution you to prepare yourselves, as some of it will be upsetting. You mustn't let it get to you or distract you in the moment, or failure is inevitable."

"No pressure," Penn comments.

"Nothing with the FIC is ever as it seems," Aster says, looking at him. "You knew that when you agreed to take this assignment. I hope you aren't having second thoughts?"

"Never."

Jess swears she sees a flicker of a smile on Aster's lips before she continues.

"The girl is physically unharmed. As far as her mental state, she is understandably distressed. Keep in mind that she had no previous knowledge of the Realm before this incident. Jess, you would be the best person to support her here."

This worries Jess more than the vague proclamation about them finding "upsetting" information. She's never struggled with her shapeshifting abilities, or picking up new useful skills, and she's not bad at getting people to tell her what she needs to know. But going beyond that and forming deeper connections with people quickly? Well, that's not so easy. There's a reason Cat is her only friend.

"When you go to find her, you should also bring a magic detecting ring, a flash drive, and a case of bottled water," Aster continues. "I foresee you will have the best chance of success if you have those items with you."

"Got it," Penn says. "Is there anything more you can tell us?"

Aster shakes her head. "Not at this time. Like I said, the future holds many possibilities. Anything more I could tell you might negatively influence what happens. But, if you're willing, Jess, I can do a reading for you, and that might help you going forward."

Jess is taken aback. Aster has spent most of the

time talking to Penn, and now she wants to do a reading for Jess? Jess had doubted at first that Aster could help them at all, and even now she's still unsure.

The offer is intriguing, though. Jess has never had a psychic reading, and maybe it could help.

"Sure, I guess. I mean, yes, I'll do it."

"Good! Come with me." Aster stands and leads Jess out of the sitting room.

"Wait, what about me?" Penn calls from behind them. "Do I get a reading, too?"

Aster laughs. "I sincerely doubt I would find any differences from the one I did for you in the eighties."

"Oh, you'd be surprised," Penn replies.

Aster just laughs as she leads Jess down the hall and into a small, darkened room. A round table flanked by two chairs stands in the center of the room, and bookcases around the edges hold thick, dusty books and are topped by candles. Jess takes a seat as Aster lights a few of the candles using magic.

"For ambience," she says with a smile, sitting across from Jess. "Now, hold out your hands."

Jess does so, and Aster takes hold of them and closes her eyes. This time, it's much sooner before she opens them again.

"You have experienced much sorrow," she says, not with pity or sympathy, but plainly, as though stating a fact. "Your experiences have made it hard for you to trust. This is understandable, but not ideal, and it is something you will need to address while there is still time."

Jess has no idea what that means, but it sounds ominous. This is turning out to be a lot more uncomfortable than she expected. She's about to ask Aster to explain, but the psychic fairy continues.

"You also take risks," she says, a somber edge creeping into her voice. "You took a big risk today with McCreed, and it paid off. Other risks may not yield such dividends. You must be cautious about the risks you take and make sure you are evaluating all potential options and outcomes."

Jess thinks Aster is judging her a little too harshly. After all, people in her line of work have to take risks, and they know there's no guarantee they'll pay off. That's just one of the hazards of the job, and one she's prepared for.

It's not like she didn't think things through earlier; yes, maybe she didn't think as much about the possible outcomes as she could have, but it still turned out fine.

"The final thing I have to say is this," Aster says. "You have been holding yourself back. Your experiences at the Academy these past few years have delivered a hit to your confidence. You don't doubt your skills, but you doubt what you can contribute to a team like this. Have confidence in your voice and contributions. You saw at McCreed's what you can accomplish when given the chance. But sometimes you need to take those chances before they're given to you. Don't wait for others to see your value; make it known."

Of all the things Aster has said so far, this hits

Jess the hardest. She hadn't been able to sum it up in so many words, but Aster has found the core of what she's been dealing with.

People at the Academy have been treating her with extra caution and trying to protect her, while claiming that the reason she's having issues is because of the Joseph incident.

It's not that the incident hasn't had an effect on her—it has—but the way they've treated her because of it has had a bigger effect. It had been so bad at some points that Jess thought she was in the wrong, that they were treating her perfectly normally. At least Cat had her back and would tell her things weren't normal. In the moment, Cat's words were somewhat reassuring, but now that she's away from the behavior, she's able to see it more clearly for herself. To have Aster reaffirm it is freeing, in a way.

Tears prick her eyes. "Thank you," she says. "I—I really needed to hear that."

Aster gives her a kind smile. "I know." She offers up a tissue, which Jess takes and dabs her eyes with, even though no tears have actually fallen.

"I hope you will consider everything I've told you today," Aster says after Jess has finished. "If you've found it helpful, you're welcome to return in the future. There is much else I can share with you when the proper time comes."

"Now isn't the proper time?"

"No, my dear, not for all of it. The universe operates on its own cycles and schedules, and it is not my prerogative to disrupt them. Besides, I believe you will find many of the insights I could offer you on your own, under the right circumstances. Truthfully, my services benefit primarily those who believe themselves lost, and I don't expect you will stay lost for long."

Jess has no idea what she means about cycles and being lost; but then again, you should never expect a straight answer from a fairy. She wouldn't be surprised if Aster is withholding information just because she thinks things might be more interesting if Jess didn't know it.

The two of them go back to the sitting room, where Penn is waiting impatiently.

"It's about time!" he says. "I was starting to think you'd both fallen into a magic mirror or something."

"Magic mirrors are for posers," Aster sniffs. "Real psychics don't use props."

"Mmm-hmm," Penn says, lifting an eyebrow. "Jess, we should get back to FIC headquarters. Lyle is probably done by now."

"Okay," Jess says. She turns to Aster. "Thank you for your help. We appreciate it."

"Yes, thank you," Penn chimes in. "What did you say those items were again?"

"A magic detecting ring, a flash drive, and a case of bottled water."

It reassures Jess that they already have one of the items, even though she's not sure how it will come into play yet.

"You should go now," Aster says. "Your friend

is waiting."

Jess picks up the roomcase and is surprised to realize Noe'or hasn't made a sound the entire time they've been at Aster's, not even when Jess left the room for her reading. Perhaps he's been napping; Jess isn't familiar with wicht sleeping patterns.

"Good luck on your mission, Jess," Aster says kindly. "Oh, and Penn," she continues, turning to him as he heads toward the door, "a word of advice: if you're going to drive a vehicle through fairy kingdom, I'd recommend choosing something less ostentatious."

"I'll keep that in mind," Penn says. Jess sincerely doubts this.

Aster smiles, her lips tilting the same as earlier. "Oh, I can't wait to see how things unfold this time around."

Penn pauses, hand on the doorknob, and turns back to Aster. "What do you mean, 'this time around'?"

"The cycles of the universe repeat in mysterious ways," Aster says. "Some elements change and fluctuate, while others remain constant." She looks to Jess, then back to Penn. "You should count yourself lucky. Not everyone is afforded a second chance."

Jess has no idea what she's talking about, but Penn's eyes widen and his face pales. Just as quickly, it colors again and he smiles, a little too widely to be believable.

"Cryptic as always, Aster. It was good to see you again." He opens the door and waves Jess out ahead of him. "Thanks for everything! See you around!" she hears him say behind her, followed by the sound of the door closing.

No sooner are they past the gate than Penn turns to Jess. "So how was your reading?"

He tries to make it sound casual, but Jess detects a hint of desperation in the question. He's afraid of something, but she doesn't know what.

"Right to the personal questions," she notes. If he's not going to tell her what's going on, she's not going to give him what he wants.

Penn seems to realize this and, to Jess's surprise, backs off.

"Well, I'm not going to pretend I'm not curious," he says, turning away and putting his hands in his pockets. "You were gone for a while. But you're right; it is a personal question. I certainly never told anyone the full contents of my reading." They approach the car and he pulls out his keys, unlocking it. "Not that it was that deep to begin with."

He says it offhandedly, but there's a bitterness to his tone that Jess has never heard before. She wonders what the psychic fairy told him all those years ago, and, more importantly, if it has anything to do with what's happening now.

* 12 *

LYLE IS ALREADY OUTSIDE WHEN JESS AND Penn arrive at FIC headquarters. They stand up from their bench as the car approaches.

"Where were you two?" they demand when Jess and Penn get out of the car. "I come out here and there's no sign of you. You could've at least left a note."

"We went to visit a friend of mine," Penn says.

"Aster, the psychic," Jess clarifies. "She shared some things that might be helpful, if we're still on the assignment."

"Well, it took a lot of negotiating and some pretty serious arguments, but the FIC is letting us continue to search for the girl," Lyle says.

"Awesome!" Penn says, grinning. "Glad we're

still on the case. We're going to find her, I just know it."

Lyle shifts their weight. "Yeah, so about the case," they say.

"What about it?" Jess asks.

"Now that the FIC knows McCreed isn't responsible, they're freaking out. This case has moved to the top of the priority list and they're pulling officers from other assignments to cover it, so we're just one of a few teams working on it now."

"Well, it's about time!" Penn says. "This should have been the top priority from the start!"

But Jess can see what Lyle is getting at.

"More manpower isn't always better," she says. "Kind of a 'too many cooks' scenario. Adding a lot more officers means we're more likely to have issues with communication, and having too many people in the vicinity where she was taken could lead to evidence being accidentally destroyed."

"Oh," Penn says, his face falling. "Yeah, that's not so good."

"On the plus side," Lyle interjects, "assembling all the additional officers and briefing them on the situation will take time, time that we're allowed to use. The other officers will be going through that process today, giving us time to arrive at the location early and check things out. Tomorrow, Mom has agreed to let us into Della's parents' apartment before any of the others, because we have the wicht. It's not ideal timing, but at least we get first crack."

"That's good," Jess says. "Hopefully, the area will be untainted enough that Noe'or will be able to pick up the scent easily."

"I'm sure he'll be fine," Penn says. "When do we leave?"

Lyle pulls another device out of their pocket. "We can leave whenever. This one isn't set on a timer. I was thinking we could get lunch first—"

Jess likes this idea, since she's been really hungry for the last hour or so, but Penn doesn't seem to agree.

"No, no, we don't want to eat here," he says, taking the device from Lyle's hands. "Let's eat in the city."

"Ohh-kayy," Lyle says, sounding wary.

Penn leads them back to the Maserati, which shifts into a less flashy black Dodge Charger with a backseat. Jess takes the roomcase out of the trunk and slides it onto the seat next to her while Lyle takes the front seat. Penn places the device on the dashboard and fiddles with it a little. It's obvious he's not sure how to make it work with the car.

"Here, let me do it," Lyle says. They take the device, tap a few buttons on the bottom, then place it back on the dashboard. "It should work now. If not, it'll just disappear and we'll go get another one and try again."

"Or it'll disappear and take the car with it," Penn says.

"Or that. But that's highly unlikely. It's not that difficult to calibrate."

"Well, I'll defer to your infinite wisdom in

operating FIC gadgets, then," Penn replies.

"Okay. Going to set it now." Lyle pushes the top button and Jess sees it start to count down. She quickly turns to look out the rear window to get one last glimpse of FIC headquarters, and has just enough time to make an internal promise to come back someday before everything starts to twist in on itself. When it untwists, they're in a parking garage.

"What's our location?" Penn asks.

"Chicago, around State Street and Eighth," Lyle says.

Penn's eyes widen and his face lights up with excitement. "Oh man, I know so many great pizza places around here! All walking distance. This is perfect!"

"What about the wicht?" Jess asks. "He should eat, too. I don't think we should take him into a restaurant, though."

Penn sighs, and the grin that had illuminated his face at the thought of pizza slips away. "Right. Okay, why don't we drive to a park, then I'll go get the food and bring it back?"

"That'll work," Jess says.

The park they end up at is a couple blocks away, and so tiny it's barely more than a fountain, a path, and some trees. Penn drops Lyle and Jess off at the sidewalk next to the park, but not before passing them each a slip of paper on which he's scratched his phone number, "just in case."

Jess is surprised to learn he even has a phone; she's never seen it. She shoves the slip of paper in her pocket, planning to use it about as frequently as Penn uses his phone, and she and Lyle walk to the nearest bench.

She sets the roomcase down next to the bench and takes a seat at one end, and Lyle sits at the other end. The weather is cool and overcast, but apparently not appealing enough to encourage park visiting. Although there are some pedestrians on the sidewalks, none venture into the tiny park, so Jess and Lyle have the place to themselves.

Now that they're alone, Jess realizes they'll either have to make conversation or sit in awkward silence as they wait for Penn to return. She's inclined to go the silent route, but there's something she needs to know.

"Why did you test me back at the house?" she asks.

Lyle sighs, evidently not surprised by the question. "I've been in this business a long time," they say. "Knowledge can save your life, especially knowing who you're working with and their strengths and weaknesses. I'd never met you before yesterday. Besides, I wanted to know if what Mom told me was true. I thought she might be bragging."

Funny, Talia never struck Jess as the bragging sort. She briefly wonders what exactly Talia told Lyle about her, then pushes that thought aside.

"And if it wasn't true? If I hadn't passed your test?" She knows she's being direct and Lyle will see right through it, but she needs to know.

"Ah, Penn told you, didn't he?" They shake their head. "He's more like a dog than a horse sometimes. Soft, eager, and easy to lead." They see the look on Jess's face. "Not that that's bad! His heart's in the right place, bless him. But you know how it is; in our line of work, you have to know what gets to people. You have to know the right buttons to push or strings to pull to get them where you need them."

Jess knows they're right, and she hates it. She hates that part of her life, hates that she's done it, too. But Lyle is being evasive, so she decides to ask outright.

"Did you intend to send me back or not?"

Lyle's lips form a tight line before they speak. "If you hadn't passed, then yes, I would have sent you back."

Jess opens her mouth to respond, but they hold up a finger to silence her.

"Before you get mad at me, let me just say this. I've been on a lot of assignments over the years. Most were successful, but some weren't. I knew this assignment would be risky, maybe even dangerous, and I couldn't in good conscience allow you to come if I felt you weren't ready." They shake their head. "I'm old now. I'm not in my prime anymore. So I have to trust that the people I'm working with can handle things themselves if needed, and they won't get themselves killed."

Lyle stares off into the distance as they say this, like they aren't seeing the park anymore but a different place, a different time. Jess recognizes that look.

"You've lost someone on a mission, too?" she

asks quietly.

Lyle nods. "Siberia, 1981. Special mission for the FIC. There were four of us. I can't share details because it's still classified, but two didn't make it out."

"What went wrong, if you don't mind me asking?"

Jess has read many books and articles on successful intelligence operations but has always found it more helpful to read about ones that failed. She feels like they offer more to learn from.

"We didn't retreat when we should have," Lyle says. "Some of our intelligence was faulty, but I thought the operation could still be salvaged. I urged the team to keep going even though we should have pulled back and regrouped."

Lyle pauses, their gaze still focused off in the distance. The pain on their face makes it clear they're not seeing the city street anymore.

"My error in judgment cost the FIC two excellent officers and the mission," they say. "I took the McCreed gig shortly after. I needed something safe, monotonous. It fit the bill."

Jess understands the older officer's strict adherence to the assignment's objectives now. What had seemed to her to be an overly rigid stance for a field that often deals in shades of gray is actually a defense mechanism. Lyle doesn't want another mission to fail.

Jess can relate to that. She also realizes, had it been anyone other than McCreed, whom Lyle is already familiar with, they never would have gone along with Jess's idea. Knowing what she knows now, she's frankly surprised they agreed at all.

Lyle looks at her and blinks, as though clearing the past from their sight. "What about you?"

Jess's throat tightens. It's been so long since she's told someone about it that she doesn't know if she can. She looks down at her hands, clasped in her lap.

"My first big assignment," she says. "It was freshman year. My—my friend Joseph and I, we were the youngest ones on the mission." She looks back up at Lyle. "Everything went smoothly at first. I thought it was going to be a success—we would find the files with the evidence and escape without anyone the wiser. But I didn't know—I didn't *realize*—that we'd been double-crossed. Joseph"—and here, her voice cracks; she can barely say his name—"Joseph double-crossed us. It wasn't his fault—the guy we were investigating had enchanted him. He'd been controlling him like a puppet for months."

Jess looks away from Lyle. She's kept it together so far, which is mildly surprising since her emotions have been so chaotic recently, but she knows seeing Lyle's reaction could tip her over the edge.

"Joseph trapped us all in a room and told us he had to kill us." Jess remembers the way Joseph's hands shook as he tried to fight the enchantment, the pain in his voice and face as the words were forced out of him.

"I thought I could talk him down...it went

wrong. The enchantment was too powerful."

"It killed him?" Lyle asks.

Jess shakes her head. "That would have been better than what happened. He broke the enchantment, but it snapped something inside him. We all thought he would be fine and he was, at first. But his mental condition deteriorated quickly. He'd have these violent episodes more and more frequently, and finally they took him away to the Realm."

She remembers how it happened, so suddenly she didn't even have the chance to say goodbye. One day he was at the Academy, and the next he was gone. No one had even bothered to tell Jess; she'd had to practically bully Miss Colleen into telling her where he was.

"He's in the hospital there," Jess says. "They can't cure him, so they've just been keeping him in this suspended time pocket to prevent him from getting worse. I don't know why they're doing that. It seems kinder to just let him go at this point." She looks back down at her hands, willing herself to keep it together.

"You two were close?" Lyle asks, and Jess nods. They had been friends since Joseph had arrived at the Academy, six months after Jess, and had started dating a few weeks before they'd been chosen for the assignment.

"Have you visited him since he was admitted to the hospital?"

Jess shakes her head. "He used to write me letters, and in every one, he would beg me not to.

He said he didn't want me to see him like that. And, truth is, I didn't want to see him like that, either. I wanted to remember the good times. Eventually, the letters stopped coming. I guess it got to the point where he couldn't write them anymore."

"That's horrible." Lyle shakes their head. "I hope they caught the bastard responsible?"

Jess nodded. "He's dead now."

Lyle looks shocked. "They really killed him?"

"Not officially," Jess says. "He was diagnosed with stage four pancreatic cancer within a month of being captured and was dead within a year. Pretty bad luck for him."

"Let me guess. Joseph's parent is the fairy of luck."

She nods. For all the luck he brought to others, Joseph sadly couldn't bring the right kind of luck to himself. Jess often wonders what things would be like if he was still around, what her last few years at the Academy would have been like. He was her best friend besides Cat, and she misses him.

A few minutes later, Penn appears, strolling up the path carrying two pizza boxes.

"I'm back!" he says, grinning as he shifts the boxes to his left hand. With a wave of his right, the bench they're sitting on transforms into a picnic table, which he sets the boxes on. "Hope you all didn't miss me too much. Now, I didn't know what you liked, so I got—"

"Less talking, more pizza," Lyle says, pulling one of the boxes in front of them, opening it, and taking out a slice. Jess pushes away her thoughts about Joseph and the failed assignment and takes a slice, too.

After they've each eaten their fill, Jess chooses a couple pieces for Noe'or She has to lean down to open the door of the case and pass them to him—he takes them quickly, without a word—and when she sits back up, she finds Penn looking at her strangely.

"What?" she asks.

"Nothing. You just seem to take an awful lot of care with the wicht. It's interesting."

"Why's that?"

He shrugs. "I've never really thought of wichts as having feelings before. That's not the view the fairies have. Watching you take care of one, it's like seeing them in a new light. It's fascinating."

"You didn't figure that out when you were pretending to be one?" Lyle asks. "Of course wichts have feelings." They shake their head. "I'll never understand how you fairies come up with ideas like that."

"Hey, don't lump me in with the rest of them," Penn says, indignant. "At least I don't think they eat humans!"

Lyle lifts an eyebrow. "Congratulations. You should give yourself a pat on the back for figuring that one out."

Jess thinks they are being a little harsh.

"At least he's taking an interest in learning now," she says. Penn looks at her in surprise. "People at school just go around spewing rumors like that and never bother to find out the truth."

Lyle fixes their gaze on her. "And how did you learn the truth?"

"We had a unit on wichts and wicht culture in Mr. Turner's advanced shifting class," she says. "It was a bit of a shock for everyone. All our other teachers only ever talked about how evil wichts were and how we should be extra vigilant when away from the Academy because they might try and attack us."

"Ah, yes. The classic 'Don't leave unless you want to be eaten by monsters!'" Lyle says. "Some things never change. The fairies are going to face a reckoning one day, mark my words. They can't keep living by these lies forever."

"If that ever happens, it'll be far in the future," Penn says. "Fairies love those little lies that make them feel better. They're like security blankets. But you can only keep a security blanket for so long before it starts to unravel."

Lyle nods in agreement, but Jess is still stuck on Penn's words. The analogy is clever, but that's not what's tripping her up. It's the way he talked about fairies. He said the lies make *them* feel better. Not 'us,' 'them.' Like he doesn't consider himself a fairy.

Now that she's drawn this conclusion, she realizes this is a recurring pattern. She doesn't think she's ever heard Penn use 'we' or 'us' when talking about fairies as a whole. He doesn't deny he is a fairy, but he isn't actively trying to identify with them, either.

It's very interesting, especially when Jess takes

into account that he never shifted into fairy form while they were in the Realm. She can't help but wonder if it's related to his exile. She files away this idea and the new information in her mind; she's not sure how, but it could be useful in the future.

Now that everyone has eaten, Penn vanishes the pizza boxes with a wave of his hand and they make their way to the nearest street. From there, Penn is able to summon his car and they set off toward the apartment where Della's family lives. They had decided it would be a good idea to case the area today before going in tomorrow.

When they reach their destination, Penn parks down the street and they approach the building on foot. They stick to the opposite side of the street to look less conspicuous, but Jess doesn't feel it will help much. At least Lyle had the foresight to suggest they each shift so they won't be recognizable, just in case the building is being watched.

They walk slowly, being careful not to look at the building at the same time, or stare too long. When Jess looks, she doesn't see anything special about it—it looks like all the other buildings on the block, older houses that have been converted into apartments. She knows Della's family lives on the second floor, but nothing about those windows stand out or give Jess any clue as to how or why she might have been taken.

Seeing Della's nondescript home makes Jess question her disappearance all the more. What made the kidnappers target her? Everything Jess has seen, heard and read about her has painted her as just a normal kid, albeit one with a fairy parent.

She's not particularly powerful, which is why she wasn't at the Academy. Her parent isn't very high in the fairy hierarchy, either. And, although it makes Jess uncomfortable to think this, there are probably easier fairy kids to kidnap. Kids who wouldn't be missed. Kids like Jess, when she was around that age.

She thinks about how scared she felt on the run, her world turned upside down, forced into a new, harsh reality with nameless enemies chasing her and powers she didn't understand. There had been many days she'd struggled to find a safe place to sleep or something to eat, and many times she'd been forced to lie, steal, or even fight to survive.

Somehow, she'd managed to push back the fear and keep going. She couldn't control her surroundings, but she could control her abilities, so that's what she did. Now, five years later, she doesn't have to worry about where to sleep or how she'll find her next meal, but even so, there are still nights where she reverts back to that terrified little girl, waking up drenched in sweat and heart pounding, convinced she's about to be caught.

She hopes it's not too late to spare Della from the same.

When they reach the end of the block, they discuss for a minute before deciding to walk around the neighborhood a bit. The streets are deserted and the clouds have only grown thicker. After about ten minutes of walking, it starts sprinkling. They each summon umbrellas, but Jess struggles to hold hers and the roomcase.

After a few minutes of struggling and readjusting as they walk, Penn notices her plight. Wordlessly, he reaches out and taps a finger to the edge of her umbrella, and it immediately lightens in her hand. She lets go and it floats in the air, bobbing along with her as she walks.

"Thanks," she says to Penn, and he only nods. It seems they are both in a pensive mood.

Lyle, on the other hand, is alert, seeming keen to take in every detail as they walk. It's a pretty neighborhood and Jess wishes they were visiting under happier circumstances so she could appreciate it more. It looks like a cool place to live; Della probably really loved it. She probably played hopscotch on these sidewalks as a child and rode her bike up and down them as a tween.

A melancholy sort of sadness settles over Jess as she thinks of all the things Della's not here right now to do. At least she still has hope; she clings to what the psychic fairy said earlier about them likely finding Della within the next few days. Then a thought crosses her mind and she stops walking.

"Wait a second," she says. "Did Aster say *we're* likely to find Della, or Della is likely to be found?"

Penn stops walking, too. "Huh. I don't remember for sure. Why?"

Jess frowns. "I thought at first that she said we would find Della, but now that I'm thinking about it more, I don't think she did." She looks at Lyle, who has stopped too, then back at Penn. "We might not be the ones to find her."

Lyle scoffs. "Well, there was always going to be a chance of that. We're lucky we weren't thrown off the operation already so some hotshot could come in and take all the glory after we found something useful. Just between us, I think Mom was just playing favorites by keeping us on."

Jess's breath catches and she feels like she's been hit. Heat rises to her cheeks. She'd suspected this all along and now here Lyle is, confirming it. Putting her on the assignment was an appeasement tactic to keep her from leaving. They were never meant to succeed. Lyle is right—Talia was probably planning the whole time to have an active officer swoop in and take over for them.

Jess knows this is part of her line of work, that there will always be other people taking credit for what she does so she can keep her cover, but this— this is nothing but a setup.

As a matter of fact, Talia probably knew the entire time that McCreed had nothing to do with Della's disappearance, and it was only because Jess had disregarded the directive by talking to McCreed and getting him to help that she is still on the assignment.

She curses herself for not seeing it sooner. Even McCreed knew! She'd dismissed it as his prejudice speaking when he said the fairies were probably behind it, but now it's looking like he may have been right all along. How ironic—the person the fairies have been calling a liar for millennia actually seems to be the only one speaking the truth.

How could Jess have deluded herself into thinking that anyone would trust her on an assignment like this, anyway? It's like her grandfather always said: if it seems too good to be true, it probably is.

Jess wants to sink to the ground and cry, or rage and beat her fists on the pavement. But the others are still here and she won't embarrass herself in front of them, so she holds it in. She forces herself to focus on what Penn has started to say.

"If we aren't the ones to find her, then why did Aster give us all that advice?" he's saying. "About objects to bring and what to expect and such. If she didn't know we would be the ones to find Della, why would she give us that information?"

Lyle shrugs. "Who knows? Maybe we do find her. Or maybe we don't but we end up passing on the information to whoever does. Or maybe Aster's just playing with us." They lift an eyebrow. "Is there any reason she might do that?"

The color drains from Penn's face and he curses. "Stupid *Back to the Future II*. Stars fall, I never should have asked about that." He shoves his free hand angrily through his hair.

"So it's possible she was just leading you along," Lyle concludes.

"I mean, it's possible, yeah. She doesn't like me much." He looks up at Jess. "But you talked to her. Did she say anything about it to you?"

Jess shakes her head, feeling worse by the

second. "No, nothing."

She sees some of the hope leave Penn's eyes and she feels like the entire mission is unraveling. How naive she'd been yesterday, upset at Lyle for testing her and Penn for going along with it, and generally being pessimistic about the assignment based on that. Now they probably won't even be able to complete the assignment.

Penn turns back to Lyle. "That doesn't necessarily mean Aster was lying. Besides, the future is malleable. It's not one hundred percent set. That means whatever she did see might not end up happening anyway, but it also means that something bad could happen, something she didn't tell us about. I'm going to operate under the assumption that us being on this mission gives it a greater chance of success than if we just give up."

"You are relentlessly optimistic, aren't you?" Lyle says.

Penn shrugs. "Someone has to be." He turns to Jess. "Jess, are you still in?"

After everything she's realized and all the lies she's uncovered, she still can't bring herself to say no. She wants to—no—she *needs* to see this to the end.

"Yes."

Penn turns back to Lyle. "What about you?"

"Let's see what our little friend uncovers tomorrow. Then we'll see."

It's not a firm yes, but it isn't a no, either. Jess doesn't know what would happen if Lyle decides to leave. Probably another fight between her and

Penn. She hopes they find something tomorrow.

"All right, we have a plan," Penn says, suddenly smiling. "Now, I think we need a pick-me-up, and I know exactly the right thing for it!"

* 13 *

PENN'S IDEA OF A PICK-ME-UP TURNS OUT to be walking the Magnificent Mile and checking out the designer stores. They leave the wicht and the car in a parking garage (Penn assures Jess that the car is temperature controlled and has sufficient air flow) and he leads the way through the city. He seems at once incredibly touristy and right at home, alternately pointing out every little sight and striding into stores like he owns them.

Jess would never admit it, but the shopping helps distract her from thinking about the mission. In each store they enter, she focuses on the clothes—the way they look, the way they feel, the way they fit. She takes them in through sight and touch, running her fingers over them, cataloging them in the back of her mind.

It's soothing, not having to think about anything other than the clothes. If the others find her behavior odd, they don't mention it, which Jess appreciates. When they finally break from shopping to get dinner, she feels as grounded as she did on that rock by Lyle's house.

They have dinner at a place on Navy Pier, make a quick stop to pick up the case of water bottles and flash drive Aster recommended, and then it's time to head to the safe house.

The FIC has houses around the world, some rented and some owned, that it uses as safe houses when needed. The house they are staying at is in a neighborhood similar to the one Della's family lives in. Instead of being broken up into multiple apartments, though, this house is all one space.

There are enough rooms for each of them, and, after Lyle takes the one on the ground floor, Jess chooses the one on the top floor. She tells the others that she's tired and is going to bed early, but in reality she just wants to be alone. And call Cat, of course. It's only been a day since they talked, but it feels like weeks.

When she's changed into her pajamas and gets Cat on the line, she doesn't make it past Cat's "Hello?" before she breaks.

"It's me," Jess says, her voice catching. "Cat, this whole thing has been a lie."

She explains some of what happened in the morning, leaving out anything confidential, then tells her Lyle's conclusion about why they are still on the assignment.

"It was never because they thought I could actually help, it was all to keep me from leaving the Academy!" she finishes. "I said I'd stay on, but I don't know if it will do any good." She swallows, and her next words are barely more than a whisper. "I'm scared I'm going to make things worse."

There. She's said it at last, voiced the fear that's been haunting her since getting in Penn's car yesterday morning. The fear that first budded after her dad's death and flowered after Joseph's accident. The fear that whispers to her in the voice of every teacher at the Academy who told her she wasn't ready but meant something else entirely.

"What do you mean, make things worse?" Cat asks. "Why would you think that?"

Though the room is warm, Jess shivers. "Something's wrong with me, Cat. I've been feeling so angry lately and I can't control it. It comes so fast, and then I do or say things I wouldn't normally. It's not right."

She doesn't mention how she cried at Lyle's house; she wants Cat's help, not to scare her.

"I'm not saying I don't believe you," Cat says, "but are you sure there isn't another explanation? I know you're under a lot of pressure on this mission. Could that be contributing to it?"

"No, it's different than that," Jess says. "I don't know how to explain it, but it feels like it comes out of nowhere and it's not rational. Penn said something earlier that set me off, and I honestly might have gone at him if Lyle hadn't shut us down. He's a *fairy*! Why would I do that?"

"Oh, I don't know," Cat says. "I seem to remember you fantasizing about punching him on multiple occasions. Maybe you were finally going to go through with it."

"Okay, first off, don't say 'fantasize,' that sounds nasty. Second off, I was never actually going to do it. I don't have that much of a death wish."

"Could've fooled me."

"Hey! You're supposed to be my friend! You're supposed to be on my side!"

Cat laughs. "I am on your side, silly. That's why I'm checking to make sure it wasn't intentional."

"It wasn't!"

"I believe you," Cat says. "I'm sorry this is happening to you, and I wish I knew how to fix it."

"Me, too," Jess says quietly. "I'm afraid I'm going to ruin everything." Then Miss Colleen, her teachers, and her mom will all see they were right to keep her off of assignments. Worse, Della, Lyle, or even Jess herself could get hurt. Penn would be fine, of course, but anything could happen to the rest of them. A bit of fairy blood doesn't make them invulnerable.

"Stop it," Cat says. "Stop talking like that. You are strong. You are capable. You are NOT going to ruin everything. Also, who cares why they put you on the assignment? They wouldn't have done it if they didn't think you were qualified, no matter what other motives they had. They don't want you to fail."

"I wouldn't be too sure."

Cat sighs. "Now I know you're just being difficult. You don't believe that."

Jess laughs. "Okay, fine. You're right. I don't believe they want me to fail, but I also don't believe they aren't just trying to control me. Happy now?"

"Yes!" Cat says. "Great, now that we've gotten that taken care of, it's time for you to help me."

Jess gives an over-dramatic sigh. "Of course. You always want something!

"Don't even with me!" Cat says in mock outrage. They both start laughing, and Jess feels some of the tension she's been holding onto start to unknot itself.

"Okay, what do you need help with?" Jess asks.

"So they're putting together the cast and crew for the next musical, and Ms. Crawford said I should try for director."

Cat loves theater and has been taking classes practically since she started at the Academy at the age of eight.

"That's awesome!" Jess says. "You should do it!"

"Well, I want to, but there's no way they'll pick me over, say, Allison or Chris." Both children of the theater fairy. "I don't want to get my hopes up for nothing. And some of the theater kids already don't like me. They don't think someone without a theater talent should be in the advanced classes."

"That's so elitist," Jess says. "I hate people like that."

"Me, too," Cat says. "I mean, I can't help being born with snow talent any more than you can help being born with your talents. And just because I have a snow talent doesn't mean I just sit around building snowmen all day. I'm a person, too. I'm allowed to like different things!"

"Absolutely," Jess says. "You'll never guess what I'm going to say—prove them wrong!"

Cat laughs. "Why am I not surprised?"

"Come on, you knew that was going to be my advice," Jess says. "Of course I think you should try for director. You'd be great at it. You've put so much into that program; you deserve it as much as anyone else."

"Even Allison and Chris?"

"Especially Allison and Chris. They haven't got anything you haven't, except a little bit of theater blood. And a lot of good that's doing them. Ms. Crawford is right. You need to try for director."

Cat laughs softly. "Okay, I'll do it."

"When are the tryouts?"

"Tomorrow after class."

Jess gasps. "Then what are you still talking to me for? You should be preparing! Go! Practice your director voice!"

Now it's a full laugh from Cat. "Okay, okay, I'll go!" She grows serious again. "Are you sure you're all right, Jess?"

Jess sighs. "I will be."

"That's good enough, I guess," Cat says. "Goodnight, Jess."

"'Night."

They hang up and Jess stares at the phone for a bit before she moves again. She goes to the bathroom to brush her teeth, then returns and removes the small bottle from her bag.

She's glad there's more than one dose, because she doesn't know how she would be able to cope with the radar sense otherwise. It seemed a little better today, maybe because she's gotten used to it, but she can feel the toll it's taking on her body. She needs that valuable sleep to make up for it.

She pours a capful and downs it. The lid is barely screwed on again before the sense of relaxation hits. She doesn't remember lying down, but suddenly she's asleep.

* * * *

At some point during the night, she feels someone shaking her. She can hear her name, too, faintly, as if someone is calling her from far down a dark road. Slowly, she rises to a state of semiconsciousness and realizes it's Penn, trying to shake her awake. She isn't conscious enough to feel annoyed by this. Some sort of muffled racket seems to be coming from downstairs, or maybe it's just in her head? She's not sure.

She's not sure, either, exactly what Penn is trying to tell her. Reality seems to have a slightly blurry quality to it, like she's still in a dream. She can tell at least that he wants her to follow him downstairs, so she gets up slowly.

Walking feels weird; her limbs are heavy, but at the same time, she feels like she's floating. She imagines this is what it feels like to be a fish at the bottom of the ocean, and the thought is so bizarre, she giggles a little. Penn gives her a strange look as they walk downstairs.

When they get to the living room, she can see what has Penn worked up. The roomcase is shaking and a loud shrieking sound is coming from it. Jess stares at it, not quite sure what is going on, until Penn waves his hand in front of her face.

"What?" she says. Her voice sounds weird and kind of far away.

"The wicht," Penn says. "He's throwing a fit and he won't tell us why. He said he'd only talk to you."

"Okay, I'll talk to him," Jess says, yawning. She walks over to the case, squats down, and peers through the door. "What's the matter?"

The banging and shrieking stops and Noe'or's face appears from the gloom. "Nasty wings," he grumbles. "They moved me and now the bright numbers are staring at me."

Jess has no idea what this means. "What?"

"The bright numbers!" He points behind her and she turns to look. She's facing the kitchen and all she sees are the countertops, the stove and microwave, the refrigerator...

"I don't see numbers," she says.

"The big red ones and the green ones!" Noe'or shrieks.

Jess looks again for numbers. It feels like her brain is moving at half speed. After her third scan of the kitchen, she finally realizes what he's talking about. "You mean on the microwave and the oven?"

"Yes. Too bright."

Jess turns back to him and tries to think. "What if...what if we move the case, over by the chair, and it doesn't face the kitchen. How about that?"

Noe'or thinks on it for a moment, and Jess feels her eyes drooping. "Fine," he says. "But it's too hot in here, and too quiet. Unnatural."

Jess rubs her eyes. "Uh...we can open a window?"

There's another pause, then the wicht says, "Okay."

Jess picks up the case and moves it by the chair. When she's done, she's surprised to see Lyle has opened the window. She didn't even notice them in the room.

Her eyes are starting to droop again and her limbs are feeling heavier. She's not totally sure she's awake right now, but if she is, she wants to sleep. "I'm going back to bed," she says with a yawn.

She thinks she hears Lyle whisper something to Penn as she goes into the hall. She's about to climb the first step when Penn appears at her side. It's so sudden it reminds her of a genie. She pictures Penn in a genie outfit singing the song from *Aladdin* and giggles.

Penn takes her arm as she walks up the steps, although she doesn't understand why. Normally, she would be annoyed, but now she realizes that even though his hand is touching her elbow, she can't feel him. No radar senses! She giggles again.

"What's so funny?" Penn asks, and his tone

sounds annoyed or mad or irritated, Jess isn't sure which. But she doesn't care!

"Can't feel you!" she says with another giggle. "Nothing, nada, zilch! I'm free!"

They reach the second floor landing and Penn stops her from going any farther. He turns her around, holding her by the shoulders. He looks like he's searching for something. "Are you on something? Drugs? Alcohol?"

Jess laughs. "You're funny! No, no, no thank you."

Penn narrows his eyes. "Something's wrong with you. This isn't normal." He turns her around and starts guiding her up the next flight of stairs.

"Normal," Jess repeats. "You're not normal. But I'm normal! Now I'm normal."

"What does that mean?"

Jess isn't sure what it means. She's not even sure what they were talking about. As she tries to remember, her foot catches on the top step and she almost falls before Penn catches her. He lifts her onto the last step and she giggles again.

"I can't feel you!" she says.

"What?" he asks, letting go of her as he steps onto the landing.

She pokes his arm. "I can feel you, but I can't *feel* you." She pokes him again and laughs. "It's funny!"

He grabs her hand before she can poke him a third time. "What is going on with you?"

Even in her half-conscious state, Jess can hear the concern in his voice.

"Don't worry," she says, patting him on the shoulder with her free hand. "It'll be okay. I'll be okay."

"Will you?"

What a funny question! Jess laughs. "Someday! Sunday. Someday, Sunday, Monday..."

She's forgotten what they're talking about again. Her eyes feel so tired...

"Tomorrow is Monday," he says, releasing her hand. "Do you mean whatever you're on will wear off and you'll be back to normal tomorrow?"

"Normal..." Jess's brow furrows. "But I am normal. I'm normal now."

It's getting harder and harder for Jess to think straight, but she remembers that much. She runs her hands up and down her arms. "No feeling. I *am* normal!"

He grasps her hands, gently tugging them away from her arms. "Jess, you are normal. You're very normal. But I think you're not feeling well right now. I'm going to help you get to your bed so you can sleep, okay?"

"Sleep..." That's all Jess wants to do. Her bed...she's not sure where it is. But he said he would help her.

He lets go of her hands and takes ahold of her arm, his grasp gentle. "Thank you," Jess murmurs as he guides her toward the doorway. "It's very nice of you..."

She doesn't remember what the nice thing was that he was doing. She tries again. "Very nice...you're very nice. Thank you...for being nice."

He stops, turning to stare at her. His eyes look sad, Jess thinks. "You don't even recognize me right now, do you?"

Jess makes an effort to open her eyes, to really look at him. Those green eyes that look so sad; that face, so familiar she must have known it for years. She knows him; she must. Why has she forgotten?

She realizes that must be why he looks sad. He thinks Jess has forgotten him. And yes, she may have forgotten his name, but she remembers who he is.

"My friend," Jess says, smiling. "You're my friend!"

His eyes still look sad. "Let's get you to bed."

He guides her across the room, and when she reaches her bed, she immediately sinks into it. The last thing she sees before the wave of slumber overtakes her is her friend crossing to her nightstand and plucking something from it.

* 14 *

LYLE AND PENN ARE ALREADY IN THE kitchen when Jess comes downstairs the next morning, because of course they are. Jess is surprised to see Penn has cooked up some eggs and sausage. He never struck her as having the patience for cooking.

When she sits down at the table, both Penn and Lyle are giving her a strange look. Lyle breaks the silence first.

"Did you sleep okay?" they ask.

"Yeah, I slept fine," Jess says between bites of food. "How about you all?"

"Fine," they both say, sharing a glance. They're acting very oddly, and Jess doesn't know why. Before she can ask, she hears a noise from the living room and remembers the wicht. She stands up quickly.

"Are there any leftovers I can give to Noe'or?" she asks Penn. "He should eat, too, before we go."

"Sure," Penn says, gesturing to the pans. "He can have the rest of that. Be quick, though. The sooner we leave, the better."

Jess finds another plate and scoops the rest of the food onto it. She takes it into the living room and finds the case next to the chair.

"Morning," she says to Noe'or, bending down and opening the door slightly. "I have food."

He snatches the plate with a quick "Thanks."

In less than thirty seconds, he's passing the plate back to her without a crumb left. She takes it and closes the door.

"We're going to leave for Della's apartment in a little bit," she tells him. "Do you need anything before we go?"

Noe'or wrinkles his nose. "Do you have any milk? Helps clear the palate."

"I'll go check," Jess says, standing up. When she turns, she sees Penn and Lyle with their heads together, whispering, but they pull apart when they see her looking. She gets a weird feeling seeing them, like deja vu, but she's not sure where it's coming from.

She goes to the fridge and finds some milk, which she pours into a plastic cup and brings back to Noe'or. She expects him to down it in one gulp, but he doesn't, taking small sips instead.

When he's finished, she takes the cup to the

sink to wash it, but Penn tells her he'll take care of it. He waves his hand lazily and the dishes start to wash themselves. Jess goes back to the table and finishes her breakfast. She's still getting a strange vibe from Lyle and Penn, but can't pinpoint why. She wonders if they received a new communication from Talia while she was asleep, but if that's the case, why aren't they telling her about it?

* * * *

It's a short drive to Della's, and Jess sits in the back seat, clutching the case in anticipation. When they arrive, they head up to the apartment, where Lyle uses a key provided by the FIC to unlock the door.

The apartment looks exactly like the photos from the file—well-kept and nicely decorated, yet still homey. But it feels wrong. The air is too still and heavy, overwhelming Jess with the feeling that she shouldn't be there. It feels wrong to be invading the family's privacy, and it feels wrong that the place is so empty.

She can see signs of life in the half-empty glass on the kitchen table, the pair of reading glasses abandoned on the side table, the neatly lined up shoes in the boot tray next to the front door. Life, frozen by loss.

Lyle is the first to break the stifling silence. "We ought to take a look around before you let out your little friend. See if we can find anything that was missed. Mom said the parents have been staying with a relative, so the evidence shouldn't be disturbed. I'll start with the bedroom, if you two want to take the kitchen."

"Okay," Jess says, and Lyle takes off down the hallway to the bedroom.

Jess sets the roomcase down in the entryway and heads to the kitchen, Penn behind her. Before she enters the room, she stops, scanning the area to see if anything looks out of place. The room is meticulously clean, the countertops spotless, every appliance gleaming like it's been freshly polished. At least one of Della's parents must be a real clean freak.

"What do you see?" Penn says from behind her.

"Nothing yet. Can you dim the light?"

"How will that help?" The skepticism is thick in Penn's voice. Jess turns to him.

"Will you please just do it?"

"Fine."

Penn clasps his hands together, then separates them, holding them up like a conductor, before bringing them down slowly. As he does, the light in the room dims until it almost looks like it's nighttime.

Jess pulls out her phone and switches on the flashlight. She crouches down and cups her hand around the edge of the light to keep the beam tight, then holds it at a forty-five-degree angle about an inch above the floor. Suddenly, every speck of dirt, dust, and hair is illuminated—along with something else.

"Look," Jess says, pointing. Penn crouches down behind her so he can see what she's spotted.

"Footprints?"

Jess nods. "Three sets. Look how the smaller set goes straight to the window, then straight back. They were probably keeping watch."

She pans her phone light from left to right and back again.

"The set with the worn soles is more active—looks like they poked around a lot, maybe searching for something? Then they sat at the table before getting back up again..." She pans the light once more.

"The big set barely comes into the room at all; they must have waited or hidden somewhere else. Probably the one who subdued Della."

There's a pause before Penn speaks. "That's impressive," he says, "but how do you know those all belong to the kidnappers?"

"Look at the rest of the floor, the rest of the kitchen," Jess says. "It's spotless. And see how orderly the shoes are lined up by the door. There's no way anyone in Della's family was wearing shoes in the house. The FIC and any law enforcement would be wearing protective shoe covers, so that leaves the kidnappers."

"Do you think the police saw the footprints?"

Jess shrugs. "If they had a forensic investigator look things over, probably. But they may not have looked too closely at this room. It's obviously not where the struggle took place." Jess switches her flashlight off and stands up. "Can you bring the light back?"

Penn snaps his fingers and the light immediately returns. Jess slips off her shoes and carefully steps into the kitchen, trying to avoid the footprints. She hears a small knock behind her and turns to see Penn kneeling at the entrance again, his hand poised above the floor. From where his knuckles hit the tile, a wave of magic is emanating out; Jess watches as it reveals the footprints, highlighting them in purple.

She turns back and starts to follow the trail of worn footprints. Their owner seems to have been poking around in the cupboards, judging by how close they get to the counters. Jess summons a glove and carefully opens a few of the upper cabinets, but nothing inside looks disturbed.

At the end of the countertop, she reaches the fridge. She turns her flashlight back on and points it at the fridge handles, which are made of stainless steel. The handle on the right is clean and polished, but the left handle is smudged with a set of fingerprints.

"Gotcha," Jess whispers, before turning to Penn, who is now behind her. "Look, they left fingerprints. The FIC will be interested in these."

"I'm more interested in what's in the fridge," Penn says. "If they were looking for something, like you said, did they find it?"

"Let's see." Jess turns off her flashlight and carefully opens the door, being sure to grasp the handle from below the fingerprints. The fridge is well-stocked and well-organized, with each container labeled and dated.

Penn lets out a low whistle. "Wow. Never thought I'd feel judged by a refrigerator. I feel like I need to go fold my socks now or something."

Jess looks back at him. "You don't fold your socks?"

"Wait, that's something people actually do?"

The surprise and bafflement on Penn's face are genuine, and it takes a second before they slide away as he realizes what's going on.

"You're playing with me," he says, smiling and pointing a finger at her. "That was a joke. You're joking with me."

Jess is about to respond, but as quickly as his smile appeared, it vanishes, replaced by a serious, unreadable expression. The change is so sudden, it catches her off guard.

What's his deal today? First the weird looks and whispering with Lyle at breakfast, and now this strange hot-and-cold behavior. Something's going on with him, but Jess can't figure out what.

"You two hungry already? Thought we just ate."

Jess and Penn turn to see Lyle in the doorway. "We were looking for evidence," Jess says.

"In the refrigerator." Lyle's raised eyebrow doesn't believe them.

"There are fingerprints," Penn says, pointing at the handle. "Jess thought they might be looking for something."

Jess can tell Lyle still isn't buying that, and it irritates her even though she knows she shouldn't care.

"There were at least three of them," she says, pointing at the ground where Penn's spell is still painting the prints with purple. "See, three sets of footprints."

"Well, at least you found something," Lyle says. "Mom will like that. I don't think Della even made it to her room; nothing seems out of place there. Let's check out the living room, I guess, then we can let out your little friend."

Something is niggling in the back of Jess's mind, something that's off, but whatever it is, it's hovering just out of reach. She follows Lyle and Penn into the living room, and they stop and survey the destruction.

It's as bad as the photos Jess saw in the file, but more unnerving in person. The frost is clearly magical—it's still as crisp and bright as the day the photo was taken. It should have melted by now, but the message—"Come and get her"—is crystal clear. She can see how it would be easy to mark this as McCreed's doing.

McCreed. The fairies. A war. And Della.

One of these things doesn't fit, and Jess knows which one it is.

"Doesn't it strike you as odd," she says to the others, "that they chose Della? I mean, we're assuming their objective was to start a war between McCreed and the fairies. So why kidnap Della to start it? She's not high-profile, she doesn't even know she's half-fae. There are loads of half-fae that are more powerful than Della, and probably way more efficient ways to start a war, too. So why her?"

Lyle taps their chin thoughtfully. "I considered that, too. It's definitely not the method I would use, I can tell you that. Maybe they chose her out of convenience. Maybe the kidnappers live nearby or something."

"Still, they had to have known she was half-fae. From her file, it didn't sound like a lot of people knew. So how did they find out?"

Lyle shakes their head. "No way to know. We'll just have to force it out of them when we find her."

"Guys, come look at this," Penn says. He's kneeling next to the frost on the floor and has a pen in his hand, which he's using as a pointer. "See how uneven the frost is over here, about half an inch thick, and right next to that it's so thin you can see the carpet through it. It's like the spell was thrown at the room, and that's not McCreed's style at all."

Jess and Lyle move closer to look. He's right; the frost looks downright sloppy up close.

"They certainly didn't put much effort into the spell," Lyle says. "Not only is it a mess, but there's not even a trick to it. If this was really McCreed's work, it would do something—change color, move if you touch it, conceal a hidden message—it wouldn't just stay frozen."

"Wouldn't they know that, if they were trying to frame McCreed?" Jess asks. "I imagine they would have planned everything out. Wouldn't they have done research and taken the time to learn McCreed's style of magic?"

"Unless they didn't have time," Penn says,

standing up. He starts pacing on the part of the carpet that's clear of ice.

"What if—this is going to sound crazy, but hear me out here—what if it wasn't planned? What if they weren't intending to frame McCreed, and that was just a side effect of their real plan?"

"Which is?" Lyle's eyebrows are raised in skepticism.

"Kidnapping Della," Penn says, turning to them. "We might be looking at this the wrong way. We assumed they took her to start a war, but if that's the case, why didn't they do a better job of it? I'm starting to think this isn't about a war at all, but about Della."

"If it's about Della, then why bring McCreed into it?" Jess asks. She thinks back to her conversation with McCreed the day before. "Wouldn't it have been easier, and raised less suspicion, if they'd made it look like she was kidnapped by human criminals, or just ran away?"

"It would," Penn says. He crouches beside the frost again, touching his fingertips to its edge. "Maybe that was the original plan, but something went wrong and they were forced to improvise. Magic always leaves traces. Maybe this isn't the evidence we're looking for. Maybe it's covering it up."

"You might be onto something there," Lyle says. "How about you try that magic detecting trick of yours? See if you can find anything."

Penn nods and moves to the center of the room. He sits on the floor, cross-legged, touches his fingertips to the carpet, and closes his eyes. Jess and Lyle step back and watch him closely, but his face gives no indication of what he's seeing. After a minute or so, it gets awkward for Jess, staring at him, so she looks away. It's another full minute before he moves, relaxing from the stiff pose and opening his eyes.

"There was a struggle," he says, standing up. "I think they expected her to come quietly, but she didn't. They struggled and stuff broke. That table, the vase." He points at the objects as he speaks. "They used magic to repair them and put the room back the way it was. They also used it to subdue her, right over there." He turns and points to the corner of the room closest to the doorway. Jess can almost see what he's describing, hear the echo of Della's shouts for help. A shiver runs down her spine.

"The frost was done quickly, like they were in a rush," Penn continues. "Three blasts, here, here, and here. Then thirty seconds to carve the message, and that's the last magic they used."

"So you were right," Lyle says. "This wasn't some carefully staged plan, it was thrown together on the fly. Which means our real question is: what kind of people cover up a kidnapping by attempting to start a war?"

Neither Jess nor Penn have an answer for that.

They don't find anything else of use in the living room, so it's time to let Noe'or out and see if he can pick up the kidnappers' trail. Jess goes to the hallway and grabs the roomcase, while Lyle goes to call Talia and update her on the group's finds. Penn moves to the doorway, where he stands with his arms crossed, watching Jess and the roomcase warily like a security guard.

Jess sets the roomcase on the living room floor and opens the door. Noe'or emerges slowly, stretching his legs. He sniffs the air, nostrils quivering, before turning to Jess.

"You got something of hers I can use to track?" he asks.

Jess turns to Penn. "Can you go grab something from her room? A piece of laundry or her pillow, maybe?"

"Sure," Penn says, not looking happy to have to take his eyes off the wicht. While he fetches the item, Noe'or walks around the room, sniffing various items, pieces of furniture, and patches of floor with seemingly no rhyme or reason.

Penn returns shortly and hands Jess a blue sweater before resuming his post in the doorway. Jess passes it to Noe'or, who buries his nose in it for about a minute. When he emerges, he passes it back to her and says, "Follow me."

She follows him out of the living room while Penn goes to fetch Lyle. Noe'or leads her out the back door and into the alley behind the house, which backs the houses down this street and the next one over. He points to the right.

"They put her in a van and it went that way," he says.

"Can you track it?"

He bends down and sniffs the gravel. "Yes," he

says simply.

"Well, I guess it's road trip time again," a voice says from behind Jess. She turns to see Penn, who must have teleported out to them.

He steps into the alley and sets his keychain down, and seconds later they're standing in front of the car again. Penn touches the hood and it changes from the Charger back to the Oldsmobile Cutlass.

Jess half expects him to make a joke, but he just says, "Let's head out."

"Where's Lyle?" Jess asks as she opens the rear door for Noe'or.

"They said they don't want to sit in a car in Chicago traffic, so they're going to stay here to debrief the other officers when they arrive," Penn says, sliding into the driver's seat. "I'll send them a summoner if we end up finding anything, and they can meet up with us."

Jess gets in on the passenger side, and once she's buckled in, the car starts moving. The rear window is open so the wicht can stick his head out, like the world's freakiest dog. Jess hopes that whatever camouflage effect Penn has on the car extends to Noe'or as well.

"I'm going to close off the front seat so it doesn't get too loud," Penn tells him. "There's a microphone in the seatbelt; just speak into it to tell me where to go." He glares at Noe'or in the rearview mirror. "And no funny business!"

"Aye aye, captain!" Noe'or gives Penn a sarcastic salute before sticking his nose out the window. "Left at the end of the alley," he says.

Penn presses a button on the dashboard and a clear plastic barrier appears between the rows of seats.

"Are there really microphones in the seatbelts?" Jess asks as they turn.

"No," Penn says, "that's just a simpler explanation than 'The car is a living thing and can hear whatever you say in it' and 'It drives itself so you don't even need to give me the directions.'"

"Oh" is Jess's response. She waits for some sort of joke to follow, but none comes. She gets another weird feeling, like there's something she should know. There's something Penn's not telling her.

* 15 *

IT TAKES THIRTY MINUTES, BUT THEY MAKE it to the highway and then past the traffic. When they reach a good cruising speed, Penn turns to Jess.

"Do you really not remember what happened last night?" he asks, his tone accusing.

Jess has no idea what he's talking about. A cold feeling settles in her stomach. "What do you mean?"

"When the wicht threw a tantrum and I woke you up?"

"You woke me up?" She doesn't remember anything of the sort.

"You really don't remember?" His eyes are searching, and he sounds like he doesn't quite believe her.

"Look, I have no idea what you're talking about," Jess says, exhaling in frustration. "Can you just get to whatever it is you're actually trying to ask? All I remember from last night is talking to my friend, then going to sleep."

Something in Penn's face hardens. "The wicht said he would only talk to you, so I went to get you. You didn't respond when I knocked, and when I woke you up, you were awake, but you were completely out of it. Nothing you said made any sense, aside from when you talked with the wicht."

It dawns on Jess what must have happened. Celia had warned her when she gave her the potion that if she was somehow woken up while still under its effects, she would be in a semiconscious state and probably not remember anything in the morning. She must have said something strange, and now Penn wants an explanation.

"I must have still been half asleep," Jess says. "Sometimes people say odd stuff when they're not fully awake."

Penn takes his right hand off the wheel and holds it out to her, palm up. A familiar small bottle appears in it. "I found this on your nightstand. This is a sleeping potion, right?"

Jess says nothing, but he seems to take her silence as confirmation.

"You know these can be very dangerous? I can feel the level of magic in this. This is not the kind of thing you want to be taking regularly; in fact, I'm surprised you were able to obtain it at all." He shakes his head. "Stuff like this can really mess with your body."

Jess snatches it from his hand before he can get rid of it. "Thanks for your concern, but you can save the lecture. It's none of your business anyway."

"Look, I only want to help," Penn says, and he sounds genuine. "If there's something wrong, something you need help with, you can tell me."

He's the last person Jess would go to in need. "I don't need your help. I said it's none of your business."

Penn's eyes grow cold and he raises an eyebrow. "Well, that's not what it sounded like last night."

"What is that supposed to mean?"

"You said some pretty strange stuff. I don't know what any of it meant, but I know you were talking about me."

"I doubt that," Jess says.

"You kept poking me and telling me you couldn't feel me. You said you were 'normal now,' whatever that means."

He's staring at her again and she knows he's looking for any sign of recognition. She keeps her expression neutral even as her stomach feels like the bottom is going to drop out. She can't tell him about the radar sense.

"I was half asleep," she says. "You can't take anything I said seriously. It sounds like nonsense."

Penn's eyes narrow. "You know, I've got a little bit of a lie radar myself. Comes from the horse abilities. I can sense emotions and I can tell you're hiding something. There's something you're afraid of."

Jess decides to stick with her denial. "Well, then your horse senses are wrong. I don't remember saying any of that, and I don't know what it means. I was half asleep. It's nonsense."

"You weren't half asleep, you were under the influence of a very strong, very dangerous sleeping potion!" Penn bursts out. "There's a difference!"

"Okay, you want me to admit I took a sleeping potion?" Jess snaps. "Fine! I took a sleeping potion! It's not illegal, and it's not any of your business anyway! So can you just drop it?"

"It is too my business!" Penn snaps. "Maybe Colleen didn't tell you, but I'm supposed to be looking out for you on this mission. It's my responsibility to make sure nothing happens to you. And part of that includes not letting you ingest dangerous substances without anyone knowing. What if you had a reaction to that stuff, and no one knew you were taking it? Or if I hadn't been able to wake you up? At the very least, you could have told one of us so we knew."

Jess crosses her arms. "I don't need to tell you my personal business, and I certainly don't need you protecting me from anything. I can look out for myself."

She's referencing her time on the run, and she can tell he catches it by the way his lips tighten briefly before he speaks.

"I know you can," he says, his tone losing its

edge, "and I'm not trying to imply otherwise. It's just that you're young, and sometimes people, when they're young, can be a bit reckless, or they think they know all about the world when they're still learning. Even I'm still learning, and Crown knows I can be reckless sometimes, too. But me and Lyle, we're here to help you and guide you. You don't have to feel like you need to hide stuff from us if you need help."

It takes Jess a good thirty seconds to process what he's said. When she does, she's insulted. So she goes for the easy target.

"Well, excuse me for 'hiding' stuff from you. Only, I had so much practice hiding as a kid that it's kind of a habit now. Little hard to break."

Penn slaps the rim of the steering wheel with both hands. "Stars fall, aren't you ever going to give that up? This isn't about that! None of this is about that!"

"Isn't it, though?" Jess asks. "Doesn't everything go back to that? You stalked me for two years and now you want me to pretend like it never happened."

"For the last time, I wasn't stalking you, I was trying to help you!"

"Like you're trying to help me now?"

There's a beat of silence before Penn turns to look her in the eyes. "I don't know what you want from me. If it's an apology, then fine. I'll give you an apology. I'll apologize for making you feel afraid and like you had to keep running. But I won't apologize for trying to help. I'll never apologize for that."

His words sound genuine, but that doesn't mean Jess trusts him.

"I don't know what you're going through, and I don't know if I'd be able to help," he continues. "But I know sometimes it helps to talk to someone, and I want you to know it's okay to talk to me, or to Lyle. I don't want you to feel afraid, or like you have to lie to us."

"Talking to you isn't going to help anything."

It's out of her mouth before she can stop it. She braces herself for the inevitable nasty response, but it doesn't come. It seems Penn fancies himself to be taking the high ground now.

"And why's that?" he asks, a frosty edge to his tone.

"Because you don't make things better, you only make them worse."

"How do I do that?" The same frosty tone.

"By...well, you always make it about you."

"Explain."

This game is getting irritating. "You've made this whole thing about you; first, by saying I was talking about you when I don't even remember it, and then making it about how you're just trying to protect me and I'm preventing you from fulfilling your duty by being irresponsible or something."

Penn is silent for a few seconds before he speaks.

"Let me explain from my perspective. I found you last night, definitely under the influence of something. You're saying I should disregard everything you said to me as nonsense, even though you were able to have a coherent conversation with the wicht and figure out what he was going on about just minutes before you started talking to me.

"Then I find out you're taking a sleeping potion strong enough to take out a fairy for a couple hours, without telling anyone. I even checked with Colleen and she had no clue. Finally, when I ask you about it, you get defensive, evasive, and lie to me." He turns to look at her. "Can you see how all of that is concerning?"

Jess misses his last two sentences. Her brain stopped processing when he said Miss Colleen's name, and she can't focus on anything else. He told *Miss Colleen* about the sleeping potion? Who does he think he is, ratting her out like that?

"You know what? I was right about you from the very beginning," Jess snaps. "Not only are you completely inept at intelligence work, you're a back-stabbing piece of fairy trash who doesn't deserve to be on this team, or any team, for that matter."

Penn's mouth drops open and he stares at her in stunned silence. Jess knows she's done for; if there's one emotion fairies do understand, it's anger. No one insults a fairy like that and lives to tell the tale. But if she's going down, she wants him to know exactly what she thinks of him.

"Real teammates have each other's backs," she hisses. "They don't rat each other out. If I was double-crossing you or endangering the assignment, then sure. Definitely tell someone. But tattling about a sleeping potion? That wasn't to help the team, that was you trying to get brownie points with Miss Colleen. It was selfish, and there's no room for selfishness on an assignment like this. Selfishness gets people killed. Ego gets people killed. Betrayal gets people killed. You may be clipping immortal, but that just means your reputation will be stained with our blood forever. And forever is a very long time."

Penn's face has gone from shocked to furious. His cheeks are the color of a stop sign and he's shaking with barely suppressed rage. His hands are no longer on the steering wheel, but balled into fists at his sides. The car is completely silent apart from the sound of both of them breathing.

"I could obliterate you right now," he says.

Jess smiles. She knew he had some hatred for her in there somewhere, and now it's finally out in the open.

"Then *do it*."

He glares at her for a solid thirty seconds, which turn into a minute, then two. Finally, he unclenches his fists and exhales deeply, his color returning, if not to normal, to a color more befitting of a person than a traffic signal.

"I won't obliterate you, Jess," he says, turning back to face the road.

All that build-up for nothing? It's not that Jess wants to be obliterated—she doesn't have a death wish—but she was expecting *something*. She doesn't understand why he's suddenly holding back.

"You won't, or you can't?" He turns to glare at her, but as he does, she remembers—"Wait a second! You can't!" She laughs in surprise and relief. "You swore on the Crown that you'd never raise a hand against me. You *can't* obliterate me!"

Penn's cheeks color again. "Oh, I could. It'd be excruciatingly painful and I'd probably be cursed for the rest of my existence, but I could technically still obliterate you, as long as I did it fast. I'm not going to, though."

"Not worth it?"

"No, it's not, but also, Nell told me not to." He looks back at the road.

This catches Jess by surprise. "Wait, *Nell* told you not to? Why?"

Penn's lips tighten into a thin line, and when he speaks, he says the words as if it physically pains him to utter them. "She thinks that, behind your petty insults and offensive name-calling, you had a point."

"A point about what?" Jess's anger has mostly drained away now, to be replaced by curiosity. Penn's other half thinks she had a point?

"The teammate thing. She thinks I shouldn't have said anything to Colleen about the sleeping potion. Said it was poor judgment, even if I was concerned for your well-being. She thinks I should have talked to you about it first."

"Oh." Jess doesn't know what to say. She feels a rush of gratitude toward Nell, whom she hasn't even met. The other fairy may have spared her life.

"Don't get too happy about it, though," Penn says, eyeing her. "She also thinks the stuff you said about me was unnecessarily cruel and offensive and merits an apology."

Jess hangs her head in shame. Nell is right; she went too far. Just because her emotions have been out of whack recently doesn't mean she should let them run wild. When she gets back to the Academy, she'll have to figure out what's happening to her, but for now, she needs to fix the situation she's gotten herself into.

"I'm sorry. Please tell Nell that she's right. I shouldn't have said any of those things; they were mean, petty, and uncalled for. I let my anger get out of hand. That was poor teammate behavior, and I'm sorry."

She looks up to see Penn staring at her, looking genuinely surprised at her apology.

"I mean it," she says. "And please do tell Nell what I said."

"She's listening," Penn says. His cheeks redden again.

"What is it? Did she say something else?"

"She said now I need to apologize. For telling Colleen about the sleeping potion, but also for threatening to obliterate you. So I'm sorry. I shouldn't have talked to Colleen first, and I should have talked to you this morning instead of waiting. Also poor teammate behavior. And the obliteration thing"—he looks away from Jess and runs his hand through his hair—"I don't know why I said that. Nell chewed me out pretty bad for it. We've never obliterated anyone. *I've* never obliterated anyone, and I certainly wasn't going to do it to you."

Well, Jess can cross that off her list of theories why Penn was exiled from the fairy world.

She believes him, too; not just because she senses no lies, but because it tracks with his personality. McCreed may've been right when he said there's no such thing as a soft fairy, but if there was, Penn would be the prime example, hands down.

"I'm really sorry," he says. "I don't want you to think—I'm not like the—I didn't mean it." He exhales, and the action seems to calm him. He looks over at her. "I don't want to hurt you. Or anyone else for that matter, but especially you."

"Why me?"

"I'm already responsible for enough suffering in your life, aren't I?" He gives her a sad smile. "I didn't even realize. I certainly don't want to be the cause of any more."

Jess feels her stomach clench with nerves, and she knows what she has to do.

"There's something I have to tell you," she says, her voice quiet.

A look of concern replaces Penn's sad smile. "What is it? Is everything okay?"

She takes a deep breath, then holds her head up and looks him in the eyes.

"The stuff I said last night, I know what it meant."

Penn's eyes widen, and she can practically see the gears turning as he recalls what she must have said. She forges on.

"This may sound crazy, but when I was on the run, running from you, I somehow developed a sort of magic radar sense to detect when you were nearby. It basically puts me on high alert, so I'm constantly in fight-or-flight mode when you're around, and I can't control it." She twists her hands in her lap. "It makes it impossible to relax or fall asleep, but the sleeping potion dampens it. That's why I took it. I don't know any other way to stop it."

She holds his gaze, daring him to laugh or crack a joke at her expense, but to her surprise, he doesn't. Instead, he looks stunned.

"Wait, so this entire time...the past seven years, this has been happening? And you never told anyone?"

Jess shakes her head. "I didn't know how to explain it without sounding crazy, or—or having people take it the wrong way. I don't even understand what it is, so how could I get someone else to?"

There's a pause before Penn responds. "I guess that's understandable. I wish you would have told me, though."

"When? During the two years I was on the run? During the years after where I thought you were a wicked, horrible person? The sense was protecting me then. If I knew where you were, I could avoid you, and then I was safe."

Penn stares at his hands on the steering wheel for a long minute before looking back at her. "And what about now? Is it still protecting you?"

Jess is at a loss. Back then, although she was annoyed at how specific the sense was, she was still grateful that she had it. It was like knowing the location of a pothole in the sidewalk when riding a bike. If you know where it is, you can avoid it.

But maybe Jess had been too quick to avoid what she was afraid of instead of facing it. Maybe she's outgrown the sense.

"I...I don't know."

She knows it's not what he wants to hear and she wishes she had a better answer, but not for his sake. She doesn't honestly know if she needs it or not, or if she even wants it if given the choice. She doesn't have the answer yet. But maybe he has answers for her.

"What would you have done, if you knew? You're a fairy—do you know why I have this power? Or how to get rid of it?"

He shakes his head. "Unfortunately, no. My best guess would be that your magic developed in ways that helped you the most in the situations you were experiencing. As a half-fae, your specific abilities aren't set at birth, but rather they develop over time, much in the same ways fairies' powers evolve as their domains change and develop. Why this is so specific and so far outside your normal abilities, I have no idea. I'm also unaware of any way to get rid of a magical ability. Believe me, if I knew, there are some I would drop in a heartbeat."

His gaze unfocuses for a few seconds, like he's reliving a memory, or maybe listening to Nell.

When he focuses back on Jess, his gaze is serious.

"If I'd known, I would have done everything in my power to help. I *will* do everything in my power to help. I don't know if there's a way to fix this, but I'll do my best to find one."

Jess shakes her head. "You don't need to bother. It's not that big a deal anyway. I can manage."

"You shouldn't have to, though," Penn says. "It's not fair that you have to live with that and can't even sleep without an extra-strength sleeping potion."

Jess doesn't know how to explain that it's only an issue because she's around him, and it could be solved instantly if he went far enough away. Unless she wanted to be cruel, which she doesn't. She's done enough of that for one day.

She's surprised to find that she feels a sense of relief, even though she hadn't wanted to tell him. At least now it's out there, and he didn't even laugh or make a bad joke about it.

"So it doesn't work on anything else?" Penn asks. "Just me?"

Well, maybe Jess was too quick to assume no joke was coming. "Nothing else that I've found," she says.

"That's bizarre."

"Thanks," Jess says sarcastically.

"Oh, no, I didn't mean *you* were bizarre. Just that the power is so specific. It's very curious."

"Not when you have it. It's just annoying."

Penn glances over with a smile starting to form

on his lips. "Yes, I can see how it would be annoying. Imagine how much more helpful it would be to sense cheeseburgers! Or the aces in a deck of cards. Or golf balls—you'd never lose one again!"

"Cheeseburgers?" Jess asks.

Penn shrugs. "I've always wished I could sense good food. I can tell you where the nearest gas station is, or the exact height and weight of your horse, or where you parked your car in any parking lot. But I don't have a food radar and it's one of the greatest sorrows of my life."

"You're sad you don't have cheeseburger radar. Wouldn't that make you hungry all the time, always knowing where food was?"

"Eh, no. I don't usually get hungry. I just like cheeseburgers."

Jess can't help it; she can see right through him and knows he's just trying to relieve the tension, but she has to laugh at this.

"What?" Penn says, looking over at her. "They're delicious!"

"No, it's not that," she says, "it's—well, you know how people always ask, if you could have any superpower, what would it be? And most people choose flight or mind reading or super strength, and your choice is cheeseburgers." She starts giggling all over again. "Cheeseburger power!"

"I happen to think it's a very reasonable ability," Penn says, aloof. But this quickly dissolves into laughter when he follows it up with "They can call me Mr. Cheeseburger!"

"But how does your cheeseburger power help people?"

Penn gasps, affronted. "My cheeseburger power is very helpful! For example, someone could come up to me and say, 'Oh, Mr. Cheeseburger, my son is very sick, and the only thing that can cure him is a cheeseburger!' Then I would be able to tell them where the nearest available cheeseburger is and save a life!"

"Ah yes, cheeseburgers—a life or death matter!" Jess has tears in her eyes at this point, she's laughing so hard.

"Hey, don't knock the cheeseburger!" Penn says. "You never know, someday you might be in need of a life-saving cheeseburger. Then you'd wish you had cheeseburger powers, too."

At this point, every repetition of the word "cheeseburger" has caused them to laugh harder until they're both clutching their sides. It's been months since Jess has laughed this hard, and it surprises her that he was the one to elicit it. If he was this version of Penn all the time, good-natured and funny without all the annoying bits, she might actually be able to stand being around him.

After about a minute of laughing, Jess realizes the car has slowed and they are no longer on the highway anymore. She stops laughing.

"I think we might be getting close," she says.

Penn drops the barrier to the backseat and shouts back to Noe'or, "Is the trail getting stronger?"

"Yes," Noe'or shouts back. "The vehicle has

been this way multiple times, without the girl, too."

The area they are driving through is mostly forested. If she'd been paying attention on the highway, Jess may have had an idea of where they're at, but she doesn't recognize anything now. They could be near the Academy, for all she knows. If Penn has a better idea, he's not saying.

She looks over to see how he's reacting to them being so close. His expression is grim and he's gripping the steering wheel tightly with both hands. He looks intense, and Jess can see now that he does care about this mission. She had doubted his motives from the start, but regardless of why he agreed in the first place, it seems he actually does care about getting Della home safely to her family. She cares, too.

For most people, these final minutes before they reach their destination would be nerve-wracking, but for Jess, a sense of calm washes over her. This is what she's trained for, what she was born to do. All of the fear and doubt is pushed to the side, and she can only focus on the road ahead and what she'll do when they arrive.

* 16 *

WITHIN A FEW MINUTES, THEY BEGIN TO SEE signs of civilization. They're approaching a town, but from what seems like the wrong direction. They're on the very outskirts, where the industrial buildings and office complexes are. Noe'or starts directing them through a maze of smaller roads until they eventually reach a larger office complex made up of several similar-looking buildings.

"This is it," Noe'or says.

After a short discussion, Penn parks the car at a different complex down the road.

"Which building is it?" Jess asks.

Noe'or points to the one farthest from the main road. It looks...ordinary. Plain. There's nothing to distinguish it from the other buildings in the complex.

At the beginning of the mission, Jess had thought, like the others, that Della was being held at McCreed's palace. When they discovered she wasn't there, Jess hadn't really considered what type of place she might be at, but she realizes she expected it to be along the same lines.

She didn't expect this plain, ordinary building that could be on the outskirts of any medium-sized town. She finds it more disturbing than if it looked like the hideout of a cartoon villain.

"What do we do now?" Penn asks, looking at her.

Jess is surprised; she expected he would want to take the lead and she would have to speak up and assert herself, but instead, he's deferring to her.

He seems to notice her surprise. "You're the one with the spy background," he tells her. "I think you ought to take the lead."

"What about Lyle?"

He shrugs. "I can summon them now if you want, but it's up to you."

Jess thinks for a moment. "Let's watch the building for a few minutes. Does your car have an invisibility mode? Can we get closer without them seeing?"

Penn grins. "Of course it has invisibility mode! And it has an even cooler feature. Check this out."

He presses a button below the volume control on the radio panel. From below the CD player, a small panel with buttons slides out. He taps a few, then puts the car in drive and pulls forward. "Now look behind us," he says.

Jess turns back to look and sees the car, still parked in the same spot. "How...is that an illusion or something?"

His face lights up with excitement as he explains. "The actual car is invisible now, but before we went invisible, I dropped an illusion projector from the bottom of the car—they attach with magnets, it's super cool—so it looks like the car is still there even when it's not. It's part of Natoi's magic, too, not mine, which is great. I mean, I can maintain a lot of magic at a time, but it's nice to have one less thing to worry about. It's also a super helpful tool for saving parking spots! You can leave and come back and your spot will still be there."

"Neat," Jess says. It's a handy little trick, and clever, too. But she can't tell him that or he'll get a big head.

"I think it's really cool," Penn says proudly. "Anyway, now that we're in super stealth mode, let's go see what we can find out."

He pulls the car forward and they exit the lot, heading toward the building. Penn enters the parking lot and they circle the edge until they are right in front of the doors.

Jess peers outside, looking for anything of interest, but all she sees is a small plaque next to the door reading "Smith and Salt Ltd."

She tells Penn what it says. "Does that mean anything to you?"

He shakes his head. "Probably a front name."

Jess agrees, but something about the name still unsettles her. They don't see any people, but the few vehicles in the lot seem to suggest the building has at least some occupants. Penn suggests they snap pictures of the license plates so he can look them up later, and they drive slowly up and down the aisles while Jess takes the photos.

When that's done, she asks Penn to try pulling around the back of the building. He obliges, and as they turn the corner, they see something that chills Jess's blood.

A white panel van is backed up to the building's rear dock.

"Do you think..." Penn can't even finish the thought.

"That's it," Noe'or says from the backseat. "I can take a sniff to make sure, but it looks how it smells."

"We have the right place, then," Penn says. There's a pause as they all stare at the van before Jess speaks.

"I think you should send for Lyle now," she says quietly.

Penn nods. "It'll be fastest if I just fetch them myself. I'll be back in an instant." Without even giving her time to respond, he disappears.

Now Jess is alone, with only Noe'or to keep her company. She should be nervous, but instead, a deep sense of calm and focus has come over her. She looks at the van, plain and unassuming. The quiet banality of it and of the building itself makes it all feel more threatening.

Jess remembers Aster saying she would find things on this mission that would be upsetting. She dismissed it at the time, but now that she's outside the building, seeing things she'd only imagined up to that point, she thinks Aster was right.

Her mind starts to wander, caught up in imagining what they might find. Since they have no idea who these people are, how many there are, or what their end goal is, the possibilities are endless. She runs through a couple scenarios, nerves mounting with each one, before she even realizes what she's doing. When she does, she puts a hard stop to it.

Instead, she uses a trick her dad taught her. She remembers the first time he shared it with her, when she was probably six or seven and just realizing what his job was and how dangerous it could be. They were sitting outside her favorite ice cream shop, and she remembers the taste of the cool ice cream and how her legs weren't long enough for her feet to touch the ground.

"Daddy, if you could get hurt at work, don't you get scared sometimes?" she asked.

Her dad set down his ice cream bowl. "Sure I do," he said. "Everyone gets scared sometimes."

"Even superheroes?"

Jess had been fascinated with superheroes at the time, especially Batman. She had Batman books, Batman action figures, even a Batman cape that she would wear around the house to perform rescue missions for her stuffed animals.

"Yes, even superheroes," her dad said. "We all

get scared sometimes; it's part of being human. But the trick is to not let your fear control you. If you only think about how afraid you are, you'll be too afraid to do anything, and you'll miss opportunities to help or make things better."

"But how do you stop being afraid?"

"You don't stop being afraid," he said. "Instead, you have to redirect your thoughts. Put things into perspective. See, you can think for hours and hours about how things might go down, and you'll come up with all sorts of nightmare scenarios. But the truth is, most of them are never going to happen, and thinking up more isn't going to help. It'll just make you more afraid."

"So what do you think about then?"

"I think about what's going to happen *after* the thing I'm afraid of," her dad said. "I think about how I'm going to have lunch and talk with my work buddies, or go home and hug my amazing daughter."

When he said that, he smiled, his brown eyes crinkling at the corners, and tapped Jess on the nose. She smiled, too.

"Whatever happens is going to happen, and it will either be worse than you expected or, more likely, better. But there are only so many things you can do to change it, and worrying about it isn't one of them. By focusing on what will happen when it's over, you're reminding yourself that it will happen, but it will also end, and then you'll move on. Does that make sense?"

Jess thought about it for a minute. "I think so."

She kicked her legs under the chair. "So if I was worried about the spelling bee at school, then instead I should think about recess, because it's afterward? Or going home and having pizza for dinner?"

"Exactly," he said. "You're a clever one, Jessie. The world better watch out."

Jess remembers giggling when he said that, feeling proud to be called clever. She doesn't feel clever now. Just lost and confused. She wishes her dad were here to advise her.

What would he think? Would he be proud? Would he be scared for her? Would he be ashamed of the choices she'd made after he died? She'll never know for sure. All she does know is, if he were here now, he would tell her to breathe and to focus on the "after."

She pictures herself back at school, the mission over. She'll see Cat again and tell her...not everything, but as much as she can. She'll have dinner in the familiar dining hall with her classmates. She'll walk through the forest at dusk to get to her dorm, and be able to sleep in her own bed again.

All this will be over, and she won't have to deal with moody Lyle, or worry about Noe'or, or have to talk to Penn. She realizes she does miss the Academy, even if she hasn't always had the best experiences there. It's the closest thing she has to a home right now, and for that, she's grateful.

With a slight whooshing sound, Penn materializes back in the driver's seat, startling her.

Lyle has appeared in the backseat, too, in the seat opposite Noe'or. Jess feels her heart rate ramp up as the sense kicks in, and a wave of anxiety hits her with such force that she has to grab the side of the car door to steady herself.

"Sorry we scared you," Penn says. Jess can barely focus on the words. "Have you seen anyone go in or out?"

Jess shakes her head. She can't speak for the shock of what she's just realized with his return. It's all because of *him.*

The inexplicable anger, the rollercoaster of emotions she's been on this whole time, it's because he's here. The uncontrollable fight-or-flight reaction she endures in his presence is playing with her emotions, too, and has been this whole time. That's why she's been so quick to anger, why her emotions have felt out of her control. She can't believe she didn't catch on sooner, until she realizes she's never spent this much time around him before.

She looks over at him, then realizes he's speaking again. She's missed what he said entirely.

"Sorry, what?"

He gives her a funny look. "I said, this might be a good place to enter. What do you think?"

Back to the assignment. Yes. The reason they're all here. She can't find anything about his plan to disagree with. "Seems as good as any."

"Doesn't seem to be much surveillance," Lyle says. They have their binoculars out and trained on the door. "Either it's well-hidden, or they're not expecting anyone to find them. I'm hoping for the latter, but we should prepare for the former."

"We can wear illusions," Jess suggests.

"Just what I was thinking," Lyle says with a nod of respect toward her. They set the binoculars down. "Cloaking us all will be difficult to maintain if we split up, so that's probably the best option. And we should split up. If we stay together, we'll attract way too much attention."

Jess nods. "We should take Noe'or, too. He can probably lead us to Della the quickest."

Lyle looks over at Noe'or. "You're right. If anyone spots him on the cameras, though..."

Jess has an idea. She summons a stack of clothes, topped with a pair of sneakers and a baseball cap. "Here, Noe'or, put these on."

The wicht takes the clothes, wrinkling his nose. "Do I have to? Human clothes are itchy."

"He could just stay here," Lyle suggests.

"Not in my car!" Penn says. "Not unless he's in the roomcase."

Noe'or sticks his tongue out at Penn before jamming the baseball cap on his head. As he puts on the rest of the outfit, Penn looks at Jess.

"Are you sure that's enough of a disguise? He's still at least two feet shorter than everyone else in the building."

"The baseball cap will block most of his face," Jess says. "He'll just look like a kid in the cameras. Our very own Bring Your Child to Work Day."

"More like 'Bring Your Demon to Work Day,'" Penn mutters with a glare in Noe'or's direction.

"Oooh, *demon*," Noe'or cackles. "Never heard that one before!"

"That's enough," Jess says, glaring at both of them.

"Jess, you should take Noe'or," Lyle says. "Penn, why don't you and I stick together, and you can do that little magic sensing thing you fairies are so good at."

"Okay," Penn says. "How will we communicate, though, if we're splitting up? If Jess finds Della first, she shouldn't have to get her out by herself."

"We can wear earpieces," Lyle says. "This isn't McCreed's palace. We don't have to worry about how things would look if we're caught. And the illusions will at least hide that we're wearing them."

They reach into their pocket and pull out a thin case, which they open to reveal three small earpieces. They pass one each to Penn and Jess. Jess fixes hers in her ear and Penn does the same.

"What should we do if we run into someone?" Penn asks.

Lyle stares at him. "Pull them out of the line of any cameras, incapacitate them, and do a touch shift. Standard protocol for a mission like this. Our goal is to get Della out safely. The comfort and safety of her kidnappers are at the bottom of our priority list."

"Oh," Penn says, eyes wide. He seems surprised, but Jess doesn't sense any reluctance.

"What about the other officers?" Jess asks Lyle. "Did you tell them we think we've found her? Are they coming, too?"

"That's part of why we took a few minutes getting here," they say. "Penn and I talked to Mom, and we convinced her to let us go in first, since we were the ones to find her. It's better to start with a small team anyway, to scope things out. Half of the officers will be assembling outside this building in"—they check their watch—"ten minutes. Then they'll breach the building and arrest anyone inside. So we have ten minutes to find Della and as much information as we can before chaos hits."

Penn cracks a grin. "Chaos has already hit," he says. "We're here, aren't we?"

Jess rolls her eyes. "We should go now. But shift first."

Lyle nods, shifting into the form of a middle-aged, average-looking woman in slacks and a blouse. Jess shifts into the form of a business man in his late 20s, which she had picked up in her first few months on the run as a kid. She has no idea who the man is, but she's taken his form enough times that he's familiar as family.

Penn's shift still looks like him, but older, with dark hair instead of blond and light brown eyes instead of his normal deep green ones. As soon as they're all shifted, they exit the car, with Jess opening the door to let Noe'or out of the backseat. She almost expects him to bolt at the sign of freedom, but instead, he just stretches for a couple seconds, readjusts his baseball cap, then follows her to the dock door.

Once they're at the door, Penn presses his ear

against it. When he doesn't hear anything, he waves Jess forward to pick the lock.

As she kneels down and maneuvers her lockpicks amongst the tumblers, she realizes that, as a fairy, he could probably unlock the door faster with magic than she can with her picks. She also realizes that he probably didn't do this at McCreed's, and again here, to give her the opportunity to contribute and test her skills. Surprisingly, she doesn't feel annoyed so much as grateful.

The door leads them to a small dock that, unlike McCreed's, looks rarely used. Jess thinks this is a good sign, as it will make for a good exit point when they leave. When they reach the metal door that leads out into the rest of the building, Penn peers through the small window and, seeing nothing, gestures the others through.

Once they are in the hallway, Jess asks Noe'or if he's picked up Della's scent, and he points down the hallway straight ahead. She glances at Lyle, who nods and leads Penn down the hallway to the left.

Jess and Noe'or set off, with the wicht keeping a quick pace. Jess scans her surroundings as they go, but there isn't much to see. The hallway is painted a drab off-white, and the generic tan doors they pass are differentiated only by the plastic placards showing the room numbers. Jess doesn't see any cameras, but that could just mean they're concealed.

It strikes her that this area of the building feels unused. The air is still, and there isn't any noise coming from the nearby rooms. With a growing sense of dread, she wonders if this is a trap.

"Hey," she whispers to Noe'or, "stop for a second. Do you smell anything...odd here? Or any people besides Della?"

The wicht stops and inhales deeply, his brow furrowed. When he exhales, his face relaxes a bit. "Don't smell any people over here. There's some on the side the others are heading to. And they've come this way. But it doesn't smell like they use these rooms."

Jess exhales in relief. "Okay. Good. Can you tell me if you smell anything strange? I...we really don't know what's going on here. Anything you might find could be helpful."

Noe'or shrugs. "Fine." He turns and sets off down the hallway again.

They make it about thirty feet before he stops again, throwing out his arm to stop her.

"Someone's coming," he hisses.

Sure enough, Jess can hear multiple footsteps coming up a hallway that intersects with theirs about fifteen feet away. Quickly, she turns to look around them. They're right next to one of the plain doors, and she tries the handle. It's locked.

She summons her lockpicks as fast as she can, listening as the footsteps approach. It seems to take too long to get the door open, but she does, and they shut it behind them just as Jess hears a squeak indicating someone has turned the corner. She presses her ear against the door, and she can actually hear their conversation.

"Well, of course they tried to limit it. But as soon as they did, then all the fairies wanted to do it, and there wasn't a good way to stop them, was there?" a man's voice says.

Jess tries to see him through the window, but she's at the wrong angle and she doesn't want to move for fear of making a noise that would give them away.

"You'd think with all that magic, they'd be able to do something about it," a woman's voice says.

Now they've moved past the window and she can see their backs. There's nothing special about their clothes, just a regular polo for the man and a light sweater for the woman. Nothing that gives Jess any hints as to who they are and what this place is.

"They could if they cared," the man continues, "but since when do they care about humans? They barely care about half-fae..." His voice fades as they walk down the hall until Jess can no longer hear it.

When she's sure they're gone, she relaxes. It's only then that she looks around the room.

The first thing she notices are the filing cabinets. The second thing she notices is that they're empty. This is disappointing, because if they kept files, she might have been able to steal some and get some helpful information.

But it gives her an idea—if the filing cabinets are empty, it means there are probably computers somewhere with information on them. If they have time after finding Della, she'll tell the others and maybe they can go back and look for those.

Carefully, she opens the door and peers out. The hallway is empty again. She and Noe'or exit the room, and he leads her down the hall.

"We're close," he says.

"Hey, do you all copy?" Jess asks. "Noe'or says we're close."

"Where are you?" Lyle's voice comes through faint but clear.

Jess looks at the number by the nearest door. "We just passed room 151, headed toward the higher numbers."

"Okay, we'll try and meet up with you," Penn says. "Tell us where you find her."

"Will do," Jess says.

They are nearing the end of the hallway when the wicht stops. He points to a door on the right that reads "MAINTENANCE."

"Through there," he says.

Jess tries the door, but it's locked, of course. She summons her picks again and has the door unlocked in less than a minute. Cautiously, she opens it and looks inside.

The room is fairly large and looks to be a standard maintenance storage area. Shelves with cans of paint and sealer line one wall, a bulky washer and dryer stand in the corner, and Jess even sees extra ceiling tiles propped against the far wall. But no Della.

"Are you sure she's here?" Jess asks Noe'or.

He nods, then starts sniffing around the room. He stops in front of the dryer and taps his finger on the door.

"She's in THERE?" Jess whispers in horror.

"That's where the scent is strongest."

Dread fills Jess's stomach as she reaches for the door handle. She doesn't know what she'll find behind it. But when she tugs at it, it doesn't budge. She tries again, to no avail.

"It's stuck...hang on a second."

She summons the ring from her mom and puts it on her finger. When she puts her hand next to the dryer door, it pulses with light. It's not just a dryer, it's some type of magic door or portal.

"I think I've found where they're keeping her," Jess says aloud so Penn and Lyle can hear. "There's some type of portal or spell that I can't get past."

"Okay, where are you?" Lyle asks.

"There's a maintenance room at the end of the long hallway, opposite the dock. I'm in there."

"I think it's this way," she hears Penn say.

"No, it's not. We came from that way. It's this way." Lyle sounds irritated.

"This place has got me all turned around," Penn says. "I think they have some sort of enchantment going that's interfering with my sense of direction. It'll be easier if we just teleport."

"How are you going to do that? You don't even know where the maintenance room is."

"I can piggyback off the connection between the earpieces and teleport us to that location," Penn says. "Jess, you need to take your earpiece out and put it on an empty spot of floor a couple feet away from anything, okay?"

"Copy that," Jess says.

She takes it out and follows his instructions, stepping back a safe distance when she's done. Everything is silent for a second before Penn and Lyle materialize in the place the earpiece had been.

"—a bad idea," Lyle finishes, looking uneasy.

There's a beat of silence before Penn turns to them. "See? Everything's fine."

No sooner do the words leave his mouth than an alarm starts blaring through a loudspeaker in the corner of the room.

A look of horror dawns on Penn's face and he lets out a curse.

"We need to find the girl and get out of here," Lyle says.

"Attention everyone," a woman's voice crackles over the loudspeaker. "This is not a drill. The building has been breached. Captains, please go to your designated areas to check for intruders. All others, please evacuate the building via your assigned exit point. I repeat, this is not a drill."

"Where is she?" Lyle demands.

Jess points at the dryer and Lyle strides over to it and tries the door. It still doesn't budge. "Penn, get over here and open this thing up. We need to move quickly."

Penn hurries over and places his hands on the door. It starts to glow and a click sounds as it unlatches. He pulls it open and they crowd around to see.

Jess doesn't know what she expected, but it wasn't what she's seeing. The dryer door is just a portal—it leads into a hallway lined with doors that looks like something out of a hospital or a laboratory. At the far end is another hallway, perpendicular to the one they're looking at. Jess wants to know where it leads, but they won't have time to look right now. Della is the priority.

"Do you think those rooms are all occupied?" Penn says, his voice filled with horror.

"Only one way to find out," Lyle says, climbing through the portal. "Come on! Quickly!"

Jess and Penn follow them through. Noe'or stays behind, and when Jess looks back, she's surprised but pleased to see the little wicht standing near the door, keeping watch.

Once Jess and Penn's feet hit the floor of the hallway, Penn waves his hand. The doors fly open at once, and exclamations of shock and surprise emit from the rooms behind them. All the voices sound young and scared.

Penn glances at Lyle. *"Now* can I rescue all the captives?"

"They're children," Lyle growls. "We're not leaving them behind. Now, go!"

At Lyle's command, Jess runs to check the room closest to her. A thin girl with curly brown hair is huddled in the corner, her eyes filled with fear. It's not Della.

"D-don't come closer," the girl says, holding her hands out defensively. "I-I'll hurt you!" Despite the threat, her arms are shaking. She's terrified.

From the hallway, Jess hears shouts as Penn and Lyle find more captives. Jess focuses on the girl. She puts her hands up. "It's okay, I'm not here to hurt you. What's your name?"

"A-Ana," the girl says.

"Okay, Ana," Jess says in what she hopes is a calming tone, "I need you to come with me. We're here to get you out of here, but we need to leave now."

"You came for me?" the girl asks, her eyes wide.

"For all of you," Jess says. "We need to hurry, though. There isn't much time."

Ana is already scrambling to her feet. Jess grabs her hand and leads her into the hallway. Lyle is guiding the other rescued captives—a motley group of other malnourished kids and teens—through the portal, where Penn is waiting on the other side. Jess lets Ana go ahead of her, then climbs through herself, followed by Lyle.

Once she's back in the maintenance room, Jess surveys the group. There are nine other kids besides Ana. She's glad to recognize Della as one of them, but the feeling is short-lived. "How are we going to get everyone out?" she whispers to Lyle.

"We're going to have to run for it," they say, starting toward the door.

Noe'or, still standing guard, holds out his hand in warning. "Wait," he says. "They're coming. Lots of them."

He's right. Jess can hear footsteps running down the hallway toward the maintenance room.

Penn steps forward, expression serious. "Everyone, get back from the door. I can drive them away."

Jess, Lyle, Noe'or and the kids all back up

against the walls as Penn steps toward the door. He touches a finger to his forehead and Jess recognizes the beginning of an illusion spell.

There are many different types of illusion magic, and each user typically has a preferred method. The method Penn's using is a type that produces more sophisticated illusions—the kind that are harder to see through. As Penn performs the motions, Jess silently wills it to work.

With a thrust of his hands, Penn finishes the spell and the door bursts open as the illusion propels itself out of the room. Shouts and running footsteps indicate that, whatever it was, it was successful. Penn turns to them.

"I'm sending them to the front of the building. We should be clear now."

"Let's get out of here," Lyle says, already standing up. They all head to the door, Jess letting the kids go ahead of her. At the doorway, she stops. It makes her nervous to suggest it, but it'll be worth it if she can find something useful.

"You guys go on," she says. "I need to see if I can find any files or anything with information on it. We still have no idea what this group is or what their goals are, and if I find anything, it could help us learn at least that much."

Lyle stops and looks back at her. At first, they look irritated, but that changes into a grudging sort of respect. "Smart thinking," they say, pulling the flash drive out of their pocket and handing it to Jess. "I would do the same. Be quick about it, though, and don't get caught."

Jess nods, taking the flash drive. "I'll meet you all outside."

"I'm coming with you," Penn says.

Lyle shakes their head. "No, no, I'm going to need your help getting everyone out. We might need a few more of your tricks, and a bigger vehicle."

"We can't let her go alone!" Penn protests.

"I'll be fine," Jess interrupts. "Go. Save the kids. I can handle this."

Lyle has already started leading the kids down the hall, Noe'or trailing behind. Jess is glad the wicht didn't argue.

Penn looks back at her warily. "Fine," he says. "Try the first hallway. We passed some offices up there earlier that could be important. And take this."

He presses something small into her hand, which she recognizes as one of the earpieces.

"I've put a cloaking spell on it. As long as you're holding it, they can't see you. But it will only last about eight minutes, so you need to be fast. I'd say shoot to be out in six or seven minutes, just to be safe."

Jess nods, closing her hand over the small object. "I'll be back soon," she promises. Penn nods, and she takes off toward the front of the building.

* 17 *

JESS PASSES PEOPLE SPRINTING DOWN THE hallways—some looking like they are ready to fight, wearing tactical gear—but she dodges them easily. It only takes a minute and a half for her to reach the offices Penn had talked about. The alarm is still blaring over the loudspeakers at such a volume that she thinks she will probably have a headache when this is over.

The first office she tries is locked. The second is unlocked, but the computer is asleep and the password is nowhere to be found. Jess doesn't have time to try hacking it, and anyway, she thinks at least one of the people in this building probably left their computer on. The third office is also a miss, but in the fourth office, she finally strikes gold—an open door and an unlocked computer.

She slides behind the desk and pulls the flash drive out of her pocket, then plugs it into the computer. First, she checks the email and downloads the ten most recent emails. Then she moves on to browsing the files. The organization uses a shared drive, so she clicks through a few of the folders in it.

There are a couple with financial information, which she figures will be helpful. While those are downloading, she clicks back into the main folder and scrolls through it again. A folder she had missed before catches her eye, titled "Recruitment." She clicks into it and finds a few different folders.

One reads "Presentations," and she clicks on that one. It's filled with slide presentations dating back at least ten years. She opens the most recent one. It takes a while to load because of the files downloading in the background, but finally it opens.

When she sees the contents, Jess starts to understand what the organization is about, and a prickle of fear crawls down her back like a spider.

The presentation is filled with hateful depictions of the fairies. It portrays them as abusers, rapists, kidnappers, and a host of other horrible things. Jess wouldn't claim to like the fairies, but this is far beyond what she thinks and feels about them.

The presentation depicts the organization as righteous seekers of justice attempting to right the wrongs committed on the human world by fairies. Their goal seems to be fighting the fairies and driving them out of the human world for good, although it's not made clear how this would be accomplished. The interesting thing is, the presentation seems to be geared toward both half-fae and humans.

When Jess has seen enough to get the gist of it, she closes the file, then downloads it to the flash drive as well. She goes back to the "Recruitment" folder and scans through it again. She notices a folder titled "Reports" and clicks into that.

The subfolders seem to be broken into geographical regions, except one. That one reads "LaMour Academy."

Time slows to a crawl. The blood in Jess's veins feels like it belongs to one of McCreed's ice automatons. She's suddenly hyper aware of her own breathing and how shallow it feels.

They're recruiting from the Academy. They have spies planted at her school. Her home. She feels sick. How long has this been going on?

She clicks into the folder. A list of files appears, all helpfully dated. The most recent one is from last month; the oldest, five years ago.

Five years. This hate group has been recruiting from her school for *five years* and no one knew. She didn't know. How did she not know? She could have been in classes with the kids being recruited, or the recruiter themself if they were posing as a student. It could be a teacher, though, or another staff member. It could be *anyone.*

Jess realizes this must be what Aster meant when she said they would find something disturbing. At least, she hopes this is what she meant. She doesn't know if she could handle anything more disturbing at the moment. Her mind is reeling as she tries to process this new information. Who is their plant? Do they have more than one? How many students have they recruited?

Jess clicks on one of the most recent files as the loudspeakers crackle in the hallway. A robotic-sounding voice, different from the earlier woman's voice, echoes through the building.

"Attention! Self destruct sequence initiating. Please clear the building. All materials will self-destruct in ten...nine..."

A *self-destruct sequence*? Jess's file loads just as she yanks the flash drive from the computer. There's no time for anything beyond a quick glimpse before she sprints out of the office. The hallways are empty, the countdown echoing off the faded linoleum tiles.

"Seven...six..."

She doesn't know where the exit is on this side of the building. She keeps running down the hallway, putting on a burst of additional speed. There has to be a way out. She has to get this information to the others.

"Four...three..."

No exit in sight. She's not going to make it. She clutches the flash drive tighter and closes her eyes. It's too late for anything else.

"Two...one..."
BOOM.

* * * *

The floor of the bus rocks beneath Penn's feet and he drops the water bottles he'd been about to hand out to the kids. They roll under the seats, but he ignores them, pushing to the front of the vehicle.

"What was that?" he yells at Lyle, before catching sight of the building through the windshield. He stops, watching in horror as smoke billows out from the roof, which is now partially collapsed and consumed by flames.

"No, no, no," he whispers.

Lyle turns and he can see them saying something, but he doesn't hear it. He shoves past them and out of the bus, tripping on the last step but pushing himself back up again.

He has to get to the building, he has to find her, he has to make sure she made it out. She did make it out. She had to.

"JESS!" He yells her name as he stumbles toward the building. It's uncomfortably hot and there's smoke everywhere, but he ignores it.

"JESS!" he yells again, louder. He's using the Call, even though he swore never to use it again, because he needs her to respond. He needs her to be alive.

Then he hears it—someone calling his name, distantly. "Penn!"

He stops, feeling someone grab the back of his shirt. "PENN!"

It's Lyle, trying to pull him away from the building. "Penn, you can't save her," they say, shouting into his ear to be heard over the noise around them. "If she's still inside, she's gone. No one could have survived that."

"No," Penn says, "nonononono, she's still in there, I can still get to her. You have to let me go." He tries to pull away, but Lyle's grip is firm.

"Penn, listen to me," they say, the despair in their voice echoing his own. "Jess is gone. You aren't going to find her. She didn't make it."

"Let me GO!" Penn yells, breaking free of their grip. He turns toward the building in time to see the entire north side of the building—the side Jess was on, the side he had told her to go to—collapse in on itself.

It's over.

Lyle is right—she's gone.

With that realization, Penn collapses too. He's untethered, falling, losing control.

And as he falls, he feels Nell rise to catch him.

His senses start to fade, like they always do when Nell takes over, until all he can feel is her. Sweet, stable Nell.

It's okay, she says. *Rest now. I'll take it from here.*

Rest. The idea swells inside him and suddenly, that's all he wants to do. Rest, and leave behind all that's happened. Rest, and let Nell take care of things like she always does. Rest, and forget the sorrow of the girl he couldn't save.

Jess.

He doesn't know if the thought came from him or Nell, but it's her name, loud and clear, and it pulls him back.

No, he says to Nell. *Not this time.*

Are you sure? Nell's concern is palpable. He knows she's worried about him, that all she wants to do is provide him with a way out. But he's done hiding from the hard stuff. Never again.

I will not rest, he tells her, *until every last one of the bastards responsible are rotting in unmarked graves.*

Then you'll rot, too.

If she says anything else, Penn doesn't hear over the screaming. Nell's consciousness dissolves away, and with tremendous, dizzying force, he slams back into his senses. He can still hear the screaming, and he realizes it's him.

He feels Lyle's hands on his shoulders, pulling him back, trying to get him to move away from the burning wreck of a building. His scream falls away, but he can still feel it under his skin. A primal song of loss and regret.

"We have to go," Lyle is saying. They are still trying to get him to move, stand up, do anything. "The kids—they're waiting for us. They need us."

Penn turns back to look at Lyle. "Jess was a kid," he says. "She needed us. I should have gone with her. I could have saved her."

There are so many things he could have done—*should have* done—but instead, he'd left Jess to fend for herself. The past couple of days, she'd awed him with her bravery and quick thinking, and he'd forgotten that she was still so young.

She'd seemed like she could do anything, but she wasn't indestructible. He should have remembered that. He should have pushed to go with her, or insisted they wait until the kids were out safely before going back for evidence.

"We didn't know," Lyle says. Tears have left trails down the old spy's face, and the show of emotion triggers another wave of despair for Penn.

Jess was Lyle's sister. They'd barely known each other, but even Penn could see how they'd bonded over the course of the assignment. He can't begin to imagine how it must feel for Lyle to have gained and lost a sibling in so short of a time.

"I'm so sorry," Penn says, clutching Lyle's sleeve. It's an attempt to convey his sympathy and solidarity, but he has no idea if it's reaching Lyle. They seem to be in another world, staring off into the flames without really seeing them.

"I know—I know you didn't have much time to get to know her," Penn continues. "But I think if you had, you two would have had a great relationship. I think she really looked up to you."

It seems so unfair that Penn was the one who'd spent more time with Jess when Lyle was her blood relative.

"I didn't deserve her admiration," Lyle says. "She deserved a proper mentor. Someone she could have stayed in touch with, who could have supported her throughout her career. She deserved better than me."

Penn stares into the flames. Their swaying motion reminds him of fields of grass, and for a moment, that's what he longs for—the simple feeling of running through a field, the sun on his back. "She deserved better than me, too."

He's made so many mistakes over the centuries, but this has to be one of his worst. "I should have known better. I should have insisted we stick together. We didn't know what else was hidden in that building; we never should have split up."

"This isn't your doing," Lyle says. "Don't blame yourself for what happened."

But Nell's words still echo in Penn's mind. *You'll rot, too.* He's as much to blame as any of the people in that building.

"I was supposed to keep her safe." It's getting harder and harder to breathe, but he's not sure if it's the smoke in the air or his own panic that's causing it. "Talia trusted me with her daughter, and I failed. I did this. I killed her."

As he says it, Aster's talk about cycles and second chances finally clicks.

Seven years ago, he was tasked to protect this girl, to keep her safe, and he failed. Three days ago, he got the chance to right his old wrongs, to heal the rift between them and help her move on.

Instead, he destroyed her.

He buries his face in his hands. Jess had been so strong, so bright; Talia's pride and joy, even though she didn't see it...

Penn may not have Aster's gifts, but he could

see Jess's potential, even as far back as his earliest encounters with her. She would have gone on to do great things, and he wishes he'd told her that. Her work on this mission had only confirmed what he already knew.

But his words would now remain unsaid. The rest of her story would remain untold. She'd been cut down in her prime, her life snuffed out so fast he'd not even noticed until she was gone.

And she is gone.

He can sense it through his magic. There are no living things left in the building.

She walked straight to her death and he told her where to go.

It's done.

* * * *

Jess opens her eyes.

She made it. She surveys the room around her, which looks much the same as it did the last time she visited it years ago. The racks of clothes are a little fuller, the styles more up-to-date, but it's still the same room she remembers from the last time she was here.

The last time she was here. Oh no.

She weaves her way through the racks of clothes to the door and pulls it open. The hallway outside is empty, each of the countless doors lining it closed tight. Jess shuts the door and sinks down against it, dropping her shift.

So this is how the assignment ends. The FIC

team will extract the kids, they'll have the debriefing, the FIC officers will take all the credit, and she'll be stuck here in the fairy world until her mom can come get her. What a loser.

She leans her head back against the door and closes her eyes. At least she won't have to be in the room during the debriefing when they find out about the mole. Miss Colleen will freak out. And she could go without seeing that horrifying presentation again, too.

Her eyes snap open. Lyle and Penn don't know about the mole or the presentation. They weren't there when she found the files and downloaded them onto...

She opens her hand, which had been clenched in a fist since she arrived. The flash drive sits in her palm. It looks so small and harmless. She closes her hand again and puts the flash drive in her pocket. She has to find a way to get it to the others.

Jess starts running through the possibilities in her mind. She could bring it to the FIC, but there's no guarantee they'd let her in. They'd probably assume she was some kind of enemy agent sent to steal their secrets. The flash drive wouldn't help. She scraps that idea. Next.

She could call her mom, explain the situation, and ask her to come get her. She shudders. The idea of asking her mom for help—no, there has to be another solution. One that doesn't cause nausea just by thinking about it. Besides, her mom rarely answers her phone anyway. Next idea.

There has to be someone else she can call. Cat,

maybe—but how will she explain this? And Cat can't help her herself; she'd have to find someone else to rescue her. Jess gets out her phone and scrolls through her contacts. Aside from Cat and her mom, she doesn't see anyone else who could possibly help. She turns off her phone and leans back against the door again. She can't even call Lyle or Penn because she doesn't have their numbers...wait a second.

She reaches into her pockets. Nothing there except the flash drive. But wait, she was wearing her other jeans that day. Standing, Jess scans the racks of clothing. She spots them on a rack about twenty feet away, hanging next to her uniform.

She weaves her way through the rows of racks until she gets to them, then digs her hands into the front pockets, searching, searching—there! With a laugh of triumph, she pulls out the scrap of paper Penn had given her. She unfolds it, revealing his phone number written in smudged pencil.

It only takes a couple seconds to type it into her phone, but she pauses before she hits the "Call" button. Is this—or rather, he—really her only option?

Jess shakes her head. Unless she wants to call her mom, this is the best option she has. She hits the green button.

Ringing, ringing—what if he doesn't pick up? She paces in a circle as she waits. Finally, a muffled "Hello?" sounds from the speaker.

"Hi, it's me, Jess," she says. *Frost.* She didn't think about how she was going to explain this.

She hears a jumble of sounds that she thinks are from him dropping the phone. Then, "Jess? Is it really you? Where are you?"

"I'm in the Realm," she says. "I have some files on the flash drive that we'll need for the briefing, but I'm stuck."

"Clip the briefing," she hears him say. "Where in the Realm? I'm coming to get you."

"I'll send you my location, hang on," she says.

"Just turn on the location setting and I can use it as long as I've got you on the line."

She follows his instructions and in less than five seconds, he's standing in front of her. She ends the call.

"You're alive," he says. The expression on his face is a mixture of shock, confusion, and relief, maybe? Jess can't get a read on it.

"Yeah," she says. "I have the flash drive; there's some really important stuff—"

"Forget the flash drive," Penn says, his eyes oddly glittering. "Forget the mission, forget all of it. You're *alive*."

Then he does the last thing Jess expects.

He steps forward and envelops her in a hug.

Jess is so surprised she can't move. Her radar sense is setting off alarm bells in her head, and it's keeping her from being able to fully process what's happening. He's hugging her, and it's not the gentle hug of a friend (which he's not), but something fiercer. Something that sings of never letting go.

Jess can hear the ragged cadence of his breathing and his heartbeat, loud and frantic. He smells overwhelmingly of smoke, which she doesn't understand. When he finally pulls away, she realizes he's dropped his shift. He looks a mess—jeans and boots covered in dust and grime, hair disheveled and even sticking up in places. But what unsettles her most is his eyes. They're still glittering, and she realizes it's from tears.

"Wait, what happened?" she asks. "Are the kids okay?" If she'd left and something happened to the kids—

"The kids are fine," Penn says. "We all made it out. But you...we thought you didn't. The building exploded and I thought you were still inside. I—we thought you were dead."

Silence fills the room as Jess takes that in.

She's never actually lost someone on an assignment, but what happened with Joseph came awfully close. It's not a leap for her to imagine the horror and distress Penn and Lyle must have felt when they thought she was killed. She knows Penn, as a fairy, doesn't feel things the same way humans do, but it still must have been a sobering experience.

"How did you make it out?" he asks. He surveys the room, the racks of clothing and neatly organized accessories. "And how did you end up...wherever this place is?"

"I call it my magic closet," she says. "Don't laugh, I was a kid when I came up with the name."

"I'm not laughing," Penn says, still surveying the room with interest. He steps toward one of the racks, touching the sleeve of a jacket Jess recognizes from their trip to the Magnificent Mile. "How did you find this place?"

"It's where I store the outfits and things I create," Jess says. "I found it by accident once and started putting things into it. Then one day I put myself into it. The only problem is, once I put myself in, I can't take myself out, so to speak."

Penn lets go of the jacket sleeve and fixes his gaze back on her. "This is where you went that final time." It's not a question.

Jess nods. She didn't want to say as much, but yes, this is how she escaped him that last time.

"I always wondered how you got away," Penn says, shaking his head. "I was so sure I had you that time. I puzzled over it for days afterward, trying to figure out how my plan had gone awry. This makes so much sense."

He doesn't sound angry, more like satisfied to finally have an answer. Jess is glad; she really didn't want to get into another argument about the past. Maybe someday in the future, they'll be able to talk about the past like this, without anger or hurt feelings.

At that, she shakes her head. What is she thinking? Once this is over, she's going to go right back to attempting to avoid Penn at all costs. Have a conversation with him? Who is she kidding?

"We have to go back," she says. "We need to get this information to the FIC team as soon as possible." She holds up the flash drive again.

"Why? What's on there?"

"A lot of things. Emails, financial reports,

recruitment data—stuff they'll want to see."

"Okay. I know they'll be focused on the kids for a bit, so we have some time before the briefing. We've got to figure out the best way to get out of here. I'll give Talia an update." He pulls out his phone and starts texting.

"No," Jess says. "They need to see this now. This group, it's bigger than we thought, and they're not playing around." She needs him to trust her on this. "They're terrorists who want to destroy the fairies."

This gets Penn's attention. He stops typing and looks up at her. "What?"

"It's all here on this drive," she says. She describes the presentation to him as best she can. When she's finished, he's staring at her in horror.

"And this group is how big?"

"I'm not sure, but they're recruiting globally. Not just half-fae, but humans too. We need to get this to my mom ASAP."

"Agreed," he says. "Let me think...there has to be a way to get you out of here without violating the Magical Transport of Minors Act. Maybe FIC headquarters?"

Jess shakes her head. "They'll make us jump through a bunch of hoops for that, and we don't have time. Here," she says, shoving the flash drive into his free hand. "Take this back to the Academy and show it to the team. Don't worry about me; my mom can come and get me later. This is more important."

It's Penn's turn to shake his head. "No way am I

leaving you here alone. Not this time."

"You have to," Jess says, insistent. "They can't do the briefing without it."

"Listen, I already lost you once today, and I'll be damned if I do it again." He crosses his arms. "Either we go together or we don't go at all. I'm not negotiating on this."

An unexpected feeling of comfort warms Jess from the inside at his words. He's not going to abandon her in the Realm. Anyone else—her mom, other FIC officers, even Lyle—would have put the mission first and left her. But not him. For the first time since she received the assignment, Jess is glad Penn was chosen, too.

"How are we going to get out of here, then?" she asks. "If we try to teleport, you'll be caught, and I don't think it's likely the Crown will grant a special exception to the Magical Transport of Minors Act."

"The Crown..." Penn thinks for a moment, then finally says, "I have an idea. I don't think you're going to like it, though."

* 18 *

"YOU WERE RIGHT," JESS SAYS. "I DON'T LIKE this idea."

It was only after they had made it out of the Closet Emporium, as Jess thinks of it, that Penn shared his plan. She thinks it's a ridiculous plan, but unfortunately, it's just ridiculous enough that it might actually work.

The first part of the plan is getting close enough to the palace for them to see who is on guard duty. That part is easy enough; they use their shifts from earlier so they won't be recognized, and Penn leads the way from the Closet Emporium to a place he knows that they can scout from.

The trek only takes them about twenty minutes, and when they reach Penn's spot, a small grove of blue- and purple-leaved trees on the edge of the palace grounds, he summons two pairs of binoculars and hands one to Jess. They're supposed to be scanning for guards, but Jess takes a brief opportunity to appreciate the palace itself.

In contrast to McCreed's palace, which is sharp and angular, the fairy palace's architecture is smooth and flowing. Tall, rounded archways make up the first level and are mimicked by the shape of the windows on the upper levels. Balconies abound, lined with fanciful wrought-metal railings depicting images of flowers, animals, and even fairies. The palace roof is made up of exaggerated peaks and valleys rendered in swooping lines, with a few spires here and there for added visual interest.

As if that's not enough, the entire building—from steps to spires—is painted in soothing shades of lavender. The monochrome look is broken up by the ample greenery that spills out of the balconies and window sills, creating shaded canopies over the archways and emitting a soft, vaguely spicy fragrance.

Jess has visited the palace a few times, usually for the solstice gala hosted for Academy students every winter. Nevertheless, it still has the power to take her breath away for a moment.

"That one," Penn says, pulling Jess back to reality. He's pointing at a fairy with curly hair. "Addison, fairy of video games."

Jess lowers her binoculars and laughs. "The gamer fairy is a palace guard?"

Penn nods. "Bit of a hothead, too. She's new, relatively speaking, so she's got a lot to prove. She'll do fine."

"Okay, if you think she's the best choice," Jess says.

She lifts the binoculars and scrutinizes Addison, committing the details of her appearance to memory, building the shift in her mind to the point where she can feel it under her skin, ready to take form.

Instead of making the shift, she drops her binoculars and looks at Penn. "Are you ready?"

He nods, and she places her hand on his shoulder.

Unlike at McCreed's, where Jess was only editing Penn's shift, this time she's building one for him from scratch. It takes a lot more effort for her to shift someone else's appearance—she would compare it to trying to drive from the passenger seat of a car as opposed to the driver's seat. Maintaining a shift on someone else also takes about three times the effort as maintaining her own shift, but because Penn is a fairy, he can at least pick up and maintain the shift himself.

Once he has the shift, she drops her hand. He rolls his shoulders and flexes his fingers, getting used to the other fairy's form. Addison also wears her wings, and he gives those a quick shake as well.

"Your turn," he says. He's watching her closely, so she closes her eyes to focus better. Then she shifts.

Her shift isn't difficult; she's had it saved for

some time now, so it's familiar. When she opens her eyes, Penn is still staring at her.

"Freaky," he says, looking uncomfortable.

"This was your idea," Jess points out.

"Just because it's my idea and it's a good idea doesn't mean I like it."

"Do you have a plan on where to enter?"

Penn points to the door nearest them. "This one should work. We just need to wait for her to pass by again so we get the timing right."

"Okay."

Penn looks at her. "Are you sure you're okay with this? The other fairies...well, you've seen them. Are you sure you want to do this?"

"I'll be fine," Jess says. "It's not really me, anyway. And we need to get back."

Penn nods, but his expression is grim.

It only takes a few minutes before Addison reappears. After she makes her way around the corner of the building, they wait for a minute before Penn cloaks them and they sneak toward the door.

Once they're close, Penn drops the cloaking spell. Jess holds her hands behind her back; Penn has an illusion running that makes it appear as though she's cuffed. He prods her in the back.

"Keep moving!" he says, his voice now an octave higher and much harsher. Jess is mildly impressed. She hadn't thought to tell him to shift his vocal cords, too, but he clearly has. The voice he's using is definitely not his own.

Jess walks forward, doing her best to appear

irritated and combative. When they reach the door, Penn bangs on it. Another fairy guard opens it from within.

"What's this about?" the other guard growls.

"Look what I found sneaking around the grounds," Penn says, pushing Jess forward.

"I wasn't sneaking!" Jess says, because she feels that's the right response for the moment.

The other guard squints at her. "Is that..."

"The one and only," Penn says, a tinge of smugness creeping into his voice. Jess has to give him credit. He's actually not awful at this.

"I'm taking him to the king and queen," he continues. "They're going to want to deal with this immediately."

The guard smiles, and not nicely. He steps out of the way so they can come in. "By all means!" he says. "I can't wait for the little punk to get what he deserves. Again."

Penn prods Jess inside. As she passes the guard, she hisses, "If I were you, I'd watch who I was calling little."

"Can it," Penn says, prodding her again.

"You tell him!" the other guard jeers.

When they make it out into the hallway, Penn hisses, "You didn't have to say anything. It's not helping."

"I'm just trying to stay in character," Jess argues. "Was that out of character?"

There's a pause before Penn says, "Well, not really."

Jess smiles in satisfaction, although she knows

he can't see it.

They make it through the winding palace hallways without incident until they approach the hallway to the throne room, when they hear the massive doors swinging open. A chorus of voices follows, and Jess stops so suddenly that Penn runs into her.

"What's going on?" he whispers.

"We need to hide."

Jess pulls her hands apart, breaking the handcuff illusion, and grabs Penn's sleeve, pulling him behind one of the wide pillars that line the hallway. They crouch down at its base just as the group turns the corner. At the lead is someone Jess knows all too well.

"That was amazing!" Sylvie says, her voice bubbly as usual. "Did you see what the queen was wearing? I loved her necklace!"

Jess shrinks back against the wall at the sound of her voice. If Sylvie or one of the other students spots them...

Jess can see Penn watching her watching Sylvie. He leans over before she can stop him. "That girl in the front. Friend of yours?"

His voice is low, thankfully, so the group can't hear him. "Definitely not," Jess whispers back as the group passes.

"Why not? She a bully or something?" Penn's attention isn't focused on Sylvie, but entirely on Jess. It's a bit unnerving.

She waits to reply until after Sylvie's group has turned the corner. "Not a bully, just annoying."

"How so?" Penn's tone isn't judgemental, just curious. Still, the probing irritates Jess.

"She's always trying to talk to me and won't leave me alone," Jess says, her tone short. *Just like you.*

"Maybe she just wants to be your friend," Penn says as they stand up.

The idea gives Jess pause. Does Sylvie just want to be her friend? Does *Penn*? The idea is so foreign it's almost laughable. Why would either of them want to be her friend? Sylvie has lots of friends already, and Penn...it's surprising he talks to her at all with their history. He's probably just trying to maintain his "nice guy" image. It would be foolish of Jess to read into either of their actions. She's not a lonely little girl craving connection anymore. Now she knows better.

"Let's just get this over with," Jess says, holding her hands behind her back. Penn waves his hand, conjuring the illusion again, and they set off toward the throne room.

Two more guards flank the double doors.

The one on the left, a tall, muscular fairy with tattoos chaining up his brown forearms, steps forward and glares down at them. "State your purpose," he says.

Penn clears his throat. "I caught this one sneaking around the grounds. Figured the king and queen ought to see him."

"What interest would the king and queen have in a lowly trespasser?" the second guard asks. "You're wasting your time. Just take him straight to the guard office and let them take care of it."

"This isn't just any trespasser," Penn says. "Look."

He nudges Jess. She's getting a bit sick of that, but she steps forward anyway.

The guards stare at her, recognition dawning, then just as quickly changing to a wicked sort of glee.

"Oooh boy, this is gonna be fun," says the guard on the left. "I knew it was only a matter of time. Let's bring him in."

The guards push the doors open and Jess and Penn enter the throne room.

The first thing that hits Jess is the light—bright and golden, like the sun has descended from the sky and come to rest on every surface in the room. Everything in the room shines, most of it gold. Like McCreed's throne room, it's not excessively decorated, but the warm, golden glow gives it a vastly different feel.

Seated in elaborate thrones are the king and queen, surrounded at a distance by an array of other fairies in bright colors. They all turn to look at Jess and Penn as they walk down the carpet toward the dais. They stop about twelve feet from its edge.

"Your Majesties," Penn says, bowing.

Jess reluctantly follows suit. She rises to see distaste and even outright hostility on the faces of almost every fairy in the room. The king and queen remain cold and impassive. Jess's eyes fall on the queen's necklace, and she has to admit Sylvie was right—it is a very nice necklace.

"What is your business, Addison?" the queen asks.

"I caught this trespasser on the grounds, Your Majesty," Penn says.

He's trying to mask it, but since Jess is so close, she can hear how his breathing rate has increased. She hopes if any of the other fairies notice, they attribute it to Addison's nerves instead of finding it suspicious.

"I brought him straight to you," Penn continues. "Not only is he trespassing, but he has also been banished from the kingdom and further ordered not to come within fifty feet of the palace. I request Your Majesties' permission to send him back to the human realm immediately."

"Oh, I'll send him back for you," one of the fairies says maliciously.

"Silence," the king says, giving the fairy a withering glare. He looks back to the two of them, his gaze impassive. "What do you have to say for yourself, Penn? Can you explain why you were violating the terms of your banishment?"

They hadn't prepared for questioning. There wasn't time. Jess has to improvise.

"Got lost," she says, cracking a grin that she hopes looks Penn-like enough. "Happens to the best of us sometimes."

"That's a load of BS!" another fairy shouts. "'Got lost'—aren't you the car fairy now? Did your GPS crap out, or your brain?"

All the other fairies start laughing at this.

"No," Jess replies loudly. "I was searching for a clever insult, but apparently you don't make those around here, so I'm forced to come up with my own."

"Enough!" the queen says, her voice raised. "I will not tolerate petty fighting in my throne room."

She looks down at Jess and her face softens slightly. "Dear Penn," she says, her voice smooth and warm, "I had hoped the next time you returned to this room, you would be bringing happy news. Is that not the case today?"

Jess has no idea what the queen is referring to. Penn hadn't given her any background going into this, so she can't even begin to guess what the queen wants from him. She's scrambling to think of how to react when the whisper of Penn's voice sounds in her ear, giving her a single word.

"No," she says, her voice firm.

Jess doesn't know what news she's denying bringing, but whatever it is, her denial has set the other fairies off. They start crowing and jeering.

"Figures!"

"What did I say? It's gonna be ten years at least!"

"We don't want you back anyway!"

The queen waves her hand and the other fairies freeze, mouths open and fingers pointing.

"Ignore them," she says. "We do want you back. The Realm will always be your home, and our gates will always be open when you decide to return."

If Jess thought Miss Colleen's stare was

invasive, the queen's is a thousand times worse. She's staring into Jess's eyes so deeply that Jess is sure she's seeing through the shift to Jess's soul. Any second now, the queen will reveal her identity and call for the guards.

But that doesn't happen. Instead, the queen folds her hands in her lap and utters a single cryptic sentence.

"You know what you need to do."

With a nod, the queen unfreezes the other fairies, but they've lost their momentum. They look around in vague confusion, which mirrors what Jess is feeling internally. It sounds like Penn can choose to end his exile by doing whatever the queen is talking about. So why hasn't he? What has the queen asked him to do?

"Addison," the queen says, her gaze focused on the real Penn now, "I grant you permission to send him back to the human realm."

If Jess thought the fairies were angry before, they're absolutely apoplectic now, yelling and shouting over each other to be heard.

"You're just sending him back?" one screams. "That's not punishment! We all know he likes it there!"

"Yeah, look at him, he even looks like one of them!" another shouts. "He's not even wearing his wings!"

"Maybe he doesn't have them anymore," a third says. "Maybe they fell off from lack of use!"

The fairies scream with laughter, falling over themselves like it's the funniest joke they've ever heard. Jess knew Penn wasn't well-liked by the fairies, but this is far beyond what she expected.

In her experience, fairies tend to be very clan-like, preferring the company of their own kind and never fighting over anything more than petty grievances. What could have happened to make them turn on one of their own like this?

Jess can't see Penn since he's behind her, but she can tell he's not taking the fairies' taunts well. She senses him shifting his weight, as though he's preparing to run, or maybe fight. Hopefully he'll be able to keep his cool long enough for them to get out.

There's a loud bang as the king slams his staff on the ground. "Silence!"

The other fairies stop twittering in an instant, as though frozen again.

"You would question the judgment of your queen?" the king demands. "She has made a decision. He will be sent back immediately. We believe this is the best course of action. Would you question us?"

The other fairies start shaking their heads and genuflecting. "No, Your Majesties," they chorus.

The king nods. The queen looks to Penn, the real Penn. "Thank you for your service, Addison. You may take him back now. Please follow the protocol upon your arrival in the human world and reread the terms of his banishment."

"Yes, Your Majesty," Penn says. He places a hand on Jess's shoulder. "Let's go."

With only that warning, he teleports them

away from the palace. Everything twists around them, and when it untwists, they're on the side of a two-lane road lined with dense trees. Jess recognizes this stretch of road; they're maybe a quarter of a mile from the Academy, just out of range of the enchantments that block teleportation within school grounds. They'll have to walk.

Jess drops her shift and takes a step forward, about to start the walk to the school, but a tug on her sleeve stops her. She turns to see Penn, shift gone and face tight.

"Wait," he says. "Can we not head there just yet? I...I need a minute first."

Jess is about to argue, to point out they've already wasted enough time and they need to get the data to the others for the briefing, but the look on Penn's face stops her. It's hollow and a little unhinged. And maybe it's just a trick of the light, but his eyes look like they're shifting colors, their normal tone interrupted by sparks and flashes of bright green. If he's losing control, she'd rather he do it out here than at the Academy.

She nods, and as soon as she does, he turns and heads into the trees, saying, "I'll be right back."

With him gone, the area around Jess is quiet except for the soft calls of birds in the woods. The road is deserted, and there's nothing else around—no other buildings or side roads, no animals or people, just Jess and the strip of asphalt stretching toward home.

Jess doesn't know what she's supposed to do until Penn gets back. Just stand here? She paces in a circle, then kicks a piece of gravel, watching it skip across the road into the trees on the other side.

She wonders what Penn's doing. Resting, maybe? He's an all-powerful fairy—surely a bit of shifting and teleportation are as simple as breathing. It barely costs Jess anything to maintain a half-shift, and she doesn't have even a quarter of the power he does. There's no way he would need a break.

Jess, on the other hand, is feeling her energy start to fade. The shifting was easy, but it took a lot to transport herself to the Realm. On top of that, the adrenaline from earlier's events is waning quickly, leaving her with only the low-level buzz of her radar sense, which is currently telling her Penn has stopped about five hundred feet behind her. Once the briefing is done, Jess knows she is going to head straight for her dorm and sleep until dinner, or longer.

She paces a little more, but Penn still doesn't reappear. She decides she might as well sit down to conserve some of her energy and is just about to do so when a loud scream pierces the air, followed by the squawking of birds.

Jess whips around to see a cloud of birds rising above the trees, their cries frantic.

Penn.

And before she can even think about it, before she even remembers that he's a fairy, she takes off into the woods toward the sound.

She can see the path he took, the broken branches and flattened leaves that indicate where his feet touched the ground. She follows it, keeping her steps quick but silent. She can sense him just up ahead, but her sense doesn't tell her if he's safe or not. What if the king and queen discovered their deception? What if one of the fairies from the palace followed them back?

Jess slows down as she approaches the spot where she can sense him. She can see a clearing up ahead through the trees, and creeps slowly to the edge, prepared to see armed guards, angry fairies, or something even worse, but instead, all she sees is Penn.

He's sitting on a fallen tree trunk, his head buried in his hands. He's speaking, or maybe humming, but the sound is so low she can't make out any words.

Jess feels uncomfortable, like she's stumbled upon something she shouldn't have. She's never seen Penn like this before, and it's unsettling, almost like—

A breeze rustles through the forest behind her, blowing past her and playing with the ends of her hair. Penn looks up, and before she can duck out of sight, he spots her.

"Jess?"

The discomfort she felt upon seeing him has nothing on how she feels now, caught spying. She wishes her powers would allow her to shrink to the size of a bug and crawl away into the foliage.

"Sorry," she says. "I heard a scream, and I thought..." Her voice trails off. She'd rather not explain what she thought, since she realizes now that it was silly of her to think he was in danger. Like there's anything she could have done to help.

"Oh," Penn says, surprise in his voice. "Sorry, I didn't mean to scare you. I just..."

His voice trails off, too, and Jess is surprised. She doesn't think she's ever seen Penn at a loss for words.

"Are you okay?"

"Yeah, I'm fine." His voice is weary, and he looks away from her. "It's just...all of this, it's a lot. I need to get my head on straight before we talk to the others."

Jess gets it, in that she understands feeling overwhelmed and needing to take a moment to process emotions. What she doesn't get is why Penn would feel that way.

He's a fairy. Fairies don't get overwhelmed. They brush things off and keep going like nothing ever happened.

Penn looks back up at her. "I'm sorry," he says. "I never should have left you in that building alone. And at the palace—I didn't realize the others were there. I thought it would just be the king and queen. If I'd known, I would have tried to find a different option. I'm sorry."

He looks away again, like he can't meet her eyes any longer.

Jess is at a loss for how to respond. Penn's behavior doesn't compute. This is not how things are supposed to go. He should be back to his usual self, she should be trying to avoid talking to him, and they should be on their way to the briefing.

Instead, he's a mess, she's trying to figure out why, and they're both in the middle of the woods trying to stop feeling.

Stop feeling.

Then it clicks.

For years, Jess has believed that the differences between fairies and humans went beyond magic and immortality, that fairies were incapable of feeling emotions like humans and half-fae. They couldn't feel loss or love, or anything complex or nuanced. Somehow, that made it easier for her to accept their existence, to coexist in this world with creatures stronger and more powerful than she could ever dream to be. It made it easier for her not to care.

Now in front of her is the fairy she cared for least. The one who chased her, who traumatized her as a child, who took two years from her that she will never get back.

The one who looks just as exhausted and distraught as she feels.

The one who wants to stop feeling, too.

Jess has to sit down. The world feels like it's spinning around her, and she has to hold her palms to the ground to steady herself. It's not true. It can't be true. All these years...but she can't deny it any longer.

Penn is capable of human emotion, and if he is, that means the other fairies are, too.

Including Jess's mom.

Jess feels sick. When she came to the Academy and discovered her mom was alive but had never visited or bothered to try and find her when she was on the run...that cut deep.

As she learned more about the fairies and started to form impressions of them, she explained away her mom's behavior as a result of fairies not feeling like people do. It wasn't a happy explanation, but it gave her a little comfort to know that was just the way her mom was.

Now, the realization that her mom has been capable of emotion—even love—this whole time, takes that scrap of comfort Jess has held tightly to for years and tears it to shreds.

It's all too much. Hunting for Della, finding out there are spies in her home, and now learning her mom could have cared enough to help her but never did—it's too much for one day.

Jess wants to find a small, dark space to crawl into and hide from the world. She wants to have a good cry and get so exhausted that she falls asleep so she can wake up tomorrow like none of this ever happened. She wants to be living a different life.

That's impossible now. She has to keep going, if not for herself, for everyone who is depending on her. She will have to do what she's always done—take the complicated emotions, put them in a mental box, and file them away to deal with later. There isn't time now.

"It's okay, right?" Penn's voice brings her back to the present. "We saved the kids. You got the evidence. We're here and we're safe. Everything's fine, right?"

She focuses on him, and what she sees chills

her. His eyes are searching like he desperately needs her reassurance, but that's not what makes her afraid.

It's the way his form is starting to blur at the edges, like it can't decide what it wants to be; the way his eyes are still doing that weird flickering, definitely not a trick of the light. And behind it all, a low hum like the buzz of fluorescent lights that has steadily grown stronger since she entered the clearing. She realizes it's coming from him.

Jess doesn't know what any of it means, but it can't be good. He needs to pull himself together.

"Penn." As his name leaves her mouth, she realizes this is the first time she's ever spoken it aloud to him. She can't use the Call, but from the way his eyes instantly lock with hers, she may as well have.

"Everything worked out," she says, keeping her voice low and steady. "We're all safe. It's going to be okay."

"I sent you into a trap. If you'd died, Talia never would have forgiven me. I never would have forgiven myself."

Her mom, caring about Jess's well-being? She'd never even reached out when Jess's dad died. She'd left her to fend for herself. No visits, no calls, no magical guidance. Radio silence. It's hard for Jess to believe that her own death would be more than a minor disturbance to her mom. It doesn't matter now, though.

"It wasn't your fault," she says. "None of us knew."

"I should have known. I'm supposed to be the responsible one, to have your backs. That's why I was on this mission, and I let you down."

His gaze drops from hers. The edges of his form are getting more unstable, and the buzzing noise is getting louder.

"You were right. I'm not cut out for intelligence work or being on a team. I failed everyone."

"That's not true." Jess keeps her voice firm, trying to keep her growing worry from showing.

"Penn, look at me."

It's slow, but he raises his head to meet her gaze. His eyes are still flickering and sparking, and it's disorienting to look at, but Jess holds his gaze.

"You didn't fail," she tells him. "You were great. The way you cast that illusion to distract the guards—that was really impressive. And when you uncovered the hidden spell residue back at the apartment; we never would have known to even look for that without you. Not to mention, it was your idea to go see Aster, and she told us the three items we needed for the assignment to be a success. That's the reason we even have evidence to catch these people. You did a lot of really great things that made this assignment turn out the way it did."

She's saying it to reassure him, but she realizes she believes it, too. Regardless of their history, she can admit his presence was helpful.

"Yeah, but I also made a lot of mistakes," he says, looking back at the ground.

"So did I," Jess says, "and I made a really big one. I made you feel like you were bad at this, for no other reason than I was angry and wanted to take it out on you. I'm sorry for that. You're not bad at this; you're just learning, like me."

"You really mean that?" He looks up at her, eyes searching but guarded. The edges of his form seem to have stabilized a bit, and though the buzzing noise hasn't receded, it hasn't gotten louder.

"Yes," Jess says. "You're clever, you're charismatic, and you're excellent with spellwork. You could be a great FIC officer if that's what you're shooting for."

Penn considers her for a few seconds before he speaks again.

"You know," he says, tilting his head, "I think that's the first nice thing you've ever said to me. Thank you."

"You're welcome," Jess says automatically, then curses internally. Regardless of what he's dealing with right now, he's still *Penn*, still the same annoying fairy who won't leave her be. She doesn't want him to misinterpret this, to think they're friends. "Don't get used to it."

Surprise crosses Penn's face, then blooms into a smile. He laughs, and the effect is instantaneous. His form sharpens, every edge and feature crystal clear again. The buzzing sound dies away, and his eyes return to normal, no longer shifting or sparking. Whatever was happening to him is over now.

"I won't." There's still a hint of a smile in his voice that irks Jess, but at least he doesn't seem like he's in danger of spontaneously combusting anymore.

"Are you okay to go back now?" He may not be concerned about the briefing, but Jess still is.

"And meet with more fairies who hate me?" he says, getting to his feet. "Let's do it."

Jess also stands, brushing a couple dead leaves off her jeans. "The FIC fairies hate you too?"

"Jess, they all hate me."

He smiles like it's a joke, but his voice says otherwise. He joins her at the edge of the clearing and they start toward the road.

"Why?" Jess asks.

"Because I'm so handsome and charming. They can't stand it."

She realizes she's not going to get a straight answer out of him, so she lets it drop.

When they reach the road, Penn does his keychain trick again, and they ride to the Academy in silence. When they get out of the car, the school feels quiet, too, and Jess imagines it's holding its breath, waiting for them.

At the front door, Penn pauses, looking over at her. "You ready for this?"

"Ready as I'll ever be," she says. She just wants it to be over.

They enter the building and Penn checks his phone.

"Everyone's in room 143," he says. "I don't know where that is, do you?"

Jess nods. "This way."

She leads the way down the hallway on the left

side of the staircase, and all too quickly, they've arrived at room 143. Jess feels like letting Penn go in first, but instead, she pushes open the door and steps inside before she can stop herself.

* 19 *

THE ROOM IS NORMALLY USED AS A classroom, but today all the desks are neatly stacked in the corners (clearly Miss Colleen's work) and a large table is set up in the center of the room, surrounded by chairs. It looks like a conference room, or a war room.

All five of the people in the room stare at Jess and Penn as they enter and take a couple of the empty seats. Finally, Lyle speaks.

"Glad you made it back," Lyle says, looking at Jess. Their tone is neutral, but the way their eyes crinkle at the corners lets Jess know their words are genuine. "That was a pretty big explosion. Took down the entire building."

"Yes," says a fairy Jess doesn't recognize, "a

shame, really. The whole building and all the evidence it contained, gone before we had a chance to examine it. What a waste."

Jess realizes she must be one of the officers from the FIC's strike team. She's tall and wearing tactical gear, with her dark hair tied back, exposing the pointed tips of her ears. Like all the fairies in their "human" disguises, she looks a little too perfect and polished to blend in. Her eyes flit from Jess to Penn to Lyle, and the look she's giving them, in combination with her words, makes it sound to Jess like she is blaming them for the building exploding.

"Everything was rigged with self-destruct spells," Jess says. "If we'd taken out anything important, it would have blown up, too."

The fairy crosses her arms. "Maybe someone should have thought about that before tripping the alarm. Someone could have grabbed the needed evidence and broken the self-destruct spell."

The three other officers are now watching in rapt attention; for what, Jess doesn't know.

"How were we supposed to know they had an alarm spell set?" Penn snaps.

Ah. Now she knows.

"If you'd followed FIC procedure, you would have caught it," the angry fairy says. "This is what happens when we send in inexperienced nobodies instead of real officers. We could have been in and out without anyone the wiser."

"*Inexperienced nobodies?*" Lyle growls, but Penn is louder.

"Oh yeah?" he says. "That alarm was set to detect teleportation. You all are so reliant on your magic, you wouldn't have lasted two seconds before one of you slipped up."

"It was YOU!" the fairy says, jabbing her finger at Penn. Her eyes gleam and her smile is triumphant. "I knew it! I knew this was your fault, wasn't I just saying that?"

She turns to the other officers, and a couple of them nod. She turns back to Penn. "I told Talia that involving you was a terrible idea, and I was right! Your bumbling mistake cost us every shred of evidence in that building!"

Penn stands up like he's about to lunge across the table at the other fairy, but Jess speaks before he has the chance.

"Not every shred of evidence."

All six pairs of eyes are now on her. Lyle, Penn, the angry fairy, and the other FIC officers. Penn sits slowly back in his seat.

"What do you mean?" asks one of the other officers. "We searched the remains of the building and everything was torched. Did you manage to smuggle something out?"

Jess nods. "I downloaded some data off one of their computers that might be helpful."

"Well, let's see it, then," the angry fairy says, crossing her arms again. "Where is it? You got it on a flash drive?"

Jess reaches toward the flash drive in her pocket, but Penn puts his hand out to stop her. "Not so fast," he says to the other fairy. "We're not showing anything until Talia is here."

Jess bristles at the word "we." Who is he to make that decision? She was the one to risk her life to get the evidence in the first place.

The angry fairy isn't happy about Penn's answer, either. "I am the lead officer on this case," she snaps. "You will hand over any relevant information when I request it, or I'll have you reported for withholding evidence and obstructing my investigation."

"Oh, give it to you so you can pretend your team found it and take all the credit? Not a chance."

There's a split second of silence before the other fairy goes off.

"You selfish bastard! You think you can just waltz in here playing your James Bond games and expect us all to applaud you like a hero? YOU'RE NOT A CLIPPING HERO! Look around you. You think anyone in this room respects you? NO! You're a JOKE to them! Everyone knows you're only here because Talia has a soft spot for you, not because you have any value. So why don't you just hand over that information and go back to the stable where you belong?"

A stunned sort of silence rings through the room. Penn's jaw tightens and his eyes flash—literally, they turn a bright, electric green for a moment—but before he can respond, a voice rings out from the doorway.

"That will be enough, Kasi," Talia says, striding into the room. Miss Colleen follows close behind. The door closes magically with a click.

"Penn has proven himself to be a capable contract officer these past few days. His teammates have proven themselves as well. If, as you said, no one in this room respects him"—Talia surveys the room, looking at each of the officers in turn—"then I would recommend they reconsider their position on the matter, as well as whether they truly want to continue with the FIC."

Silence greets these words. Kasi, the angry fairy, doesn't look like she's reconsidering, but she also doesn't look like she's about to throttle anyone like she did a minute ago. Jess considers that progress.

Talia and Miss Colleen pull up chairs. Talia's is directly next to Jess, and Jess feels weird sitting so close to this person she should know, but really doesn't. Of course, it doesn't help that she's already on edge from her radar senses. Stars, she can't wait until this is over and she can relax.

"So, if I heard correctly, you have information on the group that was occupying the building?" Talia asks, looking at Jess.

"Yes," Jess says. "I copied some information from an unlocked computer and downloaded it onto a flash drive."

"Did you look at any of the files?"

"Yes. There were financial records, emails, and"—she has to pause here, remembering the shock of discovering the truth of what the group was—"recruitment information."

"Recruitment information? They're recruiting?"

Jess nods. She doesn't think she can convey how disturbing this group is without showing them all the files. She pulls the flash drive out of her pocket. "It'll be easier just to show you."

Talia summons a laptop, which she boots up and hands to Jess. Jess plugs in the flash drive and navigates to the recruitment presentation. When she opens it, the images appear on the projector screen at the front of the room. Everyone turns to look.

As she silently clicks through the slides, Jess can feel the mood in the room darkening. The presentation isn't any less disturbing the second time around; actually, she notices things she missed the first time, like how the group emphasizes creating a "better" family and promises its members happiness and belonging. It's sickening, and she can tell the others feel the same.

When she reaches the end of the presentation, everyone is silent. Lyle is the first to speak.

"If this group is so big and powerful, why hasn't anyone heard of them before?" they ask. "You haven't heard of them, right?"

The other fairies shake their heads. Talia leans back in her chair, looking thoughtful, but doesn't seem to recognize the group, either.

"They're probably not as big as they claim they are," Kasi says.

"We'll know once we get this back to headquarters and the analysts check out that financial data," another fairy says.

"You're absolutely right, Kasi," Talia says. "This

is disturbing, but there's no need to get overly concerned until we know what we're dealing with." She turns to Jess, all business. "Is there anything else you want to show us?"

"There's one more thing," Jess says. This is the hard part, the scary part. The part she wishes she could forget she ever saw. She takes a deep breath.

"They had folders with reports on their recruiting efforts. They were labeled by region, and one of them was for the Academy. They're recruiting from the Academy."

Everyone's eyes are on her again and she wishes they weren't.

"You mean...they're here? In my school?" Miss Colleen speaks for the first time since she entered the room. Her voice quivers, reflecting the distress Jess is experiencing, and she feels an odd sort of sympathy for the headmistress. This is painful enough for Jess, having lived here full time for almost six years, but the Academy is Miss Colleen's baby. Jess has heard enough of her annual welcome speeches to know this.

"Where are the reports? Did you get them?" Talia asks.

"N-no," Jess says. "I couldn't download them in time. The power went out and the countdown started right as I went to copy them."

"So we know they have a mole—or multiple moles—here, but we don't know who they are or how many students they've recruited?" Kasi says. She doesn't continue, but Jess can hear from her voice that she doesn't think that's good enough.

"We know enough to start figuring it out," Talia says coolly. She looks back at Jess, warmth returning to her tone. "Anything else?"

"The reports dated back the past five years," Jess says. "That's the only other thing I know. There wasn't time to read any of them."

Talia nods. "That's very helpful, thank you." She turns to the other fairies and claps her hands. "Well, I think we've heard enough for one day. Jess, Penn, Lyle, thank you for your work on this mission. Colleen and I will be reconvening on the issue of the mole, and we will hopefully be able to suss them out shortly. Officers, we will have a formal debrief back at headquarters this afternoon. Thank you for your work as well. You are all dismissed."

"Wait, what about the other kids?" Penn asks. "Did you two find out where they came from? And why did they kidnap Della?"

Lyle crosses their arms. "I was wondering the same thing. We've shared what we know; now it's your turn."

Talia and Miss Colleen share a look. "I don't know how relevant it is," Talia starts.

"I want to know, too," Jess says. She ejects the flash drive and holds it up. "I risked a lot to get this, and we all took risks to find Della and rescue those kids. We deserve to know."

Talia looks at Jess and her face softens. "You sound so much like your father," she says. "He would have been so proud of you."

If Talia had stabbed her with a knife, Jess

wouldn't have been more surprised. Her dad…sometimes she forgets that her mother knew him, that they had to have known each other for Jess to be born.

Jess spent the first twelve years of her life with nothing but an imaginary version of a mother, and it's hard to reconcile that vague figure with the very real fairy sitting in front of her, and harder still to come to terms with the idea of Talia and her dad together. It's so much easier to forget, and Jess does, most of the time. To have Talia break that spell in this moment sets her off balance, so much so that it's hard for her to refocus on what Talia is saying now.

"Experiments," Talia says. "They were running experiments with the kids, all half-fae. It's not clear from the kids' testimonies what they were looking for, but we know they were studying their abilities."

"But the kids, where did they come from?" Penn asks. "Why wasn't anyone looking for them? Why didn't we notice they were gone, that there was a pattern?"

"They were runaways," Talia says. "Most were living on the street."

"So they wouldn't be missed," Jess says, sickened. Kids like her, when she was on the run.

"Right," Talia says. "Della is the only one who didn't fit the pattern; we think there was something specific they wanted her for, but it's not clear what. Whatever it was, it was worth the risk to them to kidnap someone who would be higher-profile."

"This is messed up," Penn says, shaking his

head. "Those poor kids."

"Well, the good news is they're safe now," Miss Colleen says. "They'll be able to stay at the Academy and have a home here. It'll all work out."

"We'll find the people who did this," Talia adds. "They will not escape the Crown's justice, I can assure you of that."

The other officers murmur in agreement and Talia stands, signifying the end of the briefing. Jess gets up to leave with the others. As they exit, she notices Talia pull Penn aside.

"Stay back for a moment, please," she says, but Jess is out of the room before she can hear if she says anything else.

The fairies set off toward the entrance hall, but Lyle stays behind. Jess realizes they are waiting for her.

"That was some crazy stuff," they say. "You holding up all right?"

Jess shrugs. She doesn't feel like talking about her feelings.

Lyle seems to pick up on them anyway. "Come on," they say. "Let's get you some fresh air."

Jess follows them down the hall and out the back door onto the patio. They sit down at one of the tables and Jess joins them.

"By the way, your little friend made it back to McCreed," Lyle says. "Figured you'd want to hear that."

Noe'or. In all the commotion since she'd escaped the explosion, Jess had completely forgotten about the little wicht. She'd send him with Lyle and Penn and not thought twice about him since. Tears prick her eyes. How could she be so selfish?

"Hey," Lyle says, apparently noticing her distress. "It's okay. I know you didn't get to say goodbye—"

"It's not that," Jess says, although it would have been nice to say goodbye. "He was my responsibility. I was the one who was supposed to look out for him; I shouldn't have just sent him off with you like that. What if something had happened to him?"

Lyle leans back in their seat, and Jess sees they have a smile on their face, which completely throws her off.

"What's so funny?"

"Nothing," Lyle replies. "You just remind me of someone is all. Look." They lean forward again, knitting their fingers together and resting their hands on the tabletop. "You did a phenomenal job working with Noe'or. Above and beyond. No one can argue you weren't responsible enough. I'll bet you made his whole year, too; maybe even his whole life. No one's probably ever treated him with that kind of respect."

Jess feels heat rising in her cheeks at the compliment. "You really think so?"

"When he found out he wouldn't get to see you before we sent him back, he pouted for ten minutes," Lyle says. "It's safe to say you made quite the impression."

"I didn't do anything special—"

"You did what was right," Lyle says. "I doubt Noe'or will ever forget you. And neither will his boss."

Jess shivers, remembering McCreed and his interest in her and her abilities. He didn't mention when his "future invitation" would arrive, but she has a feeling it'll be sooner than she'd like.

"Don't worry about McCreed, though," Lyle says. "He knows who our mother is. He may want something, but he won't mess with you to get it. You've got bigger things to deal with."

"The spy." The heavy weight that's been perched on her shoulders like an overly large vulture since she opened that computer file.

"No," Lyle says. "I mean your studies. Your future. Leave the spy business to Mom. I know you've got that instinct, same as me, to get suspicious of everyone and start trying to figure it out on your own. You need to bury it. You've still got the rest of your senior year left. Enjoy it!"

It's a nice sentiment, but impossible. Jess can't simply ignore what she knows.

"How?" she asks. "How can I just go to class, or walk around campus, or do anything when I know anyone I meet could be a spy?"

"You just have to," Lyle says. "You don't have any choice. Focus on the people you do trust. You know who those are, right?"

Jess nods. She trusts Cat. That's about it. Oh, and maybe Miss Colleen, but only because she knows she isn't the spy.

"Good," Lyle is saying. "Focus on those people.

Ignore everyone else. If you see anything suspicious, obviously you should say something, but don't set out looking for it. You don't want to be the one seeing spooks where there aren't any."

They reach into their pocket and pull out a card, which they pass to Jess.

"Here's my contact info. Ring me up if you ever need anything, or just someone to talk to. I'm usually always around."

Jess takes the card. "Thank you," she says, and she means it. She didn't know what to think of her half-sibling when they first met, especially after the "test," but now she realizes she's actually going to miss having the old spy around.

Lyle stands up from the table, popping their back as they do. "Well, I'd better get going," they say. "I've got a stack of novels waiting for me back home, and they aren't going to read themselves."

Jess stands up, too. "Thank you for the advice," she says, "just now and back at the park. I really appreciate it."

Lyle waves her off. "Not a problem, young one. Always happy to pass on some of the knowledge knocking around in this old brain of mine. Otherwise, what else am I going to do with it?"

"You could write your own novel," Jess suggests.

Lyle laughs. "Nobody would ever read it. If I wrote about even half the things I've seen in my life, people would say it's too unbelievable, even for fantasy! No, I'll just settle for beating you young kids over the head with my advice. Much more enjoyable anyway."

* * * *

After her talk with Lyle, Jess really wants to go back to her dorm and sleep. She knows Miss Colleen would excuse her from class; after all, she just helped save ten kids and uncover evidence of a plot against the fairies. But first, there's one more person she needs to see. She steps off the patio on the path to the Barn.

The Barn is a building Jess's mom could be proud of, meaning it's deceptive in just about every regard, from size and appearance to function. Sure, it holds the Academy's stables, but it also holds the school's gym, dance studio, and full-size theater.

When she first arrived at the Academy, Jess had questioned how it was possible for one building to be four different things simultaneously. Cat had told her, with the full sincerity of a twelve-year-old wise beyond her years, not to think about it too hard.

It's the theater Jess is looking for now, so she heads to the west side of the building, entering through the side door there. She makes her way down the aisle quietly, finding a seat on the end of the third row.

No one notices her; no one acknowledges her presence. After the intensity of the last few days and the pressure she's been under, Jess is glad for the chance to be a nameless face in the audience, watching a performance instead of living it.

Up on the stage, Cat stands tall and proud. She's reciting a monologue, something dramatic and bittersweet that Jess doesn't recognize. As she finishes, she sweeps her gaze over the theater and it catches on Jess. The smile that blooms on her face mirrors Jess's, and Jess feels a bubble of warmth rise up inside of her. She may not have much, but at least she knows Cat will always be there for her.

* 20 *

JESS IS SITTING IN MATH CLASS WHEN THE paper butterfly derails her day.

It's been a week since the debriefing, and she feels like she's been doing well; she's been showing up to every class, doing all her homework, and avoiding extreme paranoia about her classmates.

The butterfly itself isn't strange—Miss Colleen and the teachers use the enchanted paper notes instead of hand-carried ones or loudspeaker announcements—but it's strange that Jess would be receiving one. She's not aware of any teachers who would need to see her.

She unfolds the butterfly to find it's not from a teacher at all, but from Miss Colleen. It's a summons to a meeting at five in Miss Colleen's office. The only other detail given is a brief note in the headmistress's perfect cursive—"for a follow-up to last week's meeting."

Anticipation bubbles up inside Jess. She'd almost given up hope that she could contribute anything more to the case. Without being able to actively search for the spy, it's unlikely she would find them before the FIC, and it's not like she can investigate the organization between classes. Now it looks like she may get a chance to help.

She doesn't know if anyone else will be at the meeting, or if it will just be her. Her radar senses are telling her Penn is on campus and has been since mid-morning, but he's on campus frequently, so it could be unrelated. Just to be safe, though, she decides to assume Penn and at least one person from the FIC will be there, possibly her mom if she's not busy. Best to prepare for the worst.

Throughout the rest of the afternoon, Jess's anticipation makes her antsy. She can hardly focus in her remaining classes, and they seem to drag on forever. Even when classes finish, she still has two hours to kill before the meeting.

She goes for a run to use up some of her excess energy, then heads to the dining hall for an early dinner. She's outside Miss Colleen's office by 4:50 p.m. She waits on a bench until exactly five o'clock, when she knocks on the door.

Miss Colleen opens the door within a few seconds of her knock.

"Come on in, Jess," she says, holding the door open.

Jess enters her office and notices the door on the left side of the room is open. It leads to a small conference room, which she's only ever been in once before, when she first arrived at the Academy. As she expected, she's not the only one at the meeting. Rather, it seems like the meeting has already been going on for a bit before she arrived.

She sees her mom, some of the FIC officers from the debrief (Kasi is notably absent) and, as she predicted, Penn. He gives her a small wave of acknowledgement when she enters the conference room, and she nods in response. She notices messy stacks of files and paperwork are spread on the table, and most of the fairies have half-full drink glasses in front of them. Jess gets the feeling this meeting hasn't been called to share positive news.

"Okay, Talia," Miss Colleen says, clapping her hands. "Do you want to give a quick recap so Jess knows where we're at?"

Talia nods. "As you know, we are currently investigating more into the organization calling themselves 'Smith and Salt Ltd.,'" she says. "Some of our officers are out in the field hunting for more information, and the data you were able to download from that computer has been very helpful in understanding the scope of this organization."

She doesn't elaborate on this, which Jess takes as a bad sign. It must be bigger than they'd expected.

"On a different front, we have also been working to figure out who the group's mole is at the Academy," Talia continues. "Unfortunately, we haven't had much luck. We've combed through all the student records and confirmed they are all genuine. We've checked the records of everyone who works for and with the Academy to confirm their identities as well. We've found nothing suspicious so far, despite the information you saw indicating the group is recruiting here."

She pauses, and Jess doesn't understand. "So you're just giving up?"

"No," Talia says. "We're going to try a different method instead."

The other FIC officers look at each other, and Jess gets the feeling they hadn't discussed this other method before she arrived. The fairies look annoyed to have been left out of the decision, but Talia either doesn't notice or, more likely, doesn't care.

"We are going to plant our own spy at the Academy," Talia continues. "That person will go undercover as a new student and behave in such a manner that will cause the organization's mole to take notice and attempt to recruit them. If we can get an inside agent, we'll be able to find out everything we need to take this group down and get this mess cleaned up."

"I'll volunteer," one of the officers says. "I have an original shift that will work great for a student."

"No, I should do it," another says. "You're also working the Sydney case. My other case wrapped up last weekend, and besides, I have more undercover experience."

The third fairy is about to chime in when Talia interrupts.

"Actually, I'm going to have Jess do it," she says. "For one, she's already a student, so she has a better understanding of the dynamics at play here, and she also has no other commitments at this time."

"Besides school," Miss Colleen points out.

"Yes, well, we can work on that," Talia says dismissively.

When Jess guessed she might get a chance to help with the case, this was not what she'd had in mind. She'd expected to be reviewing files, maybe, or observing suspects. Not going undercover and drawing out the spy herself.

The idea excites her—she'll be using her abilities again, something that always makes her feel good—but it also makes her wary. This won't be like impersonating a wicht at McCreed's palace. She'll be living amongst and lying to people she's known for years. The thought gives her an uncomfortable feeling in the pit of her stomach.

The other fairies aren't uncomfortable by the idea; they outright hate it.

"You're giving this assignment to a high schooler?" one asks. "She hasn't even been through training! How will she know what she's doing?"

"She'll have a handler," Talia replies evenly.

"And who will that be?" the other fairy demands.

"Penn will be fulfilling that role."

When she says that, Jess finally looks over at Penn to see he's just as confused as she is.

"Now wait just a minute," he says. "How come I'm just finding out about this? You haven't even asked me if I want to do it."

Talia looks at him pointedly. "Well, do you?"

"Of course, but that's not the point," Penn says. "You didn't ask Jess, either. She should get a say in whether she does it or not."

Now Talia turns to Jess. "Jess, will you do this?"

Jess wants to say yes, but the word catches in her throat for a second. She feels put on the spot, and like she barely has an understanding of what she's agreeing to.

Penn looks at her and says gently, "You don't have to say yes. You can say no. There's always a choice."

What a concept. She can say no. This assignment—something she's been wanting for ages, and another opportunity to prove herself—could be turned down. And deep down, she kind of wants to turn it down.

She doesn't like it. She doesn't like the thought of having to lie to everyone she knows. It's one thing to avoid sharing confidential details, but it's another to impersonate someone and interact with people she's known forever day after day without being able to tell them it's really her. It's not that she doubts she can do it—she's been training for assignments like this since she arrived—but simply that she doesn't feel the desire to. That should make it simple, right? She should say no. She *wants* to say no.

But on the flip side, this is a chance to prove

herself, and it's a chance she earned because of the work she did on the last assignment. She's also burning to see how this case pans out, to find and stop this organization before they can spread any more of their poison to innocents. If she's not actively assisting on the case, she'll never find out, and if she turns down this chance, she knows she won't get another one.

So, despite her reservations, she responds, "I'll do it."

The rest of the meeting passes in a blur, or at least that's how it feels to Jess. Her mom launches into an explanation of how the assignment will work and the timing of it, the other fairies voice objections and complaints, but Jess can barely focus on any of it.

She started to get a feeling of dread in her stomach as soon as she said yes, and now she can't help but imagine what it will be like to have to lie to her teachers, her classmates, and, worst of all, her best friend. She won't be able to even tell Cat that she's on another assignment.

Talia mentions that they will tell people Jess went to the Realm for a special intensive with the FIC as a cover for her absence. She won't be able to keep in contact with Cat much at all, since she'll be undercover the whole time. She'll probably have to do make-up work for the classes she'll be missing, too, and she's supposed to be preparing for her next steps in life after the Academy—it's all so overwhelming.

The meeting is over sooner than expected.

Talia tells Jess to prepare to leave for the Realm at the end of the week, and she'll receive a detailed brief and additional training when she arrives. Jess is grateful for this, at least. She won't be unprepared. This only leaves her a few days, though.

None of them know how long she'll be undercover—it depends on what she finds and how quickly. It could be a week, or it could be the rest of the year. It's impossible to know for sure. Talia even mentioned that if the group recruits her, there could be an opportunity to act as a mole and funnel information on the organization to the FIC from the inside.

That's an even more disheartening prospect. Who knows how long that could go on for? Jess can't complain, though. All she's wanted since she arrived at the Academy has been to work with the FIC, and that's exactly what they're offering her.

She leaves Miss Colleen's office feeling numb, like she could be hit by a car and feel nothing. She should be more excited. She should be planning already, her mind running through potential strategies. But she's not. Lyle's words echo in her ears: *You've still got the rest of your senior year left. Enjoy it!*

How can she do that now?

Now that the meeting's over, she doesn't know what to do with herself. She can't talk to Cat because she's at band practice, and she can't go to dinner because she already did that. She doesn't feel like going back to her dorm so early, either.

Maybe she'll take a walk around campus instead.

She turns at the end of the hallway, not left toward the main staircase, but right toward the side staircase and the side doors, which lead out to a paved footpath. She's almost to the staircase when she hears footsteps behind her and suddenly, Penn is walking beside her like he's been there all along.

"Well, that was an interesting meeting," he says, matching her pace down the stairs. She can tell he wants her to jump in, but she doesn't feel like it.

He looks over and seems to read her emotions enough to pick up on that, because his tone softens when he asks, "You mind if I walk with you a bit?"

She doesn't really care either way, so she just shrugs. He seems to take this as a yes, and he holds the door open for her as they head outside.

The sun is making its way down to the horizon and the temperature has dropped, but it's still nice outside. Jess heads for the trail, which meanders just beyond the treeline, but close enough that it's still visible from the lawn. Penn follows, and as they enter the trees, he looks over at her.

"You okay?" he asks. "You seem a little down."

Jess shrugs again. She doesn't feel like talking about it with him, and maybe he gets this, too, because he doesn't ask her any more questions and they walk in silence for a bit.

Soon, they come to a clearing with a small shed. Jess thinks it's used for gardening supplies, but it also has a little porch attached, and the trees in this area are just thin enough that the sunset is visible through them. Jess has always liked watching sunsets, so instead of continuing on the trail, she goes over to the shed instead and climbs the couple of steps up to the porch.

Today's sunset, while still in its early stages, is going to be amazing. Jess can already tell. There are just enough clouds around to catch and reflect the light, but not obstruct it. The trees hide a little bit of the view, but add to the ambience, and she is suddenly glad she came this way.

"I didn't know this was here," Penn says. While she's leaning against the railing, he's standing at the top of the steps, his arm wrapped around the post.

The fading light catches on his hair and face, and even though he's still wearing his human form, the light makes him appear otherworldly. It would be impossible not to tell he's a fairy, despite how he tries to hide it.

"This view is incredible," he says, and Jess turns back to look at it, too.

She'll miss this when she leaves the Academy. It's probably because of all the magic around, but sunsets here hit a bit differently. She's glad she's not missing this one.

They watch the sunset for a few more minutes before Penn turns to her.

"I have something to show you," he says.

"What?"

"Here, give me your wrist." He reaches toward her, left hand outstretched.

Jess is immediately suspicious and pulls her arms to her chest. "What for?"

"I think I've found something that can help

with, ah...that extra sense we talked about," he says, running his hand through his hair. Jess doesn't know why, but the fact that he doesn't know how to refer to it either makes her feel a bit better.

"What is it?"

"It'll be easier if I just show you." He holds out his hand again and meets her gaze. "Do you trust me?"

"Not particularly," she answers before thinking. It's an honest reply, but she realizes it was a little harsh.

"You wound me," Penn says, clutching his chest. His tone is joking, but Jess can sense a sliver of truth behind it, too, and she feels a little bad.

Penn takes his hand off his chest and holds it out a third time. "Can you at least trust me for this?"

Slowly, Jess unfurls her hands from her chest. She holds out her left wrist and he takes it gently. A marker appears in his other hand, and he uncaps it with magic before using it to write a chain of symbols on Jess's wrist. She doesn't understand what he's doing or how this is supposed to help, but she's going to have to trust that it will make sense.

He's very careful as he draws each mark, and the symbols chain around Jess's wrist like a bracelet. The last symbol completes the chain, and when he draws the final line, they glow purple for a moment. That's not the most surprising part. When the glow fades, so does her radar sense.

All the tension she'd been feeling from Penn being on campus has fallen away. Her heart rate slows to normal and even her mood improves. She holds up her wrist to look at the designs closer.

"What—how does this work?"

Penn's face lights up. "So it does work? You don't feel anything anymore?"

Jess shakes her head.

"Amazing!" he says, smiling.

"What is it?" Jess wants to understand how a few lines drawn with a marker can fix this thing she's been dealing with for the past seven years.

"It's an old type of magic called sigil magic," Penn explains. "A lot of fairies don't practice it anymore, but I find it still has its uses. The symbols in this spell are ones I typically use to calm skittish horses or help engines start and run smoothly. I experimented with a few different combinations, but this is the one I thought would be most likely to work. I'm glad it did."

Jess nods as she examines her wrist. "Does it ever run out?"

Penn shakes his head. "Nope. If it seems like it's not working so well or you notice it looks faded, you can retrace it with any kind of ink. And of course, you can wash it off to stop it from working."

Jess doesn't know what to say. She looks up from her wrist to him, and he looks so genuine. It hits her that this spell probably took a lot of time to create and test.

She pictures him testing it on himself, repainting symbols in different combinations over and over again. It probably took hours. All to help her. It's not like he sees any benefit from it.

With that thought comes a realization. Throughout the mission, she'd assumed he was only participating for the thrills, but there are no thrills in developing a complex spell just to help someone you barely know. Which can only mean one thing: Penn isn't the one-dimensional, self-centered fairy she'd always pegged him as. His insistence on helping Della, and now his effort to help Jess—he didn't have to do either of those things, yet here he is.

Jess looks at the symbols wrapping her wrist again. She's seen pictures of sigils in old books in the Academy's library, but these are far more intricate, and she can tell from the careful way he drew them that Penn put a lot of time and effort into getting them right.

"Thank you," she says, looking back up at him, and she means it. Building spells like this is not one of her talents, and she never would have figured it out on her own.

Penn puts his hands in his pockets and shrugs. "It's the least I could do. I'm glad it works. That seemed to be the best combination when I tested it, but if I think of any ways to adjust it, I'll let you know."

A lump rises in Jess's throat. "Okay," she says. Then, "Why are you being so nice to me?"

He looks at her quizzically. "What do you mean? Why wouldn't I be nice?"

She looks away. "I don't know." Maybe because people don't normally help her? Maybe because, like he said, she's never been nice to him?

Maybe because she convinced herself he doesn't care, and a tiny part of her still believes he might hate her?

But she doesn't say any of that.

"I guess I thought you weren't serious. It was nice of you to say, but I assumed nothing would happen. I didn't expect, well, this." She looks back at him, holding up her wrist.

Penn takes his hand out of his pocket to run it through his hair. "I wasn't going to leave you hanging like that. Not if I could do something to help. I mean, that's what partners are for, right?"

Jess drops her hand. "Partners? One assignment doesn't make us partners."

"It's two assignments now."

Jess's heart sinks as she remembers the new assignment. She'd been so distracted by the conversation that she almost forgot, but now it's coming back to her. The information she found, all the lying she'll have to do—

"Sorry," Penn says, wincing. He must have sensed her mood change. "Didn't mean to bring that up. I know—well, I know you weren't excited when Talia volunteered you. I get it."

Jess doubts that.

"For the record, though," he continues, "I think you'll do great. You're a great spy and I know you're ready for this."

Jess cringes internally at the word "spy," but brushes it aside. "That's not it," she says, but what it is is so close, so personal, that she can't share it. If it was Cat—but she can't tell Cat, either, for different reasons.

He's waiting for a response. She looks away to lessen the weight of his gaze. "The Academy—it's my home," she says.

"And you feel like it's been invaded," he infers.

Jess can only nod. She doesn't trust herself to speak.

Penn comes to stand next to her at the railing, resting his elbows on it so his hands hang over the edge, wrists crossed.

"Hey, don't worry. We'll catch them, whoever they are, and then everything will go back to normal. You'll see."

"You don't know that for sure." Jess hopes it'll be that easy. She hopes that by finding the mole, she doesn't accidentally tear the Academy apart. But that will depend on who it is, and if what she saw is any indication—

"True," Penn says. "But you're the best one for the job. If anyone can catch them, it's you. And I'll be there to back you up. I bet this takes two or three weeks, tops."

Jess thinks that's a very idealistic goal. If they had more to go off of, sure. But all the FIC has is her word.

It's shocking they even believed that, says a voice in the back of Jess's mind. *After you didn't even tell them everything...*

Shame burns in the pit of Jess's stomach. She doesn't know why she didn't disclose the other thing she saw. She told herself that she'd glimpsed the report too quickly, that there was no time to process it and she may have misread it, but she knows that's not true. The segment of the report that she glimpsed before she ran out of that abandoned office is burned in her mind.

The spy is a student. And they aren't working alone.

Jess considers telling Penn now. She needs to tell someone, and he'll be involved in the case. At the very least, it might alleviate some of her guilt. She turns to say something to him, but he speaks before she can figure out the right way to bring it up.

"I'm excited," he says, his tone light. "I've never been a handler before. This is going to be cool."

Jess scraps her plan. He'd immediately go tell Talia, and Jess would get in trouble—if he even took her seriously. She can wait.

"Yes, desk work is so cool," she deadpans.

He nudges her with his shoulder. "Don't rain on my parade! I'm going to be the coolest handler. I'll have a headset, and a wall of monitors, and I'll learn all the lingo, too. And I'll have some cool gadgets to give you that I get to demonstrate."

"I don't think this is a 'cool gadget' type of assignment."

"Every assignment is a cool gadget type of assignment."

He is entirely too enthusiastic about this for Jess's taste, and it's not making her feel any better. "Can we not talk about this anymore?"

"Sure," Penn says.

He looks at her expectantly, waiting for her to bring up a different subject, but she doesn't. She stares out into the distance, watching the sunset, and eventually he turns to watch it, too.

About the Author

When she was younger, Rana Schenke spent way too much time reading, writing stories about quirky kids and fairies, and filming funny videos with her sisters. Now she still does all these things, but under the guise of a (mostly) responsible adult. When she's not writing, she can be found scouring thrift stores for books to add to her collection, dancing to old music in her living room, or concocting elaborate schemes with her sisters. Of the twelve states in the Midwest, she's lived in four of them. *Always A Choice* is her debut novel.

Connect with Rana on:
Instagram: @ranaschenke
Website: www.ranaschenke.com

Acknowledgments

To my early readers, especially Lyndsae, Jake, Ariana, and Kiki—when I wasn't sure how to take this story further, you showed me the way.

Ashley, your feedback and edits were invaluable. Thank you for wading through the style guide soup that was the earlier version of this book.

Without the amazing Lacy Lieffers, this book would likely still be sitting in my Google Drive. Thank you for your guidance and encouragement throughout this (occasionally messy) journey.

To my friend Anna: when I posted my first aesthetic reel for this book, you told me you've been excited about this for years and you still remember us talking about it junior/senior year. I literally have no words to describe what that meant to me. All I can say is I hope it was worth the wait.

Mao Mei, I stumbled across your LinkedIn profile almost two years ago (can you believe it??), and I'm so glad I did. Your friendship and support have meant so much to me. We may be early in our journeys, but one day we're going to dominate like the queens we are. :)

A special thank you to the enthusiastic and supportive folks on Instagram and LinkedIn. Instagram peeps, thanks for joining me on this journey!

LinkedIn friends, you were the first to hear about this book, and your kind and encouraging comments meant the world to me. LinkedIn is a place to shape your dreams into reality, and it's all because of amazing people like you.

A huge shoutout to all the library people whose behind-the-scenes work has touched every part of my writing journey. I would not be writing this today if not for them. JoCo Library, Carbondale Public Library, SM Northwest Library, Algonquin Area Public Library and their employees deserve special thanks.

Mom, you're the one who got me hooked on libraries and reading. You gave me the curiosity and courage that guided me throughout this journey, and you taught me to never stop learning and growing. Your impact is greater than you or I will ever know.

Dad, whatever the crazy idea—a flower-themed ballet, a multi-year movie project, writing on LinkedIn, or publishing a book—I've always been able to count on your support. Your enthusiasm and pride in sharing your daughters' work, although we joke about it, never goes unappreciated.

(And to all the friends of my dad who may be reading this, hello there! A big thank-you to you, too!)

To Leila: I know you're going to do amazing things one day, whether that's starting a business, performing with Cirque du Soleil, or writing your own book—or maybe all three. Whatever you do, I know you're going to kill it, and I'll always be here to cheer you on.

And to Beverly, who listened to and enjoyed my earliest stories despite their flaws. Collaborating with you has always made me stronger. May our weird, wild, and wonderful ideas never run out.

If you enjoyed this book, please consider leaving a review on Amazon and/or Goodreads!

Your honest feedback can help another reader find and enjoy the book as well.

Thank you!

Printed in Great Britain
by Amazon